Ed Cline

About the Author

ANTOINETTE MAY is the author of *Pilate's Wife: A Novel of the Roman Empire* and coauthor of the *New York Times* bestseller *Adventures of a Psychic,* a biography of contemporary clairvoyant Sylvia Browne. She is a regular contributor to the *San Francisco Chronicle* and has had articles published in *Cosmopolitan, Country Living, Self,* the *San Diego Union-Tribune,* the *Los Angeles Times,* and the *San Jose Mercury News.* May is an award-winning travel writer specializing in Mexico. She divides her time between Palo Alto and a historic California gold rush home in the Sierra foothills.

THE
SACRED
WELL

Also by Antoinette May

Passionate Pilgrim

Witness to War

Adventures of a Psychic

Pilate's Wife

Happy times!

THE
SACRED
WELL

A Novel

Antoinette May

HARPER

NEW YORK • LONDON • TORONTO • SYDNEY

HARPER

HarperCollins books may be purchased for educational, business, or sales promotional use. For information please write: Special Markets Department, HarperCollins Publishers, 10 East 53rd Street, New York, NY 10022.

FIRST EDITION

Designed by Justin Dodd

Library of Congress Cataloging-in-Publication Data is available upon request.

ISBN 978-0-06-169555-1

09 10 11 12 13 ID/RRD 10 9 8 7 6 5 4 3 2 1

To my husband, Charles Herndon, whose patience

and practicality made *The Sacred Well* a reality.

En lak ech.

You are the other me.

—A Mayan saying

THE
SACRED
WELL

1

A Storm Warning

SAGE

Yucatán, the present day

Mérida is an ancient city, sensual and sophisticated. I loved it on sight and dreamed of getting lost there, a fantasy that haunts me still.

As special guests, our wooden chairs had been placed on a small dais in the center of tiny Parque Santa Lucía. Sitting in the front row, making notes, I watched couples dance on an improvised stage. Dark-suited men darted like moths. Women in white whirled coquettishly, trays of champagne glasses delicately balanced on their heads.

I knew about balancing acts, have gotten good at them. *Not now, not tonight,* I pleaded to—to whom? Ixchel; this was her territory. *I want to have fun tonight,* I told the Mayan moon goddess. This is *my* time.

Leaning back, I fluttered a sandalwood fan against the sultry night, savoring the quaint old park with its graceful archways and lush plantings. The mariachi band sounded great: horns, violins, lots of guitars. When lightning sliced the sky I sat up with a start. A low roar echoed in the distance, barely discernable. Thunder crashed above me now. How quickly the weather changes in Yucatán. The first, fast drops of rain pelted my hair, splashed my face. Companions were already up and running. Behind us was a narrow street, beyond that our hotel. Two group members were halfway there, our leader shepherding the rest across deepening rivulets of rainwater.

I turned back to the stage and saw male dancers scatter in all directions. The women performers, gowns sodden now and clinging, looked uncertainly at one another, hands raised to trays still balanced on their heads. A goblet slid off, shattering on ancient paving stones. Mariachis grabbed their instruments and ran from the bandstand. Thunder crashed again, long and ominous.

Another fiery bolt slashed the horizon. "Sage, are you coming?" someone called to me from across the street. Hesitating, I looked again at the hotel, considered my fellow travelers, and remembered their twice-told tales. So tedious. Lost luggage in Guadalajara, leaky toilets in Taxco. I ran—in the opposite direction. The mariachis were disappearing into a cantina on the far side of the square. El Troubabor. Liking the sound of it, I hurried toward the blinking Christmas tree lights that marked the bar's lofty stone entryway. My high heels slipped on rough stones. An experienced traveler should have known better, but I couldn't resist the slinky shoes waiting so long in my closet.

Pushing open the elaborately carved wooden door, I rushed inside, glad to be out of the rain, a smooth marble floor beneath my feet. Too smooth. I slid, missed a step, and pitched forward into the dark, smoky room. An awful moment, tumbling in slow motion. I fell headlong, or would have, if a stranger's arms hadn't reached out and caught me. For the tiniest moment I relaxed against his shoulder. . . . *How good it felt to be held without being needed. How long had it been?*

"Are you all right?" the man asked in American English. He looked a little younger than me, early forties, perhaps; tall, rangy, and smiling softly. I'd never seen him before, yet felt in some crazy way that I knew him, might even have been waiting for him.

"I'm fine." I stepped back, wobbly, embarrassed. The room was filled with people, all of them looking at us. "Thank you," I gasped.

"Come, join me." He gestured toward the ornate mahogany bar where his drink waited, something dark and sparkling in a snifter.

Still shaky, I settled onto a bamboo stool, its back thickly padded with embroidered pillows. Mayan designs:

Ixchel, my favorite, alongside ferocious snouts and plumed serpents.

My reflection stared back from the cloudy mirror behind the bar. Wide eyes, wary like a startled cat. I took off my scarf, fluffed up the short silver waves its silken whimsy had failed to cover. Good haircuts are hard to come by; I was glad to have one.

"*¿Una margarita, señora?*" the bartender asked, his ring-heavy hands already busy pouring.

"*Sí, por favor.*"

"You speak Spanish?" the man beside me asked.

"*Español por tontos.*"

"*¿Tontos?*"

"Dummies—it gets me by."

The mariachis, grouped in a corner, tuned up instruments that seemed none the worse for the shower. Much of the brass was dented, the tuba tarnished, but the brave sound raised my spirits immediately. Tasting the salt from the glass's rim, I looked about the cantina: intimate, heavy with history; faded elegance, but still inviting. This was the colonial part of town, the adobe walls a good five hundred years old. I liked the ancient grillwork at the windows, the bright woven rugs scattered across the tile floor.

Studying the faded photographs on the wall beside me, I saw poignant reminders of Mexico's turbulent past. These were the heroes of the revolution: men in white with broad sombreros, bandoliers bristling with bullets, rifles ready. Young, unformed faces with fierce dark eyes. I picked up a bar napkin, jotted a few hurried notes, and looked up to see my rescuer watching me.

"This *is* a nice place to remember," he nodded. One eyelid seemed a little heavier than the other, slightly engaging, a wink waiting to happen. "The mariachis end up here nearly every night to play their own favorites. Will you be in town long?"

I shook my head. "No. Here today, Chichen Itza tomorrow, then Cancún; finally, Campeche."

"Oh, you're on a tour."

"Sort of. I'm the person who gets people to want to take tours. Now, is that a good thing?" I swirled the liquid in my glass. "I wonder sometimes."

When he looked puzzled, I explained: "I'm a travel writer. My current magazine assignment is Mexico's romantic destinations." Actually, I thought, *he* was rather romantic. Dark blue eyes, penetrating; slim hips ready for the ghost of a gun belt.

He nodded at the wall of photographs that I'd been examining. "You consider revolutionaries romantic?"

"Sometimes," I admitted, allowing a smile. "Last year I visited a museum in Chihuahua. The locals call it Pancho's Villa because the famous bandit lived there. The pistols on the bedpost are so macho."

"You like macho?"

"I used to." Forcibly suppressing a sigh, I took another sip of my drink. We were silent, listening as the mariachis trumpeted a series of old favorites, "La Golondrina," "Cielito Linda," then another melody, one I'd not heard before, a lilting, throbbing refrain that seemed to well up from the musicians' very souls. "What is that?" I asked.

"I'm surprised you don't know—'La Peregrina,' the wanderer. Story goes the governor of Yucatán wrote it for a lady journalist. Now there's something for you to write about—romantic, too."

"Why don't you tell me about it?"

He nodded at my empty glass. "Have another and you can hear all I know."

I glanced at his snifter, a dark and mysterious well. "What are you having?"

"Don Julio. Tastes smoky, a little like dark chocolate."

I watched as he drank. The liquid shimmered like a crushed topaz. My birthstone. "I'll try some of that."

At his request, the mariachis repeated "La Peregrina" for us. So lovely, but not without sadness. It spoke to me of unfulfilled longings, possibly my own.

I took the warm snifter in my hands. It was my turn to enjoy the silky smooth tequila. To me, it tasted like cinnamon and honey. "Now, about that couple," I reminded him, "the governor and the journalist."

"Their *amor de calido* happened around the time of the revolution."

"*Amor de calido*—I like that! A steamy romance." I leaned closer, flirting a little. Strange how it came back, like riding a bicycle. "What happened to them?"

He leaned forward, too. "You must have seen that big monument out on Paseo de Montejo. There was a scandal, someone got shot."

"Over the woman?" The tiniest frisson swept my body. Perhaps here was a story, fresh and new, something I could run with. How long had it been since I'd written anything that truly excited me? "Who was she?" I asked.

"An American, San Francisco, I think, but that's all I know."

"Really! I'm from there myself," I sipped the last of my tequila, thinking now of home, not quite San Francisco but close. In a few days I'd be getting off a plane. Mark would be waiting as always, leaning on his cane, faded eyes watching for me. I couldn't leave him again. This must be my last press trip.

It was time to rejoin the others back at Casa del Balam. I had an early wake-up call. The cantina's heavy door swung open, admitting a few dry-looking patrons. The rain had stopped as suddenly as it had begun.

I dug into my wallet and pulled out some pesos for the bartender. The man beside me attempted to intercept the exchange but I didn't let him.

"Leaving so soon?" he asked, disappointment apparent in his face. "I live in Mérida, I could show you the sights.

It's beautiful—the white city, they call it." His eyes met mine. "I—I'd like to know you better."

I smiled, slanting my eyes at him—how long since I'd done that? "I'm sorry," I said, and surprised myself by meaning it.

"But I haven't even introduced myself. I'm David Winslow."

"Thank you, David Winslow," I extended my hand. "I'm Sage Sanborn." I hesitated; something in his eyes held me. Admiration? Acknowledgement? *A stranger in a strange land, I could be anyone I chose to be. Do anything I chose to do. Who would ever know? More important, Mark would never know.* Tempting thoughts, almost frightening. How long since I'd been anything other than a caregiver?

Cocking my head, I glanced up at him. "Tell me, what brought you to Yucatán?"

David looked at me longer than necessary, the intent eyes momentarily evasive.

What was he hiding? I breathed an inner sigh as I realized that it didn't matter. I wasn't going to go there. What had I been thinking of? A one-night stand with a complete stranger? Foolish girls did that sort of thing. I counted myself among the grown-ups.

"You wouldn't want to know that," Winslow said at last.

I stared at the face reflected beside my own in the mirror. Intelligent, thoughtful. "Don't tell me you're a drug dealer." I laughed softly, arranging the scarf about my shoulders.

"You're getting warm."

The door opened again, admitting another small group. When two couples sitting close by went out, I allowed myself to be swept along with them. Turning, I caught a glimpse of Winslow, still sitting alone at the bar, and waved good-bye. The door closed. Laughter spilled onto wet streets as the others squeezed into a taxi. The sky was clear. The moon had come out, a slim crescent.

I cut across Parque Santa Lucía, deserted now, its ancient arches looming white and still. David Winslow was a strange one. An attractive man, *very* attractive, but what an odd sense of humor.

Strains of "La Peregrina" echoed as I crossed the narrow street. Or did I only imagine it?

2

Dos Peregrinas?

Settling into Mark's oversized chair, I savored the old leather smell. Our arrangement worked. Mark's former study had become my office. A cherrywood desk, years in his family, was more than ample for the laptop I brought to and from my apartment. I liked Mark's presence in the room, jokes tacked to a corkboard with pictures of his two sons and assorted grandkids. Paneled walls held an impressive array of his degrees and awards. The fourth wall, a window, overlooked the Los Altos foothills, amber now, dotted with live oaks.

Reaching into the carpetbag on the floor beside me, I pulled out my notes. Within minutes a travel article floated from keyboard to screen. It wasn't as though I hadn't written hundreds like it.

Having traveled nearly everywhere seeking exotic adventure, sometimes for intellectual challenge, occasionally for glitz and glamour, I've returned to Mexico, that continental boy next door, and found the excitement, the wisdom, and the elegance for which I'd been searching all along. Now isn't that a love story?

"Good work, babe. You make me want to go there." Mark stood behind me, his hand on my shoulder.

I leaned back, my cheek touching his fingers. Our cat, Mews, dozing in my lap, stirred, stretched, and leaped down. "Those government press trips, whizzing through ten towns in nine days. It's tough sorting them out." I nodded toward a jumble of table napkins and match covers on the desk before me.

Mark smiled ruefully. "Well, as they say, there's no free lunch. You're a top travel writer or they wouldn't have invited you on their junket. Now the time's come to write for your supper."

I was silent, remembering when Mark had accompanied me on my many travel assignments. London theater, rented villas in Italy, jungle trekking in Belize. Good times shared, but more than that. There was also Mark the mentor, the lawyer buddy and wannabe lover, who'd once counseled me to quit my safe little managing editor job. "What are savings for? Use them," he'd urged. "Go see the world and write about it. Just don't forget to come back."

Nearly a year later I'd called him from Hong Kong. "I'll be home in two days," I told Mark, wondering if he could detect the catch in my voice. "Would you meet me—eleven a.m., SFA?" He was there for me then, and had remained ever since—had it really been twelve years? A wannabe no longer, Mark had waited me out. We'd become a couple, a loving couple. We even had a cat together. Yes, Mark and I went way back.

"What about a martini break?" he suggested now.

I summoned a smile. Reluctantly, pressing the SAVE button, I pushed back from the computer and got up. My article could wait awhile. The nights we spent together, four each week, were marked by frosted glasses, icons of partnership and carefully fostered tradition. Our one-martini ritual, a survivor of livelier days.

It was a gray afternoon, blustery, cold, nothing like Mexico, but a fire crackled cozily in the living room. I slipped a CD into the player. "Got this in Yucatán. 'La Peregrina'—the wanderer, an old song, but new to me."

Mark listened, eyes closed. I searched his unguarded face, still handsome, but thin. Were those new lines about his mouth?

"A bit romantic, I'd say. Are you getting sentimental on me?"

"Not likely. I'm a hard-boiled newspaper dame—hadn't you heard?" I laughed, ruffling his hair. "That song is powerful. Perhaps you don't feel it because you've never been to Yucatán."

I sat down on the couch opposite his wing chair, the martini tray between us. "That song haunts me. The night I first heard it I had the most terrible dream. Guns blasting, blood, bodies. A man—it was terrible. I woke up screaming. It was barely dawn but I was so disturbed from the dream that I went out and found a taxi."

"Why? I don't get it." Mark leaned forward, pouring a martini into my glass.

I shrugged. "I can't imagine what got into me and I don't know anything more now than I did then. You know how bad my Spanish is, but the driver under-stood enough to take me to the edge of town to see a monument that someone had told me about." Pausing, I thought about that "someone," David whatever, with his heavy eyes and puzzling manner. Wouldn't my bold benefactor be surprised to know where his idle words had taken me?

Mark was smiling. "Rather a strong reaction, I'd say." Ice clinked agreeably in the Waterford pitcher as he poured me a dividend. "What was the statue of, or should I say whom?"

"Some long-ago governor."

"What did he do?"

"I wish I knew. The driver spoke almost no English and when I got back to the hotel it was time to load up. From then on it was Mayan ruins, beach resorts, pirate barricades, and finally home."

"And finally home." Mark watched with a delighted sideways smile, as though every move I made, every word I said, fascinated him. The work I longed to do in the den must wait. I couldn't leave him now; these were the moments Mark waited for.

I prepared his favorite dishes—lamb stew, spinach salad—and poured him a small glass of cabernet. Mark looked mellow when I settled him before the TV. *Masterpiece Theatre* would keep him engrossed. "I'll be back soon," I promised. "Just something I want to check." I hurried down the hall, Mews mewling at my ankles. Sitting down before the computer, I closed out the Mexico hotel story. Heart fluttering just a little, I Googled "Felipe Carrillo Puerto."

The next day I called an old friend in San Francisco. Years ago Mabs Millay and I had been roommates and reporters together on the old *Palo Alto Weekly*. We managed to stay in touch, not seeing one another often enough but always able to pick up the beat wherever we left off. Today she was full of questions that I forestalled. "I'll tell you when I see you—this afternoon, if that's okay. I'd like to use your archives."

Now, moving forward, heels sinking into thick carpet, I glanced about the posh newsroom, speculating on roads not taken. This life could have been mine—had I been a more corporate person. I wasn't, preferring to generate my own assignments, take my own chances. Mark had encouraged that from the start. What a friend he'd been—what a friend he is, I hastily corrected myself.

The room was quiet but for the muted click of computer keys emanating from roomy cubes on either side of me. Some reporters had decorated their space with artwork, others had brought in leafy plants; I saw a bud vase with a single rose on one desk.

Mabs waved from an open door. "Welcome to the *News Call*." She approached, smiling. "You look great."

"You, too. I keep reading that fifty is the new thirty. Not sure I buy it."

Mabs stood back, hands on ample hips, surveying me. "Maybe you should. How many of us can let our hair go gray and still look glamorous?" She turned, leading the way into her office.

"Very impressive," I said, admiring the stunning Bay view, the large mahogany desk. "And so orderly. You always were a neatnik. Is it fun being the big cheese?"

Mabs pushed back a shock of bright blond hair, her choice for twenty-five years. "I'm not the big cheese, but it *is* fun being Scene editor. I have a good staff." She pulled the carafe from an elaborate Krups machine, poured coffee into china mugs. "What are you up to?"

"I'm finishing an article on Mexico's romantic inns."

Mabs pushed blue-rimmed glasses over her forehead and studied me. "Is that why you want to use the archives?"

I picked up my mug, waved away the cream. "I've got a hunch about this Yucatec governor. Seems he was something of a loose cannon. The conservative establishment called him the Red Dragon with the Eyes of Jade. Looks like this wild man may have been linked to a reporter who worked here in the 1920s. Alma Reed."

Mabs's brown eyes widened. "Alma Reed is the patron saint of the *News Call*. There's a picture of her in the archives room. Come, I'll show you."

Mabs moved down the hall, threw open a door. "Alma was a pioneer woman journalist, one of the original 'sob sisters.' She wrote a column, 'Mrs. Goodfellow.' Those bleeding heart stories were great for circulation. World War One vets begging for wooden legs, dying kids dreaming of summer camp, starving widows needing operations—that kind of stuff. Readers ate it up." Mabs pointed to a yellowed newspaper picture that someone had elaborately framed. "Alma's biggest coup involved getting a law passed in Sacramento to save a kid from hanging. This picture must have been taken then." Mabs peered closer. "She looks a lot like you."

I studied Alma Reed's firm chin, her full, sensuous lips. It was an arresting face that, despite the fading newsprint, radiated vitality. "Do you really think so?"

"I do." Mabs insisted. "Something about the cheek-bones . . . no, it's the eyes, those wide, searching eyes. You're going to write about her, aren't you? It's about time someone did."

"Maybe, a paragraph or two in my article. Nothing more." A sense of longing gripped me, so intense. *If only!* Shaking my head, I explained. "I need to stick close to home. That biography I wrote—the woman psychic—did quite well. Now the CEO of a Silicon Valley company has approached me. She wants a ghostwritten autobiography."

"That's what they all want, once they've built those obscene starter castles."

"You got it. A cyber diva, but the money's good," I paused. "Her office is just five minutes from Mark's house."

Mabs's face clouded. "He's worse?"

I looked away, avoiding the pity in her eyes. "Mark's brave. First the chemo—all that gorgeous, thick, dark hair gone. Can you imagine him with a white crew cut? Mark's on radiation now. It leaves him very weak."

"Oh, Sage! That's so much responsibility. You're not even married! Why don't his kids step up to the plate? What about your own life?"

I paused, thinking of the old Mark, the brilliant, often charismatic man who'd charmed and challenged me. He was still there . . . somewhere. I looked about the room lined with filing cabinets. "There must be some Alma Reed clips buried here somewhere."

It turned out there were many clippings. Some merely crumbled fragments. Two archivists guarded them jealously. If Mabs hadn't thrown her weight around, I wouldn't have been allowed near the clips. Meticulously the archivists spread out the yellowed sheets of newspaper. "Look but don't touch." I bent over each with a magnifying glass. Four hours later, I left the *News Call* with a thick pad of notes and the choicest clippings carefully copied. I couldn't wait to begin. Taking the train back to my Palo Alto apartment, I settled into the last seat in the compartment, making a rolling office of it with papers spread around me.

Mark's radiation treatment would take another hour. I looked up at the clock in the hospital waiting room, then pulled the history book from my tote bag.

My love affair with Mexico had begun as a child enjoying beach holidays with my parents. Vallarta and Zihaut were villages then. Shorts and tees in December, damp sand between my toes, old-new friends back again from other lives, sweet brown-skinned waiters bringing us coco locos. So the loco part was missing; who cared? We kids drank like grown-ups from coconut shells. At night we played Monopoly by candlelight on someone's balcony, our parents' laughter drifting up from the pool. No one cared how long we stayed up. It was Mexico, vacation land—relaxed and gentle. Far removed from a savage past.

As I looked down at the pages, a slim figure in a sailor dress danced unbidden before my mind's eye. The thought of Alma Reed, brave but incredibly naïve, setting off for that trouble spot appalled me. It was a treacherous world then, Mexico a different place from the tourist mecca I knew.

Porfirio Díaz reigned like a monarch from 1876 to 1911, leading Mexico to a pinnacle of prosperity. Who imagined the dissidents plotting his overthrow? First Madero, a mild-mannered spiritualist; then the hell-raising bandit Pancho Villa, with his unruly army of train robbers and cattle rustlers; and finally, the brooding Indian freedom fighter Emiliano Zapata. Strange bedfellows, but within a year they'd beaten and banished Díaz. Ten years of anarchy followed—one faction fighting another to prominence only to dissolve into chaos. Zapata was lured to his death; Villa was bought off with an immense cattle ranch. Six million were dead before Álvaro Obregón's rise to uneasy dominance. Into this disaster area had stepped Alma Reed, foolhardy girl . . .

I looked up to see Mark standing before me, smiling that rare transformative smile.

"You look happy," I said.

"Why not? The technicians are pretty. They make a fuss over me."

"I should think so." I rose, helped him with his raincoat. "This is your last treatment. We should celebrate. What about lunch at MacArthur Park?" In recent months the rambling wood-frame building had been our haven. Valet parking and only three steps for Mark to climb.

"Babe, I don't think . . ." His lips smiled again; his eyes didn't.

"How silly of me. We don't need a big lunch. Let's go to my place." I squeezed his arm. "I'll fix tea while you rest and listen to music. When you're ready, I'll drive you home. We'll pick up videos to watch." I put my arm under his. "It'll be a lovely evening."

I helped Mark into my car and drove the few miles up Sand Hill Road to my apartment. It was a pretty place, close to everything and yet facing directly onto a wooded creek. I'd hardly settled him onto the couch when the phone rang.

It was Mabs, excited, insistent. "Whatever that woman's offered you, we'll pay more."

"What woman?" I looked around the kitchen door into the living room. Mark's eyes were closed. Perhaps he was already asleep. "Who's we? What are you talking about?"

"I just had lunch with Max Riley, general manager of News Call Books. He's starting a line of biographies. I suggested Alma Reed and he went for it. Why not? It's a great story and wonderful promotion for the paper. You'd be perfect for the job: I told him that you're the only one to do it justice."

Alma Reed! My heart and mind raced. Could I leave Mark? No. Could I take him with me? No, how could he possibly manage? Would his sons . . . no again. Impossible. I took a deep breath. "But I'm *not* the one to do it justice, Mabs. The research time in Yucatán is out of the question. I can't leave Mark. *I can't.* Please don't ask again."

I slid out of bed early, taking care not to awaken Mark, and tiptoed down the hall to the office. Turning on the computer, I scanned the screen. With "Romantic Inns of Mexico" out of the way, I'd pitched a variety of regional stories. Now here was an e-mail from my editor. I hoped she'd pick "Silicon Valley: Where Power Brokers Dine." So easy to write, so close to home. I murmured a prayer to the Mayan goddess Ixchel, my private deity, and clicked the mouse.

"Damn!" The last thing I expected was a brushfire:

Amp up the Yucatán section. Tell our readers why the Maya are different. Why is their state distinct from the rest of Mexico? What does this mean today? Need 1,500 words NOW.

"Double damn." On the desk before me was the tome I'd set aside to attack that morning: *The History of Silicon Valley.* Prep work for the diva bio. Now here was a New York editor already three hours ahead in time, pulling me back to a project I'd thought finished. An advertiser must have yanked an ad. *Traveling Life* was scrambling to fill the void. "Sage can do it," some editor was saying. "She's fast. She'll come through." No one ever called *me* a diva, I thought ruefully. They just took it for granted that I would come through for them. Complaints? What was the point?

I dug into my Yucatán file for notes, spread them out on the desk. The memories were fresh and vivid: trickling fountains, trailing bougainvilleas, mariachis. Yucatán, why are you so special? Why is Mérida different from the other colonial cities? *I love it, that's why!* I'd have to do better than that. *Come on, Ixchel, this time I really need you.* Within a few minutes my fingers were flitting across the keyboard.

When the first Europeans set foot on the ancient soil of the "New" World, most of the Mayan ceremonial centers had been gobbled by jungle. Only the tallest buildings still towered above the dense vegetation. Who built these cities merely to desert them? they asked, as we still do today.

All we know is that the Mayan empire—more than one hundred city-states—flourished for a millennium. During its ascendancy these magnificent people formulated the concept of the zero and devised a calendar more accurate than the one we use today. Then, as mysteriously as it began, the Mayan civilization ended. The temples, the palaces, the cities were deserted. Why?

I was really into it when Mark came in with two mugs of coffee. He'd shaved and wore the velour sweat suit I'd given him for Christmas, but his hand shook as he placed my mug on the desk.

"How's that for starters?" I asked, glancing at the screen.

"Fine," he nodded. Slowly, very carefully, he seated himself beside me.

Dear Mark, how much longer do we have together? "I'd hoped you could sleep in," I said, turning toward him. "You were so restless last night. The pills you're taking, they're—"

"They're working fine, just fine. I had things on my mind."

"What kind of things?"

"Never mind that." He leaned toward the screen, reading. "I see they've got you back on Yucatán. I never did see your pictures from the trip. Let's have a look."

It wasn't like Mark to be evasive. I double clicked on the mouse and a great pyramid filled the screen. "The Temple of Kukulkan in Chichen Itza," I told him. "Frank Lloyd Wright thought it the great wonder of the New World. Look at the stairs: they appear as wide at the top as they do at the bottom. Now look again." I clicked on another picture. "The steps widen so gradually that they give the illusion of symmetry. Chichen has such a sense of mystery and power. It's hard to explain in words—you have to see it."

"I'd like to see it," Mark said, leaning closer. "As a boy, I dreamed of being an architect, studied for a time in school, but there was so much family pressure to join the law firm."

"You'll love this," I said, clicking on another picture, this one a crumbling temple overlooking the sea. "El Castillo at Tulum. The view's spectacular, but there's something even better." I highlighted the next picture. "See the red handprints on the inner wall? Perhaps they're imprints of a living hand, maybe the builder's. I love to sit there and listen to the surf and imagine that another human is reaching out to me across time."

"I can see that you love it all," Mark commented softly. "Where are you going with the rewrite?"

"Maybe I'll add something about the old haciendas— plantation houses where the rich henequen planters lived. Yucatán's wealth came from henequen," I explained, trying the idea out on him. "Shipping drove the world in those days. Henequen twine tied it together."

I clicked on another picture. "Look at this," I pointed to a regal mansion that appeared to float above a carpet of green. The stone facade was golden, its graceful columns entwined by morning glories. "For years Hacienda del Valle was a plantation house, but when nylon replaced henequen the owners abandoned it to the jungle. Recently a big hotel chain moved in, bought the place for pennies, and restored it as an upscale inn."

Mark watched me thoughtfully from behind his coffee mug, then set it down quietly. "I want to go to Yucatán with you."

I pulled my mouth into a reassuring smile. "Why, of course, darling. One of these days we will."

"I mean *now*, Sage."

"That's impossible." I picked up the Silicon Valley history, waving it at him. "The diva's people have already sent me a contract."

"You haven't signed it, have you?"

"No, but I have given Max Riley a definite no on the Alma Reed biography."

"Then call back and give him a resounding yes. I know how much you want to do that book. I've seen you go over those clippings again and again. I'm not going to let you give it up because of me."

What was he thinking?! Mark could barely walk a block. Had he forgotten the last time we'd attempted a theater evening in San Francisco? How could he manage all the stairs in Yucatán, the ancient paving stones? "You don't realize how much research is involved. We'd be there for months. You can't—"

"I *can*. You'll run around, climb your pyramids, do your research, while I sip margaritas and read whodunits on some flowery veranda. Maybe you'll let me lure you away for a little side trip to Cancún."

"But, Mark, all your meds . . . "

"You think they don't have pharmacies in Mexico? A lot cheaper, too."

I shook my head impatiently. "You're forgetting the shots. Procrit three times a week, remember?"

"I'll find a way, Sage. I'll find a house sitter, too," he said with an aside to Mews. "Somebody who loves cats. Can you think of any other reason we can't make this trip together?"

What could I say? This was the man I loved. How little time was left for us. I'd written off the trip and the book, but could I write off Mark's courage? This was what he wanted to do despite the risk to his life.

"I'm in remission, Sage," he said, as though reading my mind. "The radiation treatments are over. My PSA count is down. What did the doctor say last week? 'Mark, you and I are going to grow old together.'" He picked up his coffee mug, clinked it against mine. "I'd rather grow old with you."

3

My *Destino*

ALMA
San Francisco, 1922

November 21, 1922, the day that changed my life forever, felt like any other. Any other, that is, with a front-page story to write and a deadline closing in. My boss, Fremont Older, towered over me as I pounded away on the big, boxlike Underwood.

"Wrap it up, Alma!" he ordered. "You're running out of time."

I attacked the stiff, sticking keys with two fingers, deaf to the other typewriters clattering around me, oblivious to the San Francisco skyline beyond my small window. Mr. Older grabbed the sheets of paper one at a time from my typewriter and scanned each. "Hey, kid!" he bellowed, and a copyboy appeared to race the page to the next room, where linotype operators in overalls stood ready.

Mr. Older took the last sheet out himself. In minutes he was back. Soon I heard the hungry presses begin to roll and roar. Breathing a sigh of weary contentment, I looked up, expecting congratulations. The story was a good one, a juicy murder trial. Instead, the editor's lean, long face looked grim.

I reached for a stack of mail. "Get a load of this." I waved a sheet of ivory stationery covered in flowery script. The scent of violet perfume wafted through the newsroom. Everyone knew my daily sob sister column, a clearing house for gift giving, was a circulation builder. I picked up the list. The Emporium had donated three union suits to the needy poor. They'd come in handy, but I wondered about the two hundred tickets to a California wildflower display. What society dame had thought that one up?

"Your 'Mrs. Goodfellow' stuff can wait." Mr. Older's tone was clipped. "Come into my office." His mouth, under the walrus mustache, looked grim. Rarely had I seen that expression and never once directed at me. I took a deep breath and rose. The managing editor of the *News Call* was a big man, well over six feet tall. I felt small as I followed him.

Many of the reporters remained lost in racing forms. They'd have a half-hour or so respite before the whole process began again for the second edition. The hot, stuffy city room was dark with smoke as we crossed to Mr. Older's office. With the paper now on the presses, reporters, sleeves pushed up under rumpled vests, were rolling cigarettes or pulling flasks from their cluttered desks. I smelled the bootleg hooch halfway across the room. A few of the men ogled me openly. At first I'd felt half naked in the new knee-length skirts, but lately I'd begun to enjoy the freedom. A little leg show wouldn't hurt anybody. Giving a little Clara Bow twist, I sailed right by. Get used to it, boys. This is the twentieth century.

Afternoon sun poured through the windows of Mr. Older's cluttered office, blazing down on his bald head. He gestured toward a chair, then sat down opposite me. His desk, as usual, was littered with papers. How did he find anything? Leaning back in his scruffy leather chair, Mr. Older lit a cigar. The tray didn't exist that could contain his ashes. They carpeted the floor, along with spilled proof sheets, crumpled newspapers, and discarded letters.

A moment or two passed in uncomfortable silence. "You could have told me," he said at last.

I looked down, feeling lower than the ink-stained rug.

"I'm glad you can still blush," he commented.

"What did you expect?" I looked up at him. "It was a chicken-egg thing. An archaeology professor at Cal told me that a group from the Carnegie Institution was going to some far corner of Mexico to survey ruins. He said they wanted a journalist to go along, someone whose writing would stir up interest, maybe get wealthy donors to cough up for future expeditions."

Sitting beneath his signed photograph of Warren G. Harding, Mr. Older regarded me coolly. Both powerful figures seemed to be judging me, finding me guilty.

"So?" my boss said at last. I looked down again. How could I describe to him, or anyone, my excitement at the prospect of such an adventure, or the wild longing I'd felt for that exotic place? Yucatán . . . I loved the very sound of it.

"The job seemed tailor-made," I explained, trying to sound casual. " 'Mrs. Goodfellow' played out on an exotic canvas."

"Perhaps," he conceded, waving his cigar in my direction like a scepter, "but why didn't you discuss the idea with me?"

There was nothing left for me to do but what I dreaded most. I would have to tell the truth.

"Mr. Older, we know the *News Call* is the best newspaper in the world, but Easterners think the sun rises and sets on the *New York Times*. The Carnegie wouldn't even consider a writer from California without their backing. Besides"—I paused, readying my riskiest salvo—"could the *News Call* afford to send me? There'd be my extra salary and expenses . . ."

"I see." He'd put his cigar aside, forgotten it, and was lighting another. "And the *Times*?"

"Ever since King Tut got dug up, archaeology's been all the rage. Every other headline is about tombs and treasure. I knew the *Times* would be right on it, so I sent clips right away—stories I did on the Fatty Arbuckle trial. The Simón Ruiz stuff, too."

"Have to admit what you did for the Ruiz kid was pretty damn dramatic," Mr. Older mused. "Ochs must have been impressed. That link with Mexico wouldn't do any harm, either. They'd love you down there, all right."

Pretty dramatic, indeed, saving Simón's life, wrecking my own . . . but now there could be a new life free from any link to Sam. I'd be far away, no chance of ever running into him, or even hearing his name. "Yes," I agreed, "the link with Mexico may have been the deciding factor—if Mr. Ochs has gone so far as to check me out with you."

"*One* of the deciding factors," he said, regarding me from beneath thick, dark brows. "What about the other, Alma?"

"I don't know what you mean."

"Come on, Alma! He's calling you Dr. Reed."

"I did take a night class in anthropology." I returned his probing glance, struggling to explain. "They need a writer, not a Ph.D. Why shouldn't I be the one?"

My face felt hot. That awful blush again. Mr. Older was so honest. I doubted that he'd ever cut a single corner, ever stretched the truth even the tiniest iota. How could he possibly understand what it was like to want something so much? Surely what I'd done wasn't so terrible. It wasn't as though I couldn't do the job. I'd be great; all I needed was a chance.

I forced myself to ask, "Are you going to tell him?"

Older regarded me through a cloud of cigar smoke. "I thought you liked working for me—for the *News Call*. You and the janitor are the only ones around here when I leave at night."

"I do like it. I love it! The paper's been everything to me—practically my home, but . . ." I hesitated, looking up at him from beneath lashes that felt annoyingly damp. "At some point everyone has to leave home. After . . . all that's happened to me here, isn't it time I got out of San Francisco?" I took a deep breath. "Maybe I don't have a degree, but archaeology fascinates me. No one knows much about the Maya. I want to learn all about them. I want to tell their story to the world. The minute I heard of the expedition, I got this funny feeling . . ."

"Okay, okay, Alma, cut the Ouija board stuff." Mr. Older raised his ink-stained hands as though to ward me away. "Maybe Anthropology 101 is a bit shy of a doctorate," he said, sinking back once again into his chair, "but no more of a disparity than the cock-and-bull stories you told me when you first came here—that paper you were supposed to have edited down on the Peninsula, for instance. No one can say you haven't got guts or a flair for fantasy."

"Imagination is good, isn't it? You tell people to use it all the time."

"No need to tell *you* that." Mr. Older's brow furrowed as he scanned the letter. "As I see it, Ochs isn't asking about your education. He wants to know—one editor to another—are you a good reporter?"

"What will you tell him?"

Mr. Older's scowling face rearranged itself into a smile. "That I've never known one better."

The street was damp, the air heavy with fog when I emerged from the *News Call* office. Euphoric, I scarcely noticed. The job was mine, I knew it. The legendary Fremont Older's recommendation would impress even Adolph Ochs. I refused to consider the warning that had followed Mr. Older's lecture: Mexico was no place for a woman, no place for *anyone* right now. He was just too darned paternal.

Threading my way past automobiles, bicycles, and horse-drawn buggies, I darted up Market to the cable car turnaround. All about me, newsboys were crying, "Extra! Extra! Read all about it!" The headline read: KILLER'S DATE SINGS. It was *my* story they were hawking, the one I'd finished scarcely an hour earlier. I thought about the newsroom I'd just left—dark, airless, noisy, crowded beyond belief. It was a dust bowl, a firetrap, a wall-to-wall wastebasket, but it had been good to me. Was I crazy to chuck it all for who knew what?

Straightening my middy dress, I anchored the cloche against the wind. This was no time to give way to doubt.

Not now, not when I still had Mama to deal with. She was sure to have a conniption fit. Maybe even call in Father O'Donohue. Crowding in among dark-suited business-men with their bowler hats and silver-tipped canes, I boarded the cable car. The brakeman smiled broadly as I sat down. No question where he stood on skirt lengths.

I picked up a discarded newspaper on the seat beside me, the *Chronicle*. Let's see what the competition has to say. . . . Attagirl! I'd scooped them on the trial. . . . Flipping open a few more pages, I idly scanned . . . "*Holy Mary!*" I muttered under my breath. A picture of Theoline. Her smug bee-stung lips pursed in a smirky smile. Surely I didn't need that today. Or any day. The caption beneath her picture announced a singing recital.

Sam would be in the audience, I knew; I could just see his proud smile, the one I'd thought reserved for me alone. I threw down the paper, determined not to let thoughts of Theoline and Sam spoil my happiness.

The cable car filled rapidly as we labored up Hyde Street. Uniformed housemaids clutching string grocery bags, workmen in overalls, a few fur-draped society ma-trons. Glad for a bench seat by the window, I watched the passing streets almost nostalgically. Vallejo. Union. Filbert. Soon I'd be far away. More and more passengers crowded in as we neared Greenwich, the car a veritable sardine can. The next stop was mine. As we approached, the bell clanged one, two, three times. Brakes screeched, the car jerked to a stop. I got up, pushed my way toward the platform, breathed in a gulp of fresh air. Waving to the brakeman, I stepped down onto Lombard Street.

It still gave me a thrill to enter the brownstone building on the corner and to climb the narrow stairs. An apartment of my own remained a badge of honor. With my first paycheck, I'd left home, fleeing to a residence club for young professional women. Once I could afford it, I moved to the tiny studio where I was living when Sam entered my life. Now here I was back in a studio, still small but perched high on Telegraph Hill with a view of the Golden Gate. I liked to stand at the window imagining myself poised on the edge of adventure.

Admiring that familiar view now, I congratulated myself once again on a dream about to come true. I turned away, glancing with a certain pride at the room—not much of a glance, really. Even with the wall bed put up it was *small*. Still, it was I who had assembled the art work, mostly calendar pictures of faraway places; I'd bought the desk, chair, and couch, a process that involved months of boring tedious budgeting.

The minuscule closet was ample for my meager wardrobe. Now, I wondered, riffling among the hangers, what would make the best impression on Mama? Surely not the flapper dress I was wearing; I shrugged that off, flinging it across a chair. Last year's suit, I finally decided. Patterned after Chanel, with slim, loose-fitting lines, it still looked chic; most important, the skirt fell discreetly to mid-calf.

Examining myself as best I could in the bathroom mirror, I pinched the suit lapels together, anchored my hat with a fancy tortoise hatpin, and set out again.

The house on Buchanan Street was the kind that springs to mind when people talk of "painted lady" Victorians. The previous spring, nearly a year after Daddy walked out on us—just went down the street for cigarettes one afternoon and never came back—my brothers got together and painted it for Mama. Orange trimmed in hunter green, it stood out amid all the others that hadn't yet ventured beyond brown or white. Mama accused the boys of being drunk. They probably were, a little. Secretly, I think, she loved the flamboyance. They were, after all, their father's sons.

When I was a small girl our home was grand. Daddy did well then. We'd had Tiffany lamps and cut-glass chandeliers, thick Oriental carpets, potted palms, crystal and silver, damask and lace. There'd even been an original Maxfield Parrish above the marble fireplace. Our family, the Sullivans, had many ups and downs. Sometimes we rode high; but, as years passed, the downs grew steeper and more frequent. All that remained now of the glory days were a few scraggly palms that no one would buy.

Daddy tried hard to climb back up, certain that each new get-rich scheme would be the one to put us over the top for good. I remember the amusement park that flourished then fizzled, 1910, I think; the theater that burned in 1915; the racetrack he almost built. I suppose that, finally, he just got tired. Mama, when she's mad, says I'm too much like him. She's wrong. Daddy didn't finish things—*I do*.

Though the house seemed large from the outside, its rooms were small, its stairs steep. Ceilings sloped in some places where a man couldn't stand erect. All ten of us kids had been jammed together in four bedrooms. I was the oldest, and the others came so fast that I can't remember a time that I didn't feel overwhelmed by babies' demanding wails and small, grasping hands. In those days each room had been crammed to bursting with diapers and baby powder, cribs, potties, and playpens. Mama loved it all, or professed to, though she was forever calling for me to help: "Feed Walter." "Dress Florence." "Change Muriel." "Go see to Prescott." "Alma! Where are you?"

Small wonder I'd fled. I kept in touch with Mama by telephone, went home for holidays and occasional Sunday suppers. It felt strange to be there now on a weekday evening, everything so quiet—quiet for the Sullivan house, anyway. Most of my brothers and sisters were married now and had growing families of their own. Only Muriel and Prescott were still at home. Prescott was in the high school band; I heard him practicing his sax upstairs. Muriel was sprawled across the parlor floor, homework spread out before her, Hawaiian love songs playing on the Victrola. I heard a kettle whistle and followed the sound to the kitchen, anxious to have it out with Mama.

Hesitating just inside the doorway, I took in Mama, her thin back turned as she faced the big black stove. Like a fading photo, I saw the old-fashioned, ankle-length dress, its severity only slightly relieved by a touch of white lace at the collar. I steeled myself as I watched her move, ram-rod straight, toward the old oak table.

Feeling my presence, Mama turned. "Well, aren't you a sight for sore eyes." She opened the cupboard, reached for two cups. "You're just in time for tea."

Mama looked me up and down, taking in the navy serge suit, lightly belted and tailored, that I thought so fashionable. "A bit mannish for my taste but I suppose it's good enough for that place where *you* work."

When I didn't take the bait, she sat down at the table. "You know, lovey, your brother Walter has an opening for a secretary in his office."

"Mama!" I exclaimed. "Not that again."

"Now don't go turning your nose up. It's a fine, decent job, a job to be proud of. I never thought a woman from our family would stoop so low as to work on a newspaper." She picked up the paper from the table, waving the front page at me. "'KILLER'S DATE SINGS'! That disgusting trial! The things you see, the stuff you write about—they just aren't fit for a lady."

I shook my head wearily. How many times had we covered this ground? "It doesn't matter now, Mama. I'm going to Yucatán—to Mexico."

"Mexico! Holy Saints!" Mama banged the teapot down on the table. "You'll be murdered in your bed! Don't you read your own newspaper?" Mama flipped through the first section. "Here, look at this." She pointed to a picture of a man with dark, brooding eyes and a thick, droopy mustache. I noted the rifle he held, the two cartridge belts across his chest. "That Pancho Villa fella is killing people right and left."

"The revolution's over, Mama." I looked down, carefully pouring tea into our cups. "Besides, I won't be anywhere near Pancho Villa. He's up north. Yucatán is a peninsula in the southeast."

Mama watched me silently. "It's Sam, isn't it?" she said at last. "The ink's not dry on your divorce papers and you're taking off for some godforsaken place that no one's ever heard of."

"It has nothing to do with Sam."

"It has everything to do with Sam. The story was in the paper last week. He and that—that singing hussy of his are getting married." Mama's voice softened. "I'm sorry, Alma, I know it's been hard. You and he know so many of the same people and all." She paused a moment, studying me over the rim of her cup. "You know I don't hold with divorce. The church is hard against it. But you never go to church anyway. You should but you don't. There's no reason you can't marry again. Of course, no Catholic man will have you, but even a Protestant husband is better than going off to some place where they'd just as soon shoot you as not."

Shooting's better than a life like you've had! I struggled to hold my tongue. "Mama, I am not going to marry anyone—Catholic or Protestant," I said at last, voice even.

"Ah, you say that now, but men are never going to let you alone. I don't want to be turning your head, but you're the prettiest of all my girls. And, even if I do say it myself, the Sullivans have always been known for their looks."

"I'm not a girl anymore," I reminded her. "I'm twenty-seven."

"You could still have a fine family. And next time it'll be different, you won't be running all over the place chasing fires and murderers. You'll be home looking after your husband and tending to your babies like a woman's supposed to."

I shook my head; there was no arguing with Mama. More than ever, I was grateful for the opportunity to get away, to change my life. I drained the cup, studying it idly. The pink roses were lovely but faded, the imported china chipped. A few scattered tea leaves remained at the bottom. Did they contain my fortune? Had I known, would it have mattered? I was ready.

4

Mouth of the Well of the Wizards

We sailed, a small party of archaeologists and me, on a freighter out of New York, on a cold, snowy morning in early January 1923.

I was odd girl out and felt it. The others, with their "doesn't everyone" approach to money, education, and privilege, were a different breed. So what? All that mattered was being there. My good fortune was still hard to believe. Not only a prize assignment, but a chance to change my life forever. No longer would I be half a couple—the unwanted half. I'd be myself. Whoever that was. Perhaps the Alma Reed I wanted to be didn't yet exist. I'd have to invent her.

The first day at sea was rough. Foam from cresting waves mixed with snow and sleet to turn the air a frothy white. Wonderful to look at but *cold*. Passengers in furs or thick overcoats jostled one another at the rail, their bright mufflers floating banners in the breeze. I shivered in my California coat as long as I could stand it, then fled below. In my small cabin, wrapped in blankets, I read about the steamy jungles of Yucatán.

As we continued southward and the temperature slowly rose, I ventured back to smell the sea. Leaning against the rail, trying to accustom myself to the slow, rolling motion of the ship, I determined to exorcise Sam once and for all. The icy fog shrouding the ship lifted, ocean swells now no more than ripples on a pond.

If allowed, I'd have spent all my time alone staring out at the sea, gray like a pewter platter, but Ann Morris wouldn't hear of it. She and Earl invariably rescued me from solitude, taking my hand, pulling me to a spot where they had spied some seabird, were sharing afternoon tea, or sat stargazing. Ann and Earl were newlyweds, their first scientific expedition together a kind of honeymoon. I couldn't keep my eyes off them, a crazy compulsion, like running one's tongue over a sore tooth. Sometimes his hand lightly caressing her bare arm drove me mad. But at other times, the love and trust in Ann's eyes as she looked at Earl brought tears to my own. Their endless glances at each other wearied me, but I wasn't weary of them. They were attractive, funny, and bright. When I was feeling blue, I wondered why a couple so complete in themselves bothered with me.

"You can't turn down a drink," Earl insisted. His light touch on my shoulder startled me. Only three days at sea and sunset watching had already become my solitary ceremony. Pale lavender shafts had just begun to pierce the flaming mélange of peach and topaz. I turned to him almost reluctantly. Earl was tall and awkward, myopic eyes dreamy behind thick glasses. "It's the real thing—not homemade hooch from someone's bathtub like you get in Frisco."

"We don't take Prohibition very seriously in *San Francisco*," I informed him. "Our mayor looks the other way. Rum runners come regularly from Canada." I thought of cliffside speakeasies down the coast, walks on the beach, night air blowing in from the sea, cold penetrating every pore. I remembered Sam's body pressed to mine inside a cocoon of heavy blankets, the taste of Scotch on each other's tongues.

"Yes!" I nodded vigorously. "A drink is exactly what I need. Whatever Captain Sanchez is pouring, I'll have a double."

Earl's eyes widened momentarily. I doubted he was used to such enthusiasm from women, at least about drinking, but his quick, broad smile put me at ease. He took my arm and led me to a makeshift bar set up near the stern. The others in our party appeared oblivious to the sunset. As usual, they talked about our destination, the "lost" city of the Maya. These archaeologists would be my news sources. They could make or break me.

I took the deck chair that Earl pulled toward me and, leaning forward, gave them my earnest look. "Chichen Itza—my editor at the *Times* insists on calling it 'that chicken place.'"

Sylvanus Morley, the expedition director, rearranged his dour face into the semblance of a smile as he passed me a drink. "I'm surprised he's interested enough to send a reporter."

"What he'd really like is for me to discover that the 'chicken place' has some kind of curse."

"Who knows, perhaps you will. Curses are à la mode these days." Ann laughed lightly, but cautioned: "In the meantime, teach the world to pronounce Chichen Itza correctly. Chee Chen Eetsa," she carefully mouthed.

Her soft voice had a cultivated, Eastern edge. Boston proper. No question about Ann's credentials. "Does it have a meaning?" I asked, turning toward her.

"A marvelous one. 'Mouth of the Well of the Itzas.' The Itza tribe lived in the area long ago. Their name is thought to mean 'wizard.'"

Just the sound of the words gave me a tingle. "When I got this assignment, I read everything I could lay my hands on about the Maya. There wasn't much. . . ." I hesitated, afraid of appearing foolish. "One theory comes up again and again: 'When Atlantis sank, Yucatán rose.' What do you think, Dr. Morley?"

"Balderdash!" Morley's drink splashed as he slammed it down on the railing. "Your Mr. Ochs undoubtedly wants a rehash of the lost continent theory, but don't let me catch you writing such drivel."

"But Sylvanus," Ann argued, brown eyes teasing—she was his pet and knew it—"nobody *really* knows."

All eight of them were talking at once, each arguing a theory. I looked from one to the other, surprised at their confusion. Perhaps these fancy-schmancy scientists didn't know much more about the Maya than I did. With a little luck, they might never guess that my anthropology degree was nothing more than wishful thinking. When the argument showed signs of subsiding, I ventured, "Has anyone tried to prove it one way or another?"

"How do you prove a myth?" Morley's tone was politely scornful, but after a moment he admitted that one man had tried. "Edward Thompson believed the Atlantis nonsense and found a couple of rich crackpots to finance an expedition. He took off for Yucatán nearly forty years ago with a wife and baby and never came back."

Startled, I looked up from my rum and cola. "He died down there?"

Morley shook his head. "To the contrary, he's very much alive. Thompson's wife and daughter returned to the States years ago, but he stayed on. They say he went native, has a Mayan family, lives in a dilapidated old hacienda—well, we'll soon see for ourselves."

It couldn't be soon enough for me. The voyage that I'd envisioned as glamorous had grown interminable. The sun baked the deck and steamed us in our berths. Back in my stifling cabin, the enormity of what I'd committed myself to hit me. This assignment was different from anything I'd ever done. What if I balled it up? I thought of Ann, just my age but cool and confident. She had it all, not only an adoring husband, but family background, a Radcliffe degree, and colleagues who respected her. Ann didn't have to prove anything to anyone.

Enough of that! I opened a fresh pack of Lucky Strikes, picked up the high school Spanish book I'd found in the attic at home, and began to study. Tried to study. It had been ten years since I'd pored over those dog-eared pages. I'd forgotten so much. The smell of diesel smoke permeated everything. The ship's pitch and toss made me queasy. I ground out the cigarette, turned another page. By the next morning I felt ready to practice on a deck hand.

"*¿Como esta usted?*"

"*Muy bien, gracias, señorita. ¿Y usted?*" he responded politely.

"*Muy bien.*"

So we were both fine. He waited politely while I searched my meager vocabulary for something more to say and came up blank. The boy smiled sympathetically and went back to scrubbing the deck.

My chief excitement came from reading *Incidents of Travel in Yucatán*. John Stephens, the intrepid author, and his artist companion, Frederick Catherwood, had encountered numerous plagues and revolutions—conditions still prevalent today. I speculated that these travel hazards might explain why his book, written some eighty years earlier, was still the only guide in print.

Politically, Mexico was a bomb waiting to go off—or maybe a series of bombs. My last day in San Francisco had been spent in the *News Call*'s morgue pouring through back issues. Mr. Older was at my side much of the time complementing what I read with his own recollections of stories behind the lurid headlines. Not a pretty picture. Porfirio Díaz, a so-called president, had reigned like a monarch for nearly forty years. For the rich, the Porfiriato was the best of times. For the poor, 80 percent of the population, it was the worst.

The eighty-year-old Díaz got himself reelected in 1910 by not counting the votes, but within a year revolution swept the country. Chaos and anarchy—ten years of it. As Mr. Older and I pored over the paper's bound volumes, I recognized many of the headlines, recalled my revulsion as one faction after another fought its way to prominence, united with another, then dissolved into violent conflict.

The most recent chapter of the decade-long holocaust was a fatal duel between the winners. Carranza's term as president was supposed to end in 1920. Obregón expected to succeed his cohort. When Carranza reneged, open warfare erupted between the two. Just three years ago Carranza had been shot by one of Obregón's officers. What next? I wondered. How long would Obregón remain president? What kind of mess was I walking into?

My eyes returned to Stephens's book lying on the table. Its illustrations, intricate lithographs, showed mysterious vine-covered pyramids and palaces, but also jaguars, snakes, and bandits. I felt scared; maybe I liked that fear. I'd signed on for adventure and that's what I would surely have.

Whatever fate had in store for me, I was eager to reach Yucatán. No bigger than a closet, my so-called stateroom was filled with books and boxes. As we traveled southward, the one porthole jammed and the air grew suffocating. I found scant relief on deck. Space was shared with twenty cows neatly tagged for Yucatán. Dazzling heat waves enveloped all of us. The sea, calm now, was an endless waste without a wrinkle, sometimes blue, sometimes green, silver white in the evening, bright indigo at dawn. At night the stars, so many and bright, looked barely beyond reach. I longed to fly to them.

A day and a night, and another day and night, and yet another passed—hot, dull, malodorous hours marked by bouts of intermittent anger. Despite the sea change and prospect of imminent adventure, I continued to think of

Sam. Nearly two years and I couldn't get the picture of him and Theoline out of my mind. Our bed, their arms and legs sprawled across the patchwork quilt that had been our wedding gift.

One morning I awakened to the awesome silence of stopped engines. Someone hammered at the door— "Breakfast served"—then a terrific blast on the whistle. I dressed quickly and hurried out on deck. Before me was a radiant stretch of beach, green coconut palms against a bright blue sky, and the long line of pink and blue build-ings that comprised the coastal town of Progreso. There was no breeze in the port city; the earth smelled damp, fecund, acid. A new smell. Despite the heat, a shiver of anticipation ran through me. Yucatán at last.

I hoped the train to Mérida wasn't an omen. Several windows were missing, while strips of tape held the re-maining ones together. Although our car was marked first class, it resembled a poultry show. Perhaps no self-re-specting Yucatecan traveled without an entourage of live fowl. I saw chickens in baskets, turkeys in sacks, geese tied in family bed linen. And then there were the pigs.

My white voile blouse, fresh and crisp an hour before, stuck damply to my shoulder blades. I unpinned my wide-brimmed hat and placed it on the rack above the worn seat, then sat down beside Dr. Morley, across the aisle from Ann and Earl. The train lurched forward, sounded a *whooooooo whoooo* warning whistle. Good-bye, Sam.

Hello . . . hello what? Did *what* matter? Surely all that counted was *where*. I was going somewhere. Excited by the staccato clack of the rails, I forgot the heat.

Picking up my notebook, I turned to Dr. Morley. "That man, the archaeologist Edward Thompson, has he discovered anything in Chichen Itza?"

"One hardly knows how seriously to take him." Morley's broad forehead knit in a frown. "Thompson's reports are intriguing, to say the least. For years the Carnegie's wanted to send someone down to investigate."

Puzzled, I looked up from my notebook. "So why haven't they?"

"The Mexicans would never allow it, even before the revolution threw the country into turmoil. Now, suddenly, here's this new reform governor issuing an invitation. As you know, ours is the first scientific expedition to visit Chichen Itza. No one knows what to make of it, or of him, for that matter."

"Really? What's the new governor like?" I asked, retrieving my hat to use as a fan.

"Felipe Carrillo Puerto?" Dr. Morley's lip curled. "He's a Bolshevik, a so-called man of the people."

I stiffened. That tone, so elitist. "You don't approve?"

"The old families know how to run the country," he assured me, leaning back in his seat. "They should, they've been doing it for centuries. Now along comes this rabble-rouser, stirring things up, making changes. Just wait and see, someone will put a stop to that in short order. Perhaps someone like Colonel Broca—"

"Who's he?"

"A hacendado who knows which side his bread is buttered on. He's sworn to put the governor and his infernal changes out of business for good."

"Perhaps it's time for change."

Morley looked at me as though I'd taken leave of my senses. "Not if it drives henequen prices up."

"Henequen?" I asked "What's that?"

"A kind of hemp. It rules the economy here," he explained. "The hacendados—plantation owners—got their grants from the king of Spain four hundred years ago. Most families hung on to them, too, a fine heritage. Those men knew what they were about, ran a tight ship, kept costs down. Now along comes this damn fool, who's breaking up their holdings, giving land to the Indians. I tell you he's not too popular in Washington."

"So much the better," I said, closing my notebook and sitting back with a sense of pleased anticipation. "Sounds like enough material for a dozen stories."

"I'm surprised you'd leave your husband for so long." Ann leaned across the aisle, her hand brushing Earl's sleeve.

"Husband?"

"I thought I heard Captain Sanchez call you *Mrs.* Reed."

"I have no husband," I answered abruptly.

I read astonishment in her wide eyes, and probably disapproval. Neither surprised me. My own family disapproved. Divorces were few and far between, even in San Francisco.

"I'm a widow," I surprised myself by saying. But then, why not?

Sam was dead to me.

5

The Red Devil with Green Eyes

Mérida charmed me—a white city turning antique ivory in the lamplight. Our party rode in vintage taxis—*fortingas,* I'd heard them called—but, all around us, horse-drawn carriages clopped through the twilight.

White mansions reminded me of wedding cakes. People crowded the streets, walking briskly, eagerly, like lovers headed for a tryst. White pants and open-necked pleated shirts set off the warm, brown skin of the men. Women looked like frothy confections, their loose-fitting white shifts worn over lacy petticoats, a profusion of brilliantly embroidered flowers spilling across bodices and hemlines. I felt warmed and welcomed, but also set apart. Could I be part of this scene? Was there a place for me here? I hoped so.

The Gran Hotel's massive doors and lacy grillwork whispered of another time, my room so voluptuous with its gold swag drapes on the high windows. A balcony overlooked a lush garden flaming with exotic blooms. Inside, the carved mahogany bed reminded me that it had been more than an hour since I'd thought of Sam.

Dinner in the hotel dining room promised to be a festive affair hosted by the government of Yucatán. I dressed carefully—satin gown drawn in about the hips by a silver sash that matched my turban. Blue's my color; the dress was the same shade as my eyes. After Dad's disappearance his big baby blues were our only legacy. All ten of us Sullivans have them—not a bad inheritance. Mine have opened plenty of doors. Now, I'd determined to interview Felipe Carrillo Puerto, the renegade reformer that Dr. Morley had described on the train. Though considered a brilliant archaeologist by many, I secretly thought Morley a pompous bore. During the trip his reactionary remarks had caused me to bite my tongue any number of times. It wouldn't do to let the old windbag know what I really thought, but, truth be told, the revolutionary leader sounded like a man after my own heart. Writing about the ruins of Chichen Itza was fine—better than fine, a dream come true. After years of sob sistering on the *News Call,* I'd created a niche for myself writing about widows and orphans. Mrs. Goodfellow was a household name in San Francisco, but I wanted more. A lot more. Instinct told me that covering the governor's cause would further my own.

I took my time, descended the curving stairway slowly while everyone watched, eyes admiring. Everyone but Felipe Carrillo Puerto. The governor had been detained by official business. His representative was a small, slight man, scarcely into his twenties. He introduced himself to us as Jorge Lopez and apologized profusely.

"You will meet His Excellency the day after tomorrow at a ribbon-cutting ceremony," he promised our group. "Afterward your party will travel his new jungle highway to the ruins of Chichen Itza."

The others murmured delightedly when told that a sightseeing trip of Mérida had been arranged for the next day, but I stepped forward. "I want to see the governor tomorrow—tomorrow morning."

"I am most sorry, *señorita*." Jorge's shiny dark eyes instantly turned regretful. "His Excellency is very busy. So many important projects claim his attention. But of course," his teeth flashed beneath a drooping mustache, "you will see him at the ceremony."

"I represent the *Times*," I reminded him, "the *New York Times*. You must be aware that many in the United States view your governor as a communist. Surely time can be found for me to speak with him alone—perhaps an hour?"

Jorge wavered for what seemed a very long time, then bowed. "I shall do my utmost, *señorita*."

The following morning, I stood in the lobby fuming impatiently while the others gaily assembled for their city tour.

"It's hopeless," Dr. Morley warned me. "Mexicans can't bear to say no, particularly to a pretty woman. Jorge never had any intention of arranging an appointment. Better come with us; you don't want to miss Mérida. It may be your only chance. Tomorrow we leave for the interior."

I did want to see Mérida very much, but the possibility of an exclusive interview with the controversial governor was too important to risk. Just then a bellman rushed in—cars and drivers waited outside. I followed the group to the curb. Everyone was getting in. One seat remained.

Drivers cranked up the engines of their *fortingas*. Forcing a confident smile, I waved them out of sight. Back in the hotel lobby, with its twirling ceiling fans and crystal chandeliers, I selected a quiet corner with a direct view of the doorway. Sinking into a high-backed velvet couch, I ordered coffee and began a postcard to Mama.

Twenty minutes later Jorge Lopez appeared, breathless. "Señorita Reed, I feared you might have gone! His Excellency has agreed to a brief interview. His car is waiting outside. I shall take you to the government office."

At five foot seven, I towered over most Mayas, but the man who rose to greet me from behind a well-ordered desk was at least six feet tall.

"*¿Usted esta journalista de New York Times?!*" he asked, surprise apparent in his voice. His dark eyebrows rose as his eyes met mine.

"*Sí.*" I nodded, returning his stare. A slow smile spread over the governor's face. It appeared that I wasn't what he'd expected either.

Our eyes caught and held. For a second or two, I felt dizzy. The world stood still, my world anyway.

"*Usted es muy amable* to—to see me." I heard myself, as though from a great distance, struggling in terrible Spanish. "I know how busy you are—*pero tengo poquito preguntas, muy poquito.*"

The governor's size as he leaned over me wasn't the only surprise. Studying him closely, I saw that his lineage was mixed. Somewhere in Felipe Carrillo Puerto's background flowed the blood of a conquistador. Though thick and coarse like an Indian's, his hair was light brown, his eyes clear green. I thought of a jungle cat, hungry and dangerous. He stepped closer with the sudden grace of that powerful animal. The governor took my hand and kissed it. "It will be my pleasure, my honor, to answer *all* your questions." His English was flawless, with only the slightest trace of an accent.

His hand still held mine. His scent was warm and musky: tobacco and leather, I thought. Backing away from the long, feline slope of him, I took the chair opposite the governor's desk.

"Where did you learn your English?" I gasped.

He shrugged slightly. "From myself."

When I cocked my head inquisitively, the governor explained. "I learned English one word at a time from a dictionary when I was a boy." He smiled depreciatively. "I know—my pronunciation is often wrong."

"On the contrary, it's near perfect," I assured him. My fingers fumbled as I opened my bag, reached for a note-book and pencil. He watched silently, his cat eyes estimating and challenging me. Delighted to abandon my fractured Spanish, I began the interview with a question about his constituency. Trite, maybe, but I had to begin somewhere.

"Fewer than a hundred hacendados—plantation own-ers—dominate everything in Yucatán," the governor explained. His words seemed to come from somewhere far away. "Until recently women of mixed blood were forbid-den to wear anything but *huipiles*. Hacienda workers could be beaten for merely looking an overseer in the eye."

I stood outside myself, watching, listening. "It sounds no better than slavery," I heard myself say.

"It *was* no better than slavery," he agreed. "Soon after the conquest of Mexico, the king of Spain gave Francisco de Montejo a—a—what do you call it—a franchise, yes, a franchise. His piece of the 'New' World was to be Yuca-tán. Perhaps you noticed the Montejo palace on your way here?"

"That large building across from the plaza?" I responded. I was back inside myself, a reporter once again.

He nodded, full lips curving in a faint smile. "You must have seen the Montejo crest, a foot planted on the head of a slave? It is repeated the length of the building. Descendants of the conquistador still live there. Do you find the architecture interesting? Much of it was built from stones stolen from a Mayan temple."

I wondered at the governor's seeming detachment, didn't believe the cool facade, not for a minute. Had his mixed blood been a political asset or a liability? What might it have cost him emotionally? "A man of the people," Sylvanus had called him, but *what* people? Clearly his Mayan background was only part of the story. Not a place to go this morning, but I determined to learn the answer. For now, a safer subject. "Cortez took only two years to conquer the Aztecs," I pointed out. "Why do you think the Maya held out so long? Why were they the last Indians subdued?"

"Ah, you've studied our history. Very good." He smiled again. This time the pleasure appeared genuine. "Indians in other parts of Mexico believed the tall, blond Spaniards to be superhuman beings. We knew better. Two sailors had been shipwrecked off the coast of Yucatán a few years before the conquest. The Maya who'd held them prisoner had no illusions."

His green eyes watched me intently. "Do you understand my English?"

"Of course!" I relaxed, smiling. Was the governor fishing for compliments? "It's excellent," I assured him, thinking how foolish my Spanish must have sounded.

He paused momentarily, his eyes again on me. "It wasn't fear of the supernatural that we fought," he resumed, "just men, superior weapons, and smallpox. As your books must have told you, the Spaniards struggled more than twenty years to vanquish the Maya while the rest of Mexico was in chains." His eyes still on mine, their expression once more appraising. "Montejo and his men considered the battle over in 1547, but, in truth, our resistance has never ended—*will* never end."

His words felt ominous. My fingers raced across the paper, trying to keep pace. I was amazed by the governor's textbook English. How many hours had it taken him to learn it? Word by word from a dictionary. Amazing! Pausing at last, I looked up to see him still watching. This time I didn't look away. "That's what you're doing now, isn't it? You're putting the Maya back in charge of their own world."

"Surely a woman as beautiful as yourself has no wish to hear such things."

"I wish to hear about you. I mean, I'd like to hear about your reforms."

Again he was silent. It seemed that several minutes passed. "Perhaps," the governor said at last, "perhaps you'd like to see a few of them in action?"

"Can you spare the time?"

"I can think of no better use for it." He was on his feet, ordering his car, canceling the day's appointments.

As we descended the marble stairs to the street, the driver was already cranking a car into motion. Felipe Carrillo Puerto opened the door with a flourish and helped me inside. It was a tan touring car, open at the sides with a canvas canopy. We would have a splendid view. When he dismissed the driver and took the wheel himself, I felt a twinge of apprehension. I'd be alone with this man. Where would he take me? He was the most powerful man in the state. The governor's mouth broadened into a boyish smile. I found myself smiling back. I liked that power.

He maneuvered skillfully through the teeming streets of Mérida, narrow lanes laid out in a time of conquistadors and carriages. As we headed out the Paseo de Montejo, the street broadened into a boulevard shaded by stately tamarinds and tropical oaks. On either side was an architectural sampler of beaux arts palaces, mosquelike mansions, and stately châteaux, shimmering together in the bright sunlight.

"A fortune has been made and spent here," he said, following my eyes, "which is all very well if the largesse is shared even in a small way. It is not and never has been."

I studied the governor's profile, trying to measure his power. This urbane, soft-spoken man had, I knew, fought beside revolutionaries in the brutal ten-year holocaust that had laid waste to most of the country. I tried to picture him on a galloping horse, cartridge belts crossing his chest, riding with Zapata or even Villa. "They say in the States that you want to change everything overnight. Dr. Morley even called you a Bolshevik. What do you have to say to that?"

He smiled at me again. "Women vote in Yucatán, did you know that?"

Bolshevik or not, I was impressed. This was a change I strongly approved. At home we'd had the vote scarcely three years. My eyes drifted to his strong brown fingers on the steering wheel. *A man in his position must have had many mistresses. He would know just how to please a woman. . . .* What had come over me?! Why would I think of such a thing?

I caught my breath, hurried on with the interview. "Your wife must be very pleased with that innovation." It was easy for me to envision the woman he would choose, a true helpmeet, someone bright, attractive, and compassionate. She, too, would be an idealist, perhaps with an agenda of her own involving the advancement of other women.

To my surprise his smile faded. "Isabel does not involve herself in politics."

Really! I couldn't imagine such a thing. It took me a minute to digest. I felt the governor watching me. "What about schools?" I asked, squeezing my pencil tightly as I pressed down on the pad. "What's your policy on that?"

"I've built a number of them, a model prison too," he replied. "Our newest project is the road linking Mérida to Chichen Itza. You and your group will travel there tomorrow. The Carnegie archaeologists are the first, but soon the whole world will come to see and understand the Mayan heritage."

"Really? Do you think anyone will ever understand it?" I asked, my voice consciously soft, not the usual brisk interview style. "I've read everything I could find about the Maya—there isn't much. I know that they could write, but I understand the conquistadors destroyed every indication of culture that they could find. That Montejo person you were talking about must have been a real zealot. I interviewed the archaeologists on the boat coming down here. They're afraid that everything was lost. What I'd like to know from you is where did the Maya come from? Why did they walk away and just abandon their great cities?"

"Why, indeed?" He shrugged. "Here we have a saying, perhaps you have heard it—*¿quien sabe?*"

His eyes were laughing. I laughed back, wondering what it would be like to kiss his mouth. "Who knows! That's the best you can do?"

"That is all I know, all that anyone knows at this time. Perhaps one day you and the others will give *me* the answers to those questions. That is why I invited the archaeologists to come here." He paused, his eyes on mine, wary but searching. "I can see that you are interested. You care about Yucatán," he said at last, "I feel it. The secrets of the Maya have yet to be uncovered; that will take time. But, perhaps for today, you would like to see what is happening in Yucatán now. May I take you to Kanasin, a newly completed village? It is not far."

I nodded happily. It wouldn't have mattered if Kanasin were on the other side of the moon.

Before long we were out in the countryside, the car bouncing from one pothole to another. How would I ever read my notes? After a time I gave up taking them, choosing instead to listen to the governor's voice and watch the play of expressions on his face as he turned to me from time to time. I wondered if he had any idea of the happiness that had taken possession of me.

Looking away, I turned my attention to the scene around us. The stately mansions had given way to clusters of round Mayan houses with palm-thatched roofs. On cloths weighted by stones, women had spread melon slices, tortillas, and beer. I saw towers of pottery and passed by bare-footed Indians bent almost double under staggering bundles of maize. Women plodded with their babies slung in rebozos. Surely a different world from the Paseo de Montejo.

Before long this teeming neighborhood was also behind us and we were alone on a dusty road. On either side, fields planted in orderly rows stretched to infinity. The crop's long, sharp bayonet leaves reminded me of cactus.

"You're looking at green gold," the governor said. "Henequen is Yucatán's blessing and its curse. The leaves are made into rope. Everyone wants it—your country most of all. The hacendados have become rich beyond their wildest dreams—but it's the Maya who continue to pay the price."

The residents of Kanasin went a little crazy when they saw their governor. Men and women cheered, children ran alongside us, showering the car with hastily gathered flowers. Someone appeared with a battered trumpet. Suddenly there were two guitars. With an impromptu concert underway, people reached eagerly for our hands, bowed, gestured for us to come into their homes, have a cup of cold water, view a new building, a freshly painted wall.

There was a school to see, a small clinic, and a park with newly planted trees. The interiors of the round, thatch-roofed houses looked almost identical—dirt floors, simple, handmade tables and chairs, pictures of saints, and hammocks. No beds, just hammocks. How did these people make love? I looked about at the many small children darting here and there. They managed somehow.

I saw the governor smile and blushed.

"We have family planning clinics in Yucatán," he volunteered.

In the United States, birth control was a hot potato that no politician would touch. Had I met a true idealist—as well as a mind reader?

Felipe Carrillo Puerto glanced at his pocket watch, exclaiming, "*Por favor!* Forgive me! You must be hungry. I know North Americans are often bewildered by our dining hours."

I smiled at him appreciatively. I was starving.

"We shall return to Mérida right away. There's an excellent French restaurant that I believe you will like."

"I'm sure I would, but isn't that a café?" I pointed to a white stucco building with a thatched roof.

"The food is very simple here, not at all what you're accustomed to."

"All the more reason for me to try it."

The governor smiled broadly as we entered the small restaurant. All conversation stopped and then quickly resumed, an excited buzz. Every eye followed us, friendly, admiring glances. I felt their pleasure and approval. The owner hurried forward, then bowed low. A few words were exchanged, not Spanish, possibly Maya. He returned quickly, smiling proudly. In his hands was a tray of hot tortillas, flat corn cakes filled sandwich-style with venison. The dish was new to me, new and delicious.

Everything around us looked sharper, clearer, brighter; the sounds, too, seemed somehow amplified. A sense of exhilaration swept over me. Feeling better than I had in weeks, I lifted a glass of dark local beer in a toast. "To the future, Your Excellency." Oh, dear, what was I saying? I meant his *political* future, of course.

"The future—I like that," he said, taking my other hand, "but please, not Your Excellency. I hope you will always call me Felipe."

I'm here for an interview, just an interview, I reminded myself. I disengaged my hand.

"Your Excellency," I crisply resumed, "all those years of slavery . . . was there nothing that anyone could do?"

"Many of us tried," he said, his face briefly registering disappointment at my withdrawal, "but it wasn't until the revolution finally reached Yucatán that the old ways were finally challenged."

"But that's so recent! How long have you been governor?"

"Just over a year."

I stared at him, amazed. "You've done so much."

He nodded, smiling, his eyes on mine. "But so much remains to be done."

That evening I sat alone in my opulent room at the Gran. Reflected in the mirror before me was the mahogany bed. So large, too large for me alone. I opened the dressing table drawer and took out my journal. "The governor seems as good as he is handsome," I wrote. "Too bad he has a wife." Children, too, I imagined, putting the journal away.

The earlier exhilaration had dissipated, leaving me depressed. How silly I'd been, how mad. The feelings that had exploded so suddenly, so inexplicably, were hopeless, unthinkable. I despised Sam and Theoline for their betrayal. It disgusted me that I should feel such desire for a man legally and morally bound to another. A bad joke had been played on me. Were the perpetrators my mother's saints or his Mayan gods? Did it matter? The irony was not amusing.

Somewhere outside I heard soft music playing. Beautiful music, melodious and passionate. I stepped out onto the balcony. Wrought-iron lamps, lemon yellow, pooled their light and shadow on a small group of mariachis standing just below. They were dressed in white and wore broad sombreros.

The men sang late into the warm tropic night. The moist air felt heavy with the scent of jasmine. I smoked a cigarette, leaning against the railing, swaying slightly to the music, studying the mariachis below: limpid brown eyes, great, bristling mustaches. Their faces were sad, their songs soulful. What were the words?

I leaned forward, straining to hear, but recognized only one: *Amor. Amor. Amor.* Sighing softly, I gave up and went to bed.

The Temple of Kukulkan

Somewhere in the distance a church bell tolled somberly. Unimpressed, the brightly plumaged birds in the garden below continued their hysterical squawking. They'd been up for hours. So had I.

Standing before a full-length mirror, I carefully knotted the tie beneath the collar of my long-sleeved blouse, then stepped back to survey the effect. I'd never worn trousers before. These molded to my full hips and thighs in a manner that seemed awfully revealing. I'd have to get used to it. White shirts and tan twill jodhpurs would be my uniform for the next six weeks.

Above me the ceiling fan whirled noisily. Though hardly past nine, the air felt hot and sticky. I recalled the cool, gray morning I'd bought my digging clothes. "They're all the rage in Egypt," the Emporium's fashion consultant assured me. She was so perfect: confident, knowing, a sophisticated San Franciscan, only slightly condescending. I remembered her crêpe de chine sailor dress shimmering in the flattering lamplight. Puce, wasn't it? Between her assurance and my eager excitement, I would have bought anything.

Now I was glad Mama couldn't see me. She had lots to say about women who wore trousers. Pulling on the high leather boots, I tucked in my pant legs. The boots helped. That woman in the mirror looked ready for anything. At least I *hoped* she did. Grabbing my pith helmet, I hurried to join the others.

Down the hall, Ann and Earl emerged from their room. As usual, Ann was à la mode. Her petite body, fashionably boyish like Theoline's, was perfect for trousers. Sam admired that look. Lots of men did. I wondered about the governor, then chided myself. What difference did it make?!

I took a deep breath and smiled at the approaching couple. Earl saluted me. Ann lightly squeezed my arm. "Isn't this the bee's knees?" she exclaimed. "We're on our way to Chichen Itza!"

Ann spoke too soon. Nothing could have prepared us for the sorry caravan of vehicles parked outside the hotel. Looking at the ancient, multicolored cars, I suspected that Felipe Carrillo Puerto had spent so much money building the road that nothing remained for state limousines. Perhaps the touring car he'd taken me out in yesterday was Yucatán's one and only. Our party surveyed the worn tires, broken lights, and cracked windows dubiously. The archaeologists hesitated, looking at one another. The governor, standing beside the lead car, watched only me. Did anyone else notice the sparks between us?

"Perhaps we should be on our way," I murmured to Dr. Morley. "Shall I ride in this one?" Without waiting for an answer, I clambered in beside the driver of the nearest car. Others followed until each vehicle was crammed with archaeologists and their gear.

It took nearly ten minutes of spirited engine cranking before our cars were under way, snorting black smoke, jolting and bouncing down the ancient streets of Mérida. The whole city seemed to have turned out to see us off. Narrow sidewalks swelled with waving well-wishers. I waved back until road dust obscured them from view.

For a time we passed through the same spiky rows of henequen I'd seen the previous day. Then, quite abruptly, the scene changed. Orderly fields gave way to tangled growth. The road, a slim ribbon, threaded its way through infinity. Distance ceased to exist in this green twilight where strangely contorted trees, towering plants, and feathery ferns crowded around us. Every growing thing, even the flower petals, exuded a warm, moist stickiness, dense and thick to breathe. Brilliantly feathered birds screeched angrily; I could imagine jaguars slipping in and out of the forest shadows.

Finally, we rounded a curve. Instead of another vista of unchanging jungle, the road stretched straight for a mile or so to a sight of breathtaking grandeur. In the distance, a great white pyramid towered above emerald foliage, at its top a square stone temple. My breath caught. There was a moment of stunned silence from everyone, then we were all crying out excitedly and pointing to the view before us.

At last we had reached the fabled city-state of Chichen Itza. I shivered with anticipation. So this was what Francisco de Montejo and the other conquistadors had seen four hundred years earlier. Their letters overflowed with superlatives, vain attempts to describe the indescribable. Would I, could I, do better? Was it possible to bring the majesty and wonder of these ruins to readers unlikely to ever see them? I vowed to do my best.

Archaeologists scrambled out of their cars, each hurrying in a different direction. I got out and stood uncertainly. There were so many mysterious mounds, like small hills, all of them covered by trees and dense shrubs. Each whispered of barbaric, splendorous times long past: ball games fought to the death, burials that heaped the dead with jewels, victory ceremonies around the pyramid before me. I stared up, awestruck by that great towering structure.

"How do you do," a white-haired man approached me, hand extended. "I'm Edward Thompson. You'll be staying at my hacienda," he explained in a thin, raspy voice that made me wonder if his vocal cords weren't shutting down.

"Alma Reed, the *New York Times*," I introduced myself.

"A reporter?" Thompson withdrew his hand. "No one told me about a reporter."

I flashed my disarming smile, searched his eyes, on level with my own. "I've so looked forward to this. I'm eager to hear all about your work. Perhaps I could also write about your house. I understand it has quite a history."

He studied me, stroking his white beard. "The house, yes; it is old. Montejo, the conquistador of Yucatán, built it. I could take you there now. My wife can get you settled."

"You're very kind, but I want to explore the ruins first." I looked about at the mystifying mounds that surrounded us. There was so much to explore. . . . What first? "I'm going to climb this pyramid," I told him, pointing to the great structure looming above us.

"Oh, no!" Thompson's eyes widened. "That's much too dangerous for a woman. You can see that it's badly overgrown. You could easily trip on roots. . . . The stones are loose. A fall could be fatal." He took my arm, "I can't allow you—the risk is much too great."

I pulled back, annoyed at his interference, but just then Felipe spoke. He had apparently detached himself from Morley and the others and stood now at my side. "Of course you must see the pyramid, our Temple of Ku-kulkan. I shall be your guide."

"Ku-kul-kan." I savored the unfamiliar word.

"He was the most powerful god, our sacred Plumed Serpent," the governor explained as we walked. "You will see his image everywhere in Chichen. Climb to the top with me and I will tell you the story." He nodded to Thompson. "Don't worry, Don Eduardo. I'll be with her every step of the way."

He was, too—walking close behind me all the way to the top. I worried about his view of my trousered bottom, but what could I do? After awhile I was too tired to even think of it. There were 364 steps, I would learn later. All were in ruinous condition, but that wasn't the worst. Instead of constructing a step deep enough to accommodate a normal foot, the Mayans had made each so shallow that one had to climb sideways like a crab. At least that's how I did it. They also had made the risers so high that I could hardly keep my chin out of the way of my knees. Trying desperately not to look down, I pulled myself up, clinging to slippery roots, hugging the steps so tightly with the soles of my feet, digging my toes in so urgently, that by the time I got to the top, my muscles felt as though they would explode.

I climbed the last step and sank wearily down onto the flat stone floor at the top. It was about the size of an average living room, at its center a square temple open on four sides. The archaeologists below were hardly more than specks but I could make out Thompson and Dr. Morley leaning toward each other, their postures tense. Were they arguing? "What do you suppose that's all about?" I asked Felipe, my breath still coming in gasps.

"It is hard to tell, where Thompson's concerned."

"Why do you say that?" I asked.

"Thompson—we call him Don Eduardo—is a strange man who prefers to stay to himself. He lost most of his hearing, some say in a diving accident."

"Where would anyone dive here?" I looked out over the tangled jungle below.

"There are many stories. Something about an old well. I have been too busy with other things to investigate the rumor." Felipe shrugged dismissively. "He and his Mayan wife have been alone so many years in this deserted place. No wonder the man is a bit eccentric."

The governor took off his jacket and spread it out for me on the stones. The small, square temple only a few feet away was open at the side to reveal an altar. A wave of revulsion swept over me as I recalled the gruesome accounts I'd read. Sacrificial victims had climbed these very steps only to be arched backward across that altar, chests sliced open, fountains of blood spurting free as their hearts were ripped out before still-seeing eyes.

I turned to the governor, reclining on the parapet beside me. His eyes on mine, he drew a silver case from his pocket. I watched his tanned fingers as he removed two cigarettes, lit them, and handed one to me. For an instant, our hands touched.

"How did you know I smoke?"

"I knew. . . . Did you enjoy the music?"

"Music?" I looked at him, puzzled.

"Last night, the mariachis."

"You sent them?"

"I wanted to think of them there beneath your window, lulling you to sleep. Do you know how much I envied them? I was watching, not far away."

"They were . . . very lovely." I turned my head to avoid his gaze. "I should like to hear the legend of Kukulkan."

"Legend? Perhaps," he speculated, "but many of us believe the story to be true. Kukulkan is said to have introduced astronomy and mathematics to the Maya. His creed was love and brotherhood."

I leaned back, inhaling deeply as I surveyed the ruins below. "Sounds too good to be true."

"It was," Felipe admitted. "Kukulkan vowed celibacy and promised to devote his . . . his energies—very considerable energies—to uniting the warring peoples."

I laughed nervously, but the governor continued. "Kukulkan was seduced by a beautiful woman. Conspirators drugged him at a ceremonial feast and he could not resist her. After his public humiliation, the god abandoned everything and sailed away in a flaming boat. Some say

Kukulkan's heart flew out of his body and merged with the sun. At any rate, he never returned."

I didn't know how to reply. The theme struck too close to home. Try as he might, Kukulkan had been unable to suppress his virility. The man beside me also seemed mythic, idealistic, already something of a god to the people he'd helped to free.

The governor's eyes searched mine.

This time I didn't look away. "I understand that you're married."

"Yes."

"No doubt you have many children."

"I have four."

Hardly a handicap in Mexico. I wondered if the governor's idealism extended to his private life. Such an attractive man would have many temptations. I resolved not to be one of them.

Stubbing out my cigarette, I sat up. "If Kukulkan was so peace-loving—why the killing?"

"Some blame the Toltecs, a warrior race from the north, for introducing blood sacrifices." He paused, looking at me. "Now I believe that Kukulkan will change again and, this time, it is you who will fulfill his plan."

I looked at the governor in amazement. What was he talking about?

He smiled at my surprise. "Why are you here if not to tell the world of the Maya's glorious past?"

"Is that good?" I asked, voicing an issue that had begun to nag at me. "Archaeologists are one thing, meticulous scientists, most of them. But eventually, there will be tourists. This is an old place, a sacred place. Imagine it overrun with strangers, people who don't know or understand its mysteries. Yucatán will change."

"Yucatán *must* change. The dependence on henequen has to end. Tourism will be our salvation, an industry without smokestacks."

I looked at him uncertainly, fearful of sounding foolish. "Chichen Itza has such a sense of power. I feel somehow as though the old gods never left." Hesitating, uncertainly, I ventured, almost whispering. "What—what if they're here now, watching?"

"You mean the curse?" Felipe's voice was gentle as he searched my face. "You can speak freely. I am aware of the talk. I have heard the old *brujas*, the witch women. Many of them . . . well, how else can I say it? They are ignorant. They live in the past and still forget it. The thought of archaeologists digging into secrets, the idea of strangers exploring the sacred city, frightens them. They no longer remember that Chichen Itza was a commercial center as well as a ceremonial one. Ek Chuah, the Mayan god of commerce, would welcome tourists and the trade they will generate for our artisans."

Looking out at the monuments of cold stone protruding here and there from the vast sea of jungle, I tried to imagine what Chichen Itza must once have been.

As though reading my thoughts, the governor conjured up the ancient scene. "Down there," he pointed to the tangled, vine-covered courtyard below, "vendors would have hawked sandals, knives, blankets, and weavings brought from South America. Can't you just imagine the noise they must have made?" I could indeed. Watching the governor, listening to his melodious voice, my imagination caught fire. The site came alive as I smelled the rare spices, saw the flash of precious jewels. "There would have been cages of hairless dogs—over there, I think"— he pointed toward a clearing below—"chattering monkeys, too, and parrots squawking words."

"Mayan swear words?" I suggested.

"Very probably." He laughed. "Parrots are parrots, but here there would also have been feather merchants, goldsmiths, healers, and scribes."

"Too bad some storyteller isn't around today to tell us what happened," I lamented. "Why did they build this great city, this fantastic city, only to desert it?"

"Perhaps one day you, little *peregrina,* will find the answer to that riddle."

"*Peregrina*?"

"Pilgrim. Is that not what you are? A traveler who will all too soon return to your own far-off land."

"Yes," I assured the governor, ignoring the challenge in his eyes. "I *will* be returning home very soon, just as soon as the expedition is over."

Hunac Ceel's Legacy

Edward Thompson and his hacienda had seen better days. The old house, built some three centuries earlier, must once have been splendid. By 1923, it was falling to ruin; still, the slight man with his trim white beard reigned there like a king—or at least a *don*. That's what everyone called him, Don Eduardo. As American consul to Yucatán and the Carnegie's man there, it was expected that he would assist the expedition, but from the beginning, I sensed his reluctance.

There wasn't room in the hacienda for everyone. Dr. Morley, after one look at Don Eduardo's careless ménage, pets and servants' children roaming at will, announced that he'd stay in a thatched hut out back. Two archaeologists decided to bunk with him. Ann and Earl were eager to set up housekeeping in a smaller cottage at the edge of the tangled mass of bougainvillea and morning glories that passed for a garden. The other members of the team went off to survey the estate's numerous outbuildings.

I was about to follow when Don Eduardo stopped me. "We can find something for you inside." Nodding to his wife, Celestina, Don Eduardo spoke a few words in what I took to be Maya. Apparently she didn't speak English, or even much Spanish. Celestina's brown button eyes regarded me sullenly. I smiled brightly. Unimpressed, she flounced from the room, bare feet slapping angrily at the red tile floor. A few minutes later, when a servant appeared to show me to my new quarters, I couldn't believe my luck.

The large, sunny room had high-beamed ceilings and louvered windows overlooking an inner courtyard. Jaguar skins covered the floor. A variety of religious paintings—Ascensions, mostly—stared beatifically down from the adobe walls; very old, I judged, probably museum quality. At the far end of the room was an immense carved armoire. Such a splendid antique would command a fortune in San Francisco. I tried to picture the women who would have accepted such elegance as their due. The mansion must have been a showplace when the Montejo family owned it.

The hacienda's spacious *sala,* an architectural legacy from some Spanish castle, served as our dining room.

Sitting down at the carved mahogany table that first evening, I ran my hand lightly over the scuffed woodwork recognizing classic Mayan images—jaguars, sunbursts, and snakes. The workmanship was marvelous. I was living in an art gallery.

There were twelve of us at the table, all struggling to hear and be heard. The large room, its high ceilings filled with echoes, didn't lend itself to easy conversation. Ordinary chitchat degenerated into shouting matches: " 'Better,' did you say? *Better* or *butter*?" Don Eduardo, seated at the head of the table, watched the young archaeologists wistfully, faded eyes straining as he looked from one to the other. The governor had mentioned a diving injury. How much of the conversation could the old man follow? Poor fellow. His adventures were over, theirs just beginning.

I liked the hacienda, with its cool adobe walls and tile floors, loved the bright bougainvillea spilling over the arched entrance. But the lady of the *casa* showed no such exuberance. Celestina spoke only when necessary. Sometimes I caught her watching me in the dining room, suspicion in her eyes and perhaps fear. What was that about?

The staring made me uncomfortable. So, after a sumptuous breakfast of Spanish omelets and mangoes, while the others drifted off to their individual projects, I tracked the *señora* to her domain. Breakfast hardly over, she was already preparing for *comida,* the midafternoon feast that comprised our main meal. I watched, curious and admiring, as short, chunky Celestina bustled about the great baronial kitchen. Though three women waited on her, she tasted everything herself, stirring, discarding, innovating.

I'm a reporter. I can get anyone to talk, I reminded myself. Moving in close, I pointed to the meat simmering in a rich sauce. "*¡Muy bien!*" I praised. Following her surprisingly rapid movements about the *cocina,* I questioned, "*¿Como se dice?*" Celestina's Spanish faltered, she substituted Maya. "*Pok chuc,*" the proud cook pointed to the pork marinating in orange juice and a tomato-cilantro paste.

"*Pok chuc,*" I dutifully repeated, wondering if learning Maya might be a one-dish-at-a-time project.

"*Voy a ensenar a cocinar,*" she declared, brandishing a meat fork.

Teach me to cook? I doubted that. "*Gracias, no hay tiempo,*" I demurred, retreating. "*Mas tarde.*"

Hurrying down the hall, I noticed a heavy mahogany door slightly ajar. Curious, I stepped inside and found myself in a large room, each wall lined floor to ceiling with shelves. Despite two whirling ceiling fans, I could smell mold. So this was Don Eduardo's famous library. I'd heard about it from Dr. Morley, knew that the elderly archaeologist had been collecting rare volumes and manuscripts for years. They were said to be kept in precise order, each listed carefully with a full account of everything that pertained to it. Looking about, I saw hundreds of books, comfortable leather chairs with thick cushions, and long reading tables. This clearly was a sanctuary, probably off limits.

My eyes traveled to a large carved desk where the owner sat watching me like an owl. Would he sense a kindred spirit? I hoped so. To my relief, Don Eduardo rose to his feet. He was smiling. Taking down a hand-tooled leather volume, he held it out to me. *The True History of the Conquest of New Spain,* a first edition of Bernal Díaz del Castillo's classic! At dinner, I'd thought my host looked old. Now, in his shining eyes, I glimpsed the young adventurer who'd come to Yucatán forty years earlier.

We talked for possibly an hour about books, bantering back and forth. Did I admire Thackeray? "Yes! *Vanity Fair* is my favorite; I like Becky Sharp."

"Becky Sharp, really! Most find her disagreeable," he said.

"Not me! Becky Sharp got what she went after and didn't worry too much about what she had to do to get it."

"Hmm, you like that do you? What do you think of Kipling?"

"I love *The Jungle Book*—especially Shere Khan."

"Really . . ." Don Eduardo pulled out his pipe, lit it thoughtfully. The conversation trailed as he puffed silently, eyes on me.

"I could show you about the ruins," the archaeologist offered at last.

"The ruins, yes," I nodded, "I'd like that very much." Remembering Felipe's enigmatic remark, I added, "Isn't there a well somewhere about? I'd like to see that too."

Don Eduardo's eyes widened. Or did I imagine it? "Well! Who told you about a well? What well?"

"*The* well," I said moving toward him. "Surely you don't want me to go searching for it by myself all alone in the jungle."

Green parrots squawked as they glided through the forest canopy above us. It was tough going. The trail, hacked back only days before, was already overgrown. Vines dangled from tree branches like gorged pythons exhausted from the heat.

Don Eduardo gallantly pulled aside branches, often taking my arm to guide me over exposed roots or steep rocks, but the trek was difficult for him. At one point he stopped and mopped his brow with a bandana. "It's my knees, Alma. I'm all right, it's just my joints," he apologized. "I wasn't always like this. You should have seen me on these trails even five years ago."

"I can imagine," I said. *But I couldn't.*

We passed shapeless mounds, hillocks of shrub-covered earth, with only an occasional glimpse of cut stone to suggest the ancient grandeur of Chichen Itza. Many, perhaps hundreds, of these untouched banks, large and small, were engulfed by undergrowth. Vines pushed through temples, distorting, demolishing what remained.

Emerging at last from a tangle of growth, we were abruptly confronted by an immense gaping hole with craggy, perpendicular sides. A circling hawk looked balefully down at the still, green water far below. The stagnant air reeked of decomposing vegetation. I took a deep, gasping breath, instinctively shrinking back from the edge. "What—what is this place? Something terrible happened here, I can feel it."

"I thought perhaps you knew." Don Eduardo regarded me now, his eyes searching. "This is the sacred *cenote,* a natural well formed by collapsed limestone. The Maya believed it to be a gift from the gods."

"A gift? It looks . . . evil."

"Evil? Perhaps, to some. But you should know that rain was life itself to the Maya." His narrow shoulders contracted in the suggestion of a shrug. "The gods had to be served. Many, mostly young women, were thrown into this well as sacrifices to the snout-nosed rain god, Chac. It was always hoped that one would return to the surface bringing blessings and prophetic messages from the gods."

I looked at the torpid water below. "I can't imagine that many did."

"I've heard of only one," Don Eduardo admitted. "Hunac Ceel, an ambitious commoner from Mayapan."

I sat down a few feet from the *cenote*'s rim, settling back against the crumbling remains of a low wall. "Tell me about him."

Slowly, painfully, Don Eduardo eased himself down beside me. "The story goes that Hunac was a rebel. He resented the ruling alliances of the city-states, Mayapan, Uxmal, and Chichen Itza. Chichen always seemed to come first. Why should his own Mayapan take a back seat to anyone?

"Hunac's big chance came when Mayapan's high priests organized a pilgrimage to the *cenote*. They were tired of fighting among themselves. Nothing they did satisfied anyone for long. A few human sacrifices seemed a small price to pay for Chac's guidance. Victim after victim was hurled screaming into the well. After a few frantic splashes, the water's murky surface remained still. Not one emerged from its depth. The god remained silent."

I shivered despite the blistering sun. "How barbaric! The well looks so deep. What did they expect?"

"Surely not what they got," Don Eduardo chuckled dryly. "Suddenly, there was Hunac Ceel, a nobody whose opinions had been ignored, bounding forward, shouldering the others aside, and diving into the well. The crowd edged forward in stunned silence. Such an act was beyond belief."

The *don* leaned back against a rock, clearly relishing his tale. "At last the volunteer victim emerged. 'I have spoken to Chac!' Hunac cried, his voice a roar from the depths below. The people listened, speechless, to the divine message: Chac had decreed that Hunac Ceel was to be not only Lord of Mayapan but the entire Yucatán Peninsula."

"That's quite a story. What happened next?" I wanted to know.

Don Eduardo shrugged. "What could the priests do with a man so divinely inspired, but allow him to fulfill his destiny? A supreme opportunist, perhaps, but still a prudent man, Hunac left nothing to chance. Just as he'd prepared himself for the plunge by learning to dive, he insured Mayapan's supremacy by importing Toltec mercenaries, expert archers. That combination of sagacity and force proved invincible. Hunac's dynasty, the Cocoms, lasted two hundred and fifty years."

"You mean this is a true story—not a myth?"

Thompson smiled at my surprise. "Perhaps Hunac Ceel's feats have been exaggerated—who can say?—but his descendant, Nachi Cocom, was very real. He was Yucatán's last ruler, the chief who held out longest against the conquistadors. Your friend, the governor, is directly descended from him. I'm surprised he hasn't told you."

8

Secrets

Felipe's modesty charmed me. It would have been easy for him to slip his own impressive lineage into our discussions of the Maya. As a newspaper reporter, I was accustomed to politicians interested only in promoting themselves. But this man, I was learning, was full of surprises.

The day after my conversation with Don Eduardo, I returned to the hacienda with the others from a morning of exploration. We anticipated a hurried lunch before spending the afternoon at the ruins. To my surprise— to everyone's surprise—Felipe was waiting in the *sala*. Dressed in crisp white trousers and a matching guayabera shirt, neatly pleated, he clearly expected to dine with us.

Felipe's beautiful green eyes glowed at the sight of me. How could the others not notice? How, for that matter, could they fail to see my flaming cheeks? This unexpected meeting wasn't at all what I wanted, yet my heart raced with pleasure.

Don Eduardo greeted the governor cordially. "Such a delightful surprise! You must visit us more often."

"I should like to," Felipe replied.

I saw Ann and Earl exchange a quick glance; he winked, she raised a delicately arched brow. Sylvanus and the other archeologists appeared coolly polite.

"Come," Don Eduardo nodded to Felipe, "you must sit at my right." Then he took my arm and led me to the high-backed chair at his left. "This setting becomes Mrs. Reed, does it not?" he asked Felipe once everyone was seated.

All eyes were on me. I wanted to disappear into the tapestry behind me, but Felipe was unperturbed. "Indeed it does," he agreed, "but Mrs. Reed is always lovely. Any setting would become her." He smiled at me as if we were alone. "Are you finding material for your newspaper story?" he asked.

"Ann—Mrs. Morris—is showing me the ropes. She and the other archaeologists"—I gestured widely, hoping to draw the others into this dreadfully personal conversation—"believe that there are many ruins to excavate in Chichen Itza. It may take years."

"It may," he replied.

No one spoke. All eyes turned to the governor. Were they waiting for a speech? What a relief when servants arrived with large platters of *pok chuc*.

Ann broke the silence, her light, cultivated voice echoing through the room, perhaps a bit louder than usual. "My favorite Mayan dish!" she exclaimed to Felipe.

"I like it, too," he replied, "but *pok chuc* really isn't Mayan. It was introduced by Chinese merchants so long ago that Yucatecans take it for granted, imagining that it has always been here."

I thought of my first day with Celestina. She, for one, had assumed the dish was Mayan. No matter, at least people were talking about something other than me. *Thank you, Ann.*

Sylvanus regarded Felipe coolly. "Some of us find your reforms ill-advised. For whatever reason, you've chosen to turn your back on your own Spanish antecedents. By enfranchising thousands who hold no property, mere laborers with no upbringing or education, you're opening the way to chaos. Do you consider it responsible to allow these people to vote on significant issues?"

"Entirely responsible. Yucatán is the land of the Maya, the legacy of the native people who fought valiantly against usurpers—enslavers."

"I would hardly call your Spanish founding fathers enslavers."

"No, I don't suppose you would," Felipe said, "yet the Maya are my true people."

Earl Morris leaned forward, earnest and engaging in his wrinkled digging clothes. "You don't understand, old man. None of us holds with that sword-and-cross thing. We're scientists. That's why we're here. We want to uncover and reconstruct the temples and statues so people can learn about the Maya and their heritage."

Felipe nodded, a soft smile playing about his lips. "The people of Yucatán welcome you for that. But no one can replace what was lost. What matters most today is that the descendants of the Maya, once treated so brutally, now have the opportunity to move forward with dignity and equality. Their voice will bring forth a new Yucatán."

While some murmured agreement and others shook their heads, I listened to Felipe's every word. The governor's egalitarian goals were similar to my own—much like my column in the *News Call*—but played out on a far grander scale. He was a great man, I felt it. Felipe was already making a difference in countless lives and would go on to even greater deeds. I could help him; we could work together on the many egalitarian issues that mattered deeply to us both. If only it were I at his side.

Felipe's eyes were back on mine again, warm, tender, searching eyes. I looked away. It could never be.

In the days that followed, the governor drove to Chichen Itza often. Whatever his excuses, he came to see *me*. I knew it and worried about the effect of this blatant madness on his career, but feared even more for myself. I'd come to Yucatán to regain my life, not ruin it. Everyone in our party must have been aware of my situation. I imagined them secretly laughing at me. All but Ann.

Now that I had come to know Ann, I saw how wrong I'd been to dismiss her as a New England snob. Ann was a true friend, looking out for me socially, glossing over my gaffes, smoothing my way with the others. All the while she casually taught me the very real world of archaeology—how to spot pottery shards in the rubble, dust them off, oh, so carefully, then piece them together, Humpty Dumpty style, fragment by fragment.

Not trusting myself to be alone with Felipe, I stayed close to Ann, day after day, as we roamed through the jungle, recording the remains of the ancient citadel of Chichen Itza. It wasn't easy. Ancient seedlings had rooted where roofs and walls had collapsed. Vines infiltrated stone, shattering whatever might have remained intact when ceilings toppled. The jungle had engulfed untouched hillocks, large and small. Generations of trees had grown and fallen into decay and all that remained were shapeless, earth-covered mounds with only an occasional glimpse of cut stone to suggest ancient splendor. Not only did I help to document the known standing buildings, but I also helped ferret out the unknown mounds. Dank underbrush and tangled trees blocked us at every turn. Progress was measured in inches as machetes cleared our path.

So work filled my days. At night, I wrote. The harder I had to concentrate, the less time there was to think about Felipe. At least, that was my theory. How could this enigmatic stranger have banished Sam so quickly? No more did I long for my former husband's touch. I rarely thought of him. Yet here I was allowing an even more impossible relationship to permeate my imagination. Felipe has a wife; what's more, he has children, I reminded myself again and again. Our situation was hopeless.

It saddened me to think of leaving Yucatán, yet the days passed quickly, until only a week remained of my stay. That evening, I adjourned to the library, settling down before a little mahogany table, to transcribe my rough field notes into the journal that I kept. Much of what I'd written concerned Don Eduardo. What a life he'd led. Among the old archaeologist's papers, I found a photograph, faded yet curiously arresting. The young Don Eduardo, I realized with a start, an idealistic intellectual with his whole life ahead of him. Mama would have called him well bred. His features were patrician: broad, unlined brow, narrow, high-bridged nose, eyes inquiring, almost imperious behind rimless glasses.

I put the snapshot off to one side. Just beneath it was an article, yellow with age. Publication in *Popular Science Monthly* must have been quite an achievement for a student. I could imagine the controversy generated by the article, "Atlantis: Not a Myth." His premise, a link between the Yucatán Peninsula and the lost continent, triggered just the attention he was seeking.

I imagined Don Eduardo's two benefactors, one a founder of the American Antiquarian Society, the other a guiding light of the Peabody Museum of Archaeology and Ethnology at Harvard, cut from the same cloth as Hunac Ceel's high priests. Kingmakers. In one clever coup, they ensured their protégé both a free hand and a salary by using their political clout to get him appointed U.S. consul to Yucatán. So there he was, just twenty-five, the youngest consul in United States history, setting out with his wife and baby daughter to explore Yucatán. . . .

"Hard at work, Alma?"

I looked up, startled. Don Eduardo was at my shoulder—he'd come into the library without my hearing him. "You've had quite a career," I observed, closing the journal. "It's hard to imagine it all."

My host laughed ruefully. "You *can't* begin to imagine it all. Back then, in 1885, Chichen Itza was accessible only by jungle footpath. On the night we arrived, I stumbled over the remains of the hacienda's previous owner—killed by bandits, no doubt. We never did find out."

Don Eduardo turned away, staring off into space. Was he reliving some other wild adventure? The old archaeologist knew something that he wasn't telling; I felt it. I'd have to gain his trust . . . but how? On the desk before me was a large folio. Absently, I turned the pages. Suddenly one piqued my interest. It was a drawing, intricately detailed. Two entwined serpents biting a knife blade. Deep green . . . jade. I was reminded of the *cenote,* its waters beautiful but sinister.

"I've not seen this before. Is it a drawing of a real knife? Did someone find it here in Chichen Itza?" I asked, turning eagerly toward him.

"Of course not!" Don Eduardo's hoarse voice was an angry croak. "It's not real, merely a hieroglyph I copied." He shut the folio firmly and placed it in a drawer, which he locked, pocketing the key.

"I've seen so many hieroglyphs these past few weeks. This doesn't look like any of them."

"Do you fancy that you've seen everything at Chichen?"

"Of course not," I exclaimed. "I'm sure there are many wonderful things that only *you* know about. I could help you tell the world about them. Is it fair that Dr. Morley and these new young archaeologists will soon be famous? People will think that *they* discovered Chichen Itza, when really—"

Just then a servant entered carrying two cups of frothy hot chocolate on a dented silver tray. Don Eduardo seated himself across from me at the little mahogany table. For a time, we silently sipped the rich Mexican chocolate, laced with brandy.

I stared into the cup as though it were a crystal, speculating about the mystery shrouding my host. Though invariably polite, he remained guarded. Once or twice he seemed to evade the other archaeologists' questions about the site.

Softening my voice almost to a whisper, I looked up at him. "I could make you famous, Don Eduardo. You've worked here all alone for so long. Isn't it time the world knew what you've been doing? There's something you want to tell me—I know there is."

He sat silently for a long time. I wondered if he would answer at all.

"What if there *were* something more," Don Eduardo said at last, "something no one knows. . . ." He sipped his chocolate thoughtfully. "I shouldn't have mentioned it— there are others involved, others who would be greatly affected."

"I've only one week left here. . . ." I struggled to keep my voice low, wheedling. What if this was a real scoop. My heart started thumping. I *knew* it was a scoop.

Don Eduardo set the cup down; his eyes met mine. "Yes, I'm quite aware of that, but I need time. We shall see. Let me think about it. Yes, Alma Sullivan Reed. Perhaps I do have a story to tell."

9

The View from the Top

SAGE
Chichen Itza, present time

Alma Sullivan Reed had captured my imagination.
Often I felt her at my side as I explored the ruins of
Chichen Itza. After reaching the park gate ahead of everybody one morning in May, I showed my pass and hurried in. The Temple of Kukulkan was my citadel. Others
climbed the pyramid, of course. Almost every tourist
who came to Chichen Itza regarded a picture snapped at
the top as obligatory, but they rarely lingered.

Settled into a secluded nook at the rear of the temple,
the stone wall as a back rest, I looked out at the neatly
clipped grass stretching far into the distance. The morning onslaught of tourists entering the park reminded me
of ants as they trailed their way across the carpet, inching
slowly onto one ruin or another. Inevitably they would

find their way to Kukulkan Temple, the famous pyramid that bears his name.

When I'd brought my laptop to the pyramid I found that it aroused too much attention. People distracted me by asking questions: "Are you an author?" "What are you writing?" Now, jotting things down in a notebook, I was quickly dismissed as just another journal keeper. Climbers exchanged smiles and nods, the camaraderie of Kukul-climbing, before beginning the slow tortuous descent. Alone much of the time, I found the pyramid's top ledge a perfect place to sort out Alma's life and sometimes my own.

Though Mark appeared to be having a pleasant time, I felt an occasional twinge of guilt at my enjoyment of hours spent alone researching the archaeological site. Happily, unexpectedly, he'd seemed to thrive in Yucatán. Mark had acquired a painted cane and covered surprising distances with it, but reading remained his passion. He devoured mystery novels and spent hours in the hammock strung for him across the cottage's tiny patio.

My preliminary research had gone well—almost as if Alma were guiding me. Now, just heading into our third month in Yucatán, I'd begun a tentative outline of the biography. Hacienda Chichen, our hotel, selected on the Internet for its close proximity to the archaeological park, was, in fact, the former home of Edward Thompson, Chichen Itza's first scientific investigator. Carnegie archaeologists had lived in the very cottage where we were staying. A few faded photographs of early expeditions hung in the lobby. The young archaeologists looked so serious. Did they ever have fun?

Putting aside my notebook, I studied the array of ruins stretching far as I could see. The Temple of a Thousand Columns. The Ball Court. The Sweat Lodge. El Caracol. In the past month I'd explored all of them, trying always to imagine the place as Alma had seen it. Ann Morris, one of the early archaeologists who'd been with Alma at the site, had written a book for children about the Carnegie excavation of Chichen Itza. It was full of pictures that bore little resemblance to the vast park now spread before me. All the ruins—save for the Temple of Kukulkan—had been covered then by dense brush, acres and acres of tree-covered mounds. I marveled at the excavation job, but wished I'd been there first—had seen what Alma Reed and Felipe Carrillo Puerto had seen.

Glancing at my watch, I saw that it was nearly noon. Soon it would be time to go back to the cottage. I'd rouse Mark, probably drowsing, and the two of us would stroll the short distance to Hacienda Chichen's dining room. We ate most of our meals at the elegant old manor house— so often that the hotel mariachis had begun greeting us with my new favorite song.

By now I'd learned "La Peregrina" by heart and found myself humming as I looked over my notes. What a song, what a subject, and what better place than a temple top to work. Among the old photographs in Ann's book was a picture of Alma climbing Kukulkan. She was alone, a tiny grasshopper clinging to the pyramid steps, but it was easy for me to picture her coming here with Felipe. I imagined them sitting together on the same ledge where I now sat, below them not manicured lawn but teeming jungle. If Alma could have known what was in store for her . . . would she have run a mile or seized the moment? The latter, I decided. Wasn't that what I was doing?

My eyes strayed to the pyramid's grassy edge, where the top of a Panama hat was emerging above the stone step before me. Another tourist. Slowly, very slowly, a face and shoulders appeared. A tall, rangy man in jeans and a white guayabera shirt pulled himself up the last of the stairs. Panting slightly, he stood before me.

"I believe you're humming our song."

I looked up in amazement. "I beg your pardon?"

" 'La Peregrina,' " he explained. "I'm David Winslow. We've met before." Dropping to a low stone wall beside me, he smiled regretfully. "You don't remember."

I saw amusement in his eyes and relaxed. Something about him *did* look familiar.

"A rainy night in Mérida."

I looked again. Blue eyes, heavy-lidded, dreamy, possibly teasing. Of course! The man who'd caught me when I stumbled, the music. It was my turn to smile. "I could hardly forget the drug dealer who practically saved my life."

"I wouldn't go that far."

I paused, looking at him, remembering that night and what had followed. "I would. Alma Reed—the journalist you told me about that night. What an incredible woman! I've spent the last four months researching her for a biography. It's the best thing I've ever done, I can feel it; and none of it would have happened if you hadn't turned me on to her story."

"So that's what you're doing in Yucatán. I thought I saw you here in the park three or four times. Yesterday I was sure that it was you standing by the Temple of a Thousand Columns, but by the time I got there you were gone."

"Could be. I walk the park every day before climbing up here to work." I paused, watching him curiously. "How in the world did you know me?"

"How could I forget the silver fox that got away before I could even get her phone number?"

Silver fox! I liked that. Who was this guy? "What's kept you in Yucatán so long?" I asked.

"I rent a house in Piste. It belonged to the Carnegie's original dig foreman. His family's kept it all these years. You may have seen it—a big place with high walls around it, pink and orange bougainvillea spilling over everything. It's been modernized, of course, had to be; I have my lab there."

"Your lab! Are you making the stuff yourself?"

He smiled sheepishly. "I shouldn't have let that drug stuff go on so long. It's not what you think. I'm a neurotoxicologist."

"A scientist! What are you doing in Yucatán?"

"Collecting urine samples."

I tried not to look as surprised as I felt. "I'd imaged something more exciting, perhaps dangerous."

"I thought that might be the case," David smiled. "Maybe I liked it that way. The truth is so prosaic. I work for NIH—National Institutes of Health." He smiled again, this time shrugging wryly. "My lab's anything but a drug den, but let me show it to you. We can have lunch at a nice little place nearby. I've a jeep parked at the edge of the park. It wouldn't take ten minutes to get to Piste."

"I have another idea," I said, meeting his eyes. "Why don't you have lunch with my partner and me? We're staying at Hacienda Chichen. It's even closer."

"That's Don Eduardo's old hideaway."

When I looked at him in surprise, he smiled. "Our conversation piqued my curiosity as well. I've done a little poking around myself since we talked, heard some interesting stories. That Don Eduardo was some *bandido*."

"Some might say that, but he met his match in Alma Reed."

From below a cry rang out, and then another. "Señora Sanborn! Señora Sanborn!"

I jumped to my feet, moved to the pyramid's ledge. Looking down I saw two young men from the Hacienda Chichen. They stood directly below, their arms waving frantically.

"¡Por favor Señora! Come down! ¡Es muy mal!"

From there on, things happened fast. David's hand on my arm as we descended the short, steep steps. Me stumbling, lurching forward; David steadying me. Treacherous stairs, so many of them. Finally on the ground, running, running the short distance to the cottage. Mark lying on his back in the center of our small patio.

Despite the heat, his body was covered by a thick blanket. The hotel staff was clustered about, talking in low voices, watching anxiously. A doctor was taking Mark's pulse, a New Yorker we'd met at dinner only the night before.

I sank down beside him. Relief flooded Mark's face as he saw me. He smiled, a shaky smile, his eyes wide and frightened. "Sage, I can't move my legs. I can't *feel* my legs."

I took his hands, held them tightly in mine. "Darling, darling, I'm here now. Everything will be all right."

But would it, *could* it? I turned to the doctor, who responded: "We've got to get him out right away, get him to a hospital."

"I'll take care of that."

I looked up; it was David. I'd forgotten he was there. Now I saw him standing just beyond the huddled group of onlookers. He was holding a cell phone. I kissed Mark and started to get up but he grasped my hand. "Don't leave me, Sage."

"I won't leave you. I won't ever leave you, Mark."

The doctor hurried to David's side. The two talked quietly. I couldn't hear them, nor could I hear the words David said into the phone.

A few moments later the doctor was back. "Your friend has arranged for a helicopter and alerted the hospital in Mérida," he said. "They'll be ready for Mark. The copter should be here soon. They'll take you with him."

"Did you hear that, darling?" I bent over Mark, kissing him again. "Everything's going to be all right."

The next hour was a blur. I moved quickly about the cottage, pulling together our passports, Mark's medications, my laptop and notes, a few pieces of jewelry, shoving them all into a bag. The hotel staff would have to pack the rest and ship it to me. The bill, yes, I'd need to see to that. What else? So many details. Did I have everything? Already, I could hear a distant whirring sound.

"Sage——" Mark was calling, his voice so fearful. Poor darling, how would he bear it? How would *we* bear it?

The helicopter circled overhead, sweeping palm branches in all directions, the noise deafening. As it landed two men jumped out. Someone lowered a stretcher.

I tried to thank everyone, hugged some, hurriedly shook hands with others, half of me attending to details, the other half watching as if it were all happening to someone else. Grabbing my shoulder purse and the small bag, I hurried toward the helicopter. Mark was already inside and I had one foot on the step when someone touched my shoulder. I turned to see David. "Oh!" I half sobbed, "you did all this. How can I ever thank you?"

He kissed me lightly on the forehead. "Just let me know how it goes with Mark."

The rotor blades were slowly turning.

David took my hand, placed a business card in my palm. "Drop me an e-mail," he said, closing my fingers about the card. "Promise?"

"I promise." I turned quickly, running up the steps.

The helicopter was already rising as I buckled myself in. The cottage with its pretty little garden was receding from view, Hacienda Chichen growing smaller. We were above the park now, hovering briefly over the Temple of Kukulkan. How close it looked. Would I ever see it again? The helicopter banked. I reached out involuntarily to brace myself. A sudden gust of wind and the business card slipped from my fingers, fluttering out the open window, falling, falling, who knew where.

Another Life

ALMA
Chichen Itza, 1923

An ecru envelope waited beside my plate the next morning. It was addressed to Madame Alma Reed.

"Madame?"

I turned to Don Eduardo, seated near me at the breakfast table.

He looked up from a plate piled high with *huevos rancheros,* the highly spiced fried eggs we'd come to look forward to each morning, savoring them with tortillas and beans. Don Eduardo leaned forward, straining to be heard above the breakfast din. "Alejandra del Valla fancies herself more French than Yucatecan."

Indeed. I tore open the envelope. The script was written in violet ink. I'd never seen anything to equal the fine flourishes, loops, and dashes. But what did they say?

"I'll spare you the effort," Don Eduardo offered, glancing at the note. "Our neighbors to the south are inviting you to spend tomorrow at their hacienda. They request that you enjoy *comida* with them."

"Just me? Why would they do that?"

"Curiosity, perhaps. The del Valle women no doubt find life tedious in the back country." He smiled at my puzzlement. "The lady journalist and her connections must intrigue them. Maybe they want to size her up."

"My connections?" Then it hit me. I felt my face flush and hated it. "You mean Felipe, don't you? They've heard how often he comes here." Angrily, I slammed down the invitation. "How dare they! I've no intention of going."

One bushy gray eyebrow lifted slightly as Don Eduardo regarded me in mock surprise. "You'd allow a little gossip to interfere with so splendid an opportunity? The del Valles are among the most prominent hacendados in the state. Theirs is a showplace, something you may wish to write about." His pale eyes took on a speculative glint. "Are you only interested in one side of a story? I assumed journalists were required to have open minds."

Reluctantly, I picked up the invitation.

A uniformed chauffeur called for me promptly at ten. Behind him, parked in front of Don Eduardo's *casa,* was an open touring car, its polar white paint sparkling in the sun. I straightened my straw sailor hat. It was hard not to be intimidated. I wished Ann were going with me.

As though reading my mind, she moved to my side. "You look fine." Her pretty hands, roughened now from hard work, smoothed the folds of my middy blouse ever so slightly. "What is it that Don Eduardo says Mexicans all like—*mas grande, mas prestigio, mas personalidad*? You've got them all—why, you're the cat's pajamas!"

"You're sweet," I said, and meant it.

Acutely aware that the whole digging crew had assembled to watch my departure, I took a deep breath and stepped down on to the drive, sauntering now, almost slinking, as I'd seen the Nob Hill debutantes do. Taking the chauffeur's white-gloved hand, I stepped into the car. The leather seats, deliciously soft, smelled of lemon and money.

The del Valle fortune was obviously grounded in the green gold Felipe had described to me the day we met. I passed through acres and acres of henequen, felt enveloped, almost smothered, by the sweet, heavy smell. Men worked close to the narrow road, cutting the stalks and binding them. Their white shirts and trousers clung damply to their bodies. I could see sweat trickling down their faces. Then finally the spiky crops gave way to luxuriantly manicured grounds. What a contrast to Don Eduardo's tangled garden that scarcely differed from the nearby jungle.

The *casa*, standing majestically at the end of a long drive, was a washed gold with fluted white columns encircled in a graceful web of purple morning glories. As we approached, the carved mahogany door swung open and two women floated out onto the colonnaded veranda. One wore jade green chiffon with a matching plume secured by a jeweled headband. The other was in lavender voile, on her head a tiny cloche. I never doubted for an instant that her matinee-length pearls, the largest I'd ever seen, were real. Their skirts flared ever so slightly about their knees as they moved toward me. Each might have stepped from the pages of *Vogue*. Doña Alejandra and Valencia del Valle, mother and daughter. And, for once, the cliché proved true. Doña Alejandra did look like Valencia's older sister.

What do you say about people so rich they don't even know what rich means? I expected to hate the del Valles, but couldn't. They wore their attributes like old beach clothes. What really interested them was me. *Me!* The Felipe connection was part of it, of course. Don Eduardo was right. That's why they invited me in the first place. Perhaps they hadn't expected to like me any more than I did them, but somehow that changed almost from the beginning.

Taking my hands, they drew me into the *sala*. Where to look first? My eyes darted from the antique furniture to the polished silver and then to the Impressionist paintings. I couldn't imagine what it would be like to live in such a place. "Your home, it's like a jewel," I exclaimed, "everything so perfect."

"*Ma cherie,* this is nothing!" Doña Alejandra said, her soft, heavily accented voice apologetic. "This is our . . ."—her long tapering fingers fluttered as she searched for a word—"our camp. Ricardo, *mi esposo,* needs always to check on things at the hacienda. Sometimes Valencia and I come with him for an outing, a little—how do you say—pique-nique, but our real home is in Mérida. I hope you will visit us there one day."

"Mama copied a Swiss chalet right to the last detail," Valencia said, taking my arm as an old friend might. "It's on Montejo Boulevard, *una casa blanca.* Perhaps you have noticed."

Indeed I had. The largest house on Mansion Street and for certain the most unusual. I nodded. "It's—how do you say—*fabuloso.*"

They laughed delightedly as though I'd truly said something fabulous. It was infectious. I found myself chuckling with them.

"Is there anything more beautiful than the sound of women's laughter?" In the doorway behind us stood a tall, graceful man with a clipped mustache that matched his thick, silvery hair. "Ricardo del Valle," he introduced himself, bowing. "You honor us with your presence, Señora Reed."

"He's come to kidnap you," Doña Alejandra warned.

"I thought you might enjoy a brief tour of the hacienda."

Valencia rolled her eyes. "And I thought you'd never want to do anything so boring." She took a languid puff from her jade cigarette holder.

"But I would," I assured him. "I'm curious to see everything."

Smiling, Don Ricardo took my arm. "I imagined you would be."

The chauffeur drove while *el grande patron* sat beside me in the touring car pointing out the sights in effortless English. He'd fine-tuned it at Harvard, I learned. Hacendados invariably studied abroad. Both Don Ricardo's wife and daughter had been educated in Paris. Valencia, home for her debut, planned to take voice lessons in the fall in Florence with several of her friends.

"Surely there are fine schools closer to home. Why not Mexico City?" I wondered.

He shook his head disdainfully, flicking the ashes from his cigar. "We don't consider ourselves part of Mexico. The culture in the capital is still so new, so raw."

"Like the United States?" I suggested.

"Perhaps," he admitted, his eyes smiling at me, "but with a difference. We hacendados must be realists. Our land is dependent on the whims of your government. When your country sneezes, Yucatán gets pneumonia."

"May I quote you on that?"

"If you like, though I'm sure it's been said before." He pointed a slim, well-manicured finger at a large adobe building. "This is our *casa de maquinas,* the machine shop. It's where the henequen grown on our hacienda is processed."

In an instant the chauffeur had braked the car, rushed around, and opened the door for me. Don Ricardo took my arm, leading me past a horse-drawn cart filled with freshly picked green leaves and up a short flight of shallow cement stairs to a loading platform. Threading my way through tall stacks of henequen, I entered the moist, cavernous factory. Don Ricardo shouted explanations as he pointed out various features, but I could hear little but the deafening roar of conveyer belts. All around me men, naked to the waist, stood at a series of stations cutting, tying, and twisting the henequen stalks. Ceiling fans did little to alleviate the heat or the smell: sweat, horse manure, and the heavy, cloying odor of henequen. I could feel the first trickle of my own sweat trailing down my back. What would it be like to spend one's life working in such a place? Too dreadful to imagine. I was ashamed of my eagerness as I followed Don Ricardo outside into the fresh air.

The car wove its way through a grove of mango trees, then entered a clearing. Don Ricardo indicated a substantial adobe building, the overseer's house. Beyond were perhaps three dozen Mayan-style houses, round, white-washed, and thatch-roofed.

As the car came to a stop I heard children's voices coming from a long, low building to my right. "*¿Como esta usted?*

Muy bueno, gracias," the dialogue repeated again and again in unison.

"Our school," Don Ricardo explained. "We employ a teacher for our workers' children. The only prerequisite is that they learn Spanish."

"I'm surprised so few of the Maya do."

"Some still fight the war of independence in their heads."

Next to the school was a larger building. "Our company store," Don Ricardo explained. "We stock everything our workers could desire here."

"But how do your workers pay for those things?"

"They find us most generous. We offer unlimited credit."

"And hold them forever in your debt—right?"

"My dear," he gently chided, "Even our esteemed governor's ideal society can't change human nature. Surely you must realize that."

What could I say? The hacienda's clean, well-maintained workers' settlement wasn't unlike Felipe's model village. Yet no one threw flowers at Ricardo del Valle's car.

Doña Alejandra and Valencia, seated on the veranda, waved as we pulled up before the *casa.* "A swim would feel very good now, *sí*?" Doña Alejandra called out.

Wouldn't it! I got out of the car, my red-and-white middy dress sticking to my body, the linen fabric hopelessly wrinkled.

"¡*Perfecto!* Our pool is waiting for you."

"Enjoy yourself, *muchachas*," Don Ricardo waved as he drove off.

I tried not to look as astonished as I felt. What kind of world was this? No one I knew had their very own pool. "I'm sorry, I didn't think to bring . . ."

"Of course you didn't," Doña Alejandra tucked her arm into mine. "We always keep plenty of bathing costumes on hand for our guests. Come and see which one you like best. We've laid them out for you in the guest cabana."

Plenty! The del Valles could have stocked a small store. I chose a blue-and-white-striped one, quite daring. The bathing skirt ended several inches above my knees. Mother and daughter nodded approvingly as I held it up.

"Very well, then, this is the one I'll wear." I took off my hat and felt tangles of hair slip loose, spilling down my back.

"Golden brown, such a lovely color," Doña Alejandra said.

Valencia stroked a tangled strand admiringly. "It reminds me of honey in the sun, but Mama and I were wondering why you choose to wear it long."

"Valencia!" her mother chided. "Where are your manners?" Doña Alejandra smiled at me apologetically. "Nosy—is that the word you use? Valencia has too much nose. She thought a career woman from San Francisco—"

"Would be more *au courant*?" I finished for her. "I've been admiring yours—both of yours." I had, too. Short, chic, shiny. How slim and white their throats, so gracefully exposed. "Did you get your cuts in Mérida?"

"No, in Paris. Bobbed hair is all the rage there."

"In San Francisco, too. It's just that my husband—my late husband—preferred long hair."

"Many men do." Doña Alejandra agreed. "Ricardo was shocked when I got off the ship after my last trip to Paris." She touched a sleek black wave. "He professed not to know me."

"But I think a woman should be independent. A truly modern woman doesn't allow a man to decide how she should wear her hair. Don't you agree?" Valencia asked.

"Definitely." I thought of Felipe and wondered about his wife's hair.

The pool felt deliciously cool. My swimming, learned as a kid at the YWCA, was limited. Doña Alejandra and Valencia reminded me of graceful dolphins. They could dive too. Gentle, tactful teachers, they soon had me doing it as well.

When we emerged from the pool I found that one of the del Valle servants had washed and pressed my clothes. My middy looked crisp as the day I'd bought it at that little shop on Powell and O'Farrell. A maid towel-dried my hair and arranged it in an artful sweep; small tendrils deftly twisted with a curling iron escaped gracefully here and there.

Comida was served in a splendid dining room, its maize-colored walls glowing like molten gold. A crystal chandelier glittered in the late afternoon sun while two ceiling fans whirled quietly. Throughout the many courses, the del Valle family plied me with questions about life in San Francisco. They professed to be fascinated by my adventures covering murders and robberies. I didn't tell them about the dreary obituaries I also wrote or the flowery wedding stories that bored me to tears.

"How could you leave all that to come here?" Valencia asked. "Yucatán is the end of the earth."

"I was thrilled to come," I told her. "The Carnegie team is beginning to uncover all kinds of exciting ruins."

"Those old stones," Valencia sniffed. "There isn't a house around here that isn't built on the ruins of some old thing, but it's not the Forum. Next summer Papa plans to charter a yacht in Portofino and sail to Greece. That's where the real ruins are."

I put down my fork to protest but Doña Alejandra interposed. "What do they say—'familiarity breeds contempt'? We've all grown up among the old Mayan buildings and take them for granted. Next time you come we'll have to show you the temple in the back garden. When Valencia was a little girl she used to have tea parties there."

Too soon the sun was setting. It was time for me to leave. While Don Ricardo summoned the car, his wife and daughter walked with me to the room where I'd left my hat and bag.

"I hope you'll come back," Doña Alejandra said. "We're expecting friends, the Mendozas. Carlos is most handsome. I think you would like him. I know he would like you. Won't you come and spend the weekend with us?"

"I can't," I told her, my regret genuine. "The survey's almost over. I'll be leaving in just a few days."

"You're leaving Yucatán! I had no idea." Impulsively, Doña Alejandra took my hand. "Perhaps—oh, how can I say this—perhaps it is best that you go. I hope you understand how I mean that." Her voice dropped almost to a whisper. "He is not for you, *ma cherie*."

My heart began to thump. I knew she wasn't talking about Carlos whatever his name was. "Of course not!" I responded. "The governor is a married man."

"In our country that is not always an obstacle. There is the *casa* and all too often the *casita*."

I met Doña Alejandra's eyes squarely. How sad she looked, but only for an instant. Perhaps I'd imagined it. "That sort of life would be impossible for me," I assured her.

"Of course it would," Doña Alejandra agreed. "But now that we've met you—it's easy to understand what fascinates a man like him. The governor's wife is a simple woman, a peasant. They married very young. He's come a long way—I'll give him that. She has not. Her entire life centers about her children and the Church."

"You don't like him, do you?"

"I did—at first," Valencia broke in. "The governor is very handsome, one would hardly guess his background, and then he *is* a hero. Did you know he rode with Zapata? Imagine them, '*¡Tierra y Libertad!*'" Her gold slave bracelets tinkled as she flung her arms wide.

"Valencia!" her mother reproved sharply. "Enough of that nonsense, the *tierra* he wants is ours. The man is a bandit. He was in prison twice."

"In prison?" I echoed, looking from one to the other.

"Surprised?" She regarded me, one sleek brow raised. "Obviously there is a great deal about Felipe Carrillo Puerto that you do not know." Doña Alejandra's arch expression faded. Her voice dropped: "The final chapter has yet to be written. It will not be pretty. Colonel Broca's faction is growing—get out now, get out while you still can."

11

Encounter with Kukulkan

I took the brandy that Don Eduardo had poured for me and stepped to the far end of the veranda. There must have been a thousand stars that night and nothing to do but count them. How many would it take to put my life in order?

"Wishing for your prince, Alma?" Earl asked, calling me back to the table. "You needn't look far."

When I refused the bait, Ann, curious, turned to her husband. "Who are you talking about?"

"Our governor, of course. He's crazy about her."

"Oh, Earl! Such talk. He's married."

Earl watched me, frowning slightly. "Too bad. He seems like a fine man."

"He *is* a fine man," Don Eduardo affirmed, looking up from his liqueur. "He was a hard-working boy, a standout from the start. Then the priest of Valladolid took a liking to him, loaned him books, filled his head with ideas. Once Felipe had read the French rationalists, nothing could stop him. He's come a long way since then and helped many. It's been a lonely road; few have ever helped *him*."

"Why are the good ones always taken?" Ann asked, smiling at Earl.

"It's getting late." Earl's yawn convinced no one.

"About time we turned in," Ann said as they rose, almost in unison, moving toward their small stone bungalow.

Because of the full moon the jungle creatures were especially noisy. I imagined them calling to one another. "Find me! Find me! . . . Here." The moon, heavy with promise like a ripe mango, lit the pathway. I saw Earl's arm, at first around Ann's waist, drop lower, caress her hips. I sighed softly.

"Would you like another brandy, Alma?" Don Eduardo asked.

I rose abruptly, setting the rattan rocker in motion. "No, thanks, there's something I'd like to look for in the library—if I may?"

"Of course, my dear. Perhaps I can assist you."

"Maybe. Is there anything about the Mayan god Kukulkan?"

Don Eduardo smiled broadly. "I've an excellent image—a temple rubbing, and also a book of legends collected by an early *padre*. Perhaps I can translate for you; the Spanish is pretty archaic."

Ann and Earl faded from view. I heard a screen door slam.

Don Eduardo located the temple rubbing almost immediately and spread the parchment scroll out on a mahogany table. Kukulkan was a formidable figure wearing a gorgeous crown of quetzal feathers and nothing else. I barely suppressed a gasp at the god's phallus.

"I assume this is some sort of cartoon," I said, ignoring the frank amusement in the archaeologist's eyes.

"Not at all. Kukulkan was reputed to have been extremely well endowed." Don Eduardo pulled a book from the shelf. "According to this," he said, tapping the worn leather volume, "the god appeared out of nowhere, sent from heaven, it was thought, to unite the warring tribes. He vowed to remain celibate until peace was achieved."

"Felipe told me some of that. The high priests didn't like him."

"To put it mildly. In their eyes, floral tributes would never replace blood sacrifices. Kukulkan was changing everything. He had to be destroyed. The wily priests waited for a feast day when all would be watching. The god's drink had been laced with mushrooms." Don Eduardo's eyes were on me now, watching intently. "At Kukulkan's arm stood a beautiful, seductive woman and, under the influence of the powerful aphrodisiac, he—"

"I can guess the rest. He hated himself in the morning, right?"

"Indeed, he was consumed with guilt," Don Eduardo agreed. "His self-imposed vow broken, Kukulkan turned his back on palaces, power, everything. Standing naked on a snakeskin raft, the broken hero drifted eastward until a mysterious explosion ignited his craft. Legend has it that the god's heart soared up from the flames and united with the sun."

"What a sad story. It reminds me a little of King Arthur."

"Arthur had Camelot."

"You don't think Felipe can turn Yucatán into a Camelot?"

"That remains to be seen." Don Eduardo's eyes probed mine curiously. "I understand you're something of an idealist yourself."

I returned his stare, puzzled. "What are you talking about?"

"That boy in San Francisco. Simón, wasn't that his name? Simón Ruiz."

"How did you hear about him?" My voice sounded strained even to my own ears. What else did he know? Were all my secrets about to be exposed?

"From Felipe. He came by this afternoon—hoping to see you—but of course, as usual, you were off in the jungle with Ann."

"How does he know about Simón? I've never told anyone here."

"A politician can find out anything. You know that. He
must be very interested in you, my dear."

I felt my face flush. "How dare he have me investi-
gated?" I asked indignantly. "Maybe Señora del Valle is
right about him. She says the governor is a dreadful man,
a convict."

"Really?" Don Eduardo raised a thick, gray eyebrow.
"Did the *señora* tell you why he went to prison? Years ago
Felipe operated a one-boy hauling service. Once, while
picking up a load of henequen, he saw a woman being
whipped by an overseer. When he tried to help her, they
were both dragged off to jail."

"Surely not at the del Valle hacienda?"

Don Eduardo shook his head. "Ricardo del Valle
was never that bad, though there has been a lot of
scrambling lately to bring their operation into the
twentieth century. I'm sure they wanted you to see
those improvements as much as they wanted to see
you."

"And the governor's second offense?"

"That was a real prison term. His old enemy Colonel
Broca saw to it—two years for translating the Mexican
constitution into Maya."

What could I say to that? Sylvanus Morley had sneered
at the governor when he'd called him "a man of the

people," but those words described Felipe perfectly. Despite myself, I admired him more than ever.

I had awful dreams that night. Kukulkan—or was it Felipe?—stood before a cheering audience. People tossed flowers. Or were they . . . mushrooms? It was raining mushrooms! So many, pelting me from every side. Fearful, no place to turn! The god figure saw me, held out his hand. Safety so close. I leaned toward him but could scarcely move my legs. So heavy. I pressed forward and slowly began to climb. I looked up at the god, my arms outstretched. It was Felipe. I knew he would help me, if I could only reach him. I felt heavy, languorous. Such an effort to lift my legs. Moving slowly forward, I had almost reached Felipe, his hand just beyond my grasp. I stumbled, fell downward, slipping and sliding among the mushrooms. They were big and sticky. I looked up, saw the god figure now far in the distance, standing all alone atop a flaming volcano.

My own cry awakened me. Frightened and uncertain, I stared at the morning light filtering through an open window. Who or what had I seen? Dressing quickly, I slipped into the kitchen for coffee. I gulped the drink down, anxious to forestall any effort to prevent me from entering the jungle alone. No food, no conversation this morning, I wanted to be by myself, outside, away from everyone, somewhere quiet where I could think about the dream. It remained so vivid. Was there a meaning, a message for me?

Wild green parrots squawked raucously as they buzzed the jungle path. Following the narrow trail for about an hour, I made my way far beyond the pyramid, past many mounds that the Carnegie team had marked for further excavation by later archaeologists. The next day was to be our last at the site. Much remained to be done, but I wanted this morning for myself. Beside a fallen temple a blue-crowned motmot flashed its tail, swinging it from side to side like a pendulum. As my eyes sought to penetrate the emerald canopy above, I marveled once again at the jungle's relentless force. Despite daily efforts to keep the bush at bay, Chichen Itza lay uneasily before the jungle juggernaut. Tree-size roots extended through roofs, walls, and subterranean chambers, tearing apart massive stones. Strangler vines crept along balustrades, corbeled arches, binding statues of gods, enshrouding figures of dead monarchs in leafy winding sheets.

Admiring the plumage of an orange parrot perched far above me, I lost my footing and fell headlong across the crude path. An unexpected hint of blue off to the side caught my eye as I pulled myself up. Clambering to the top of an embankment of fallen stones, I glimpsed a cavern all but obscured by foliage. I pushed aside a thick branch and gasped at the unexpected beauty beyond. Inside the grotto, a small *cenote,* a sinkhole filled with fresh water, was illuminated by shafts of sunlight, sparkled pure turquoise. How different this little pond was from the fearsome well of sacrifice. Yet, I remembered, all *cenote*s were thought to be sacred.

The sun was high; sweat gathered between my breasts and trickled down my thighs. How beguiling the pool, so incredibly blue, invitingly cool. Impulsively, I pulled off my boots, shirt, and trousers. My chemise and step-ins clung damply to my body. I'd hiked far beyond the survey site. Who would ever know?

I peeled off everything and slid into the water. The pool was shallow, reaching just below my breasts. Sighing happily, I leaned against the mossy wall. The lush, moist jungle enfolded me. It smelled of growing things. The cold water tingled between my legs, my nipples hardened with the feel of the sun. I felt like the first woman in the world, perhaps the only woman. But where was the only man? I thought of Kukulkan. The one who seduced him in the legend had been wicked, but perhaps she couldn't help herself. He was so powerful. What would it be like to have a god for a lover? Their union had been known, observed. Perhaps she hadn't minded, perhaps it even heightened her pleasure in those wonderful, awful moments.

I closed my eyes, imagining the scene. Kukulkan watching me, smiling, his eyes glittering green. In an instant, he was beside me in the pool, hot and eager, running his heavy hands over my skin with surprising tenderness. I tasted the salty sweat on his lips, felt myself weakening in his arms, surrendering. Why had I resisted? We were made for each other.

The Case for Simón Ruiz

The sun, directly overhead, beat down, penetrating my every pore. The jungle was quiet, as if saving its strength, even the raucous birds were silent. Don Eduardo's reference to Simón Ruiz had awakened memories. A rock tossed idly—or not so idly—into a pond. Now, as I returned to the *casa,* walking alone through the emerald heat, its ripples came at me from all sides. Shimmering, steaming.

I hadn't thought of Simón in quite a while, hadn't allowed myself to think of him, but San Quentin still haunted me. I was the only woman allowed to cover death row. Male reporters vied for the assignment. They loved the excitement, the drama, the bylines. I craved professional success, too, as much as any of them, but I also saw the prisoners' terror and desolation, felt their sense of waste and abandonment. "I won't go back," I'd tell myself after each visit. But every week I did.

Then one day Warden Johnston called me into his office. "We're having a hanging," he said, handing me an invitation as if to a party. "Want to come?" Johnston explained that the condemned man was actually a boy, a sixteen-year-old Mexican national who spoke no English.

My antenna was up. "No English! Did he have an interpreter?"

Johnston shrugged. "Guess not." He looked away, not meeting my eyes. "No one explained his death sentence either. The boy learned of it by chance. During a prison vaudeville show, he asked another Mexican con why they were sitting in the balcony rather than with the other prisoners. 'It's death row up here,' someone told him. 'My sentence was life!' he argued. You should have heard the guards laughing. When the kid figured it out, he screamed—got so bad it broke up the show."

The imagined scene sickened me. That poor boy might not have known his fate until they dragged him to the scaffold. Would they have bothered to tell him even then? Or might they have just slipped the noose over his head? I insisted on seeing the boy for myself. Johnston shrugged. "It's a waste of time, Mrs. Reed. He's as good as dead. No one cares about a Mexican."

A Mexican, yes. A stranger in a hostile land. Hopeless as it sounded, *I* cared. Perhaps there was something that I could do. At least I could try. I was beginning to see the hint of a story; national or not, the "man" facing death was only sixteen.

Reluctantly, Warden Johnston showed me to the small room where condemned men met their visitors. While waiting for the warden to locate a Spanish-speaking guard, I stared idly out at the prison garden. Winter wind wailed forlornly through bare rosebushes. It had rained all day. The view from the window looked as bleak and desolate as the high gray wall beyond.

The thought of Prescott, my younger brother, sprang to mind when I saw Simón Ruiz. The two were about the same age, though Simón was smaller. The Mexican boy was slight, with large, luminous eyes. Shy friendliness shone through despair as he spoke slowly and precisely, desperate to breach the gap between us. The interpreter, reluctantly pulled from his break, directed my questions brusquely. Yet, as the slow, tedious process of question, translation, answer, translation progressed, a prickly sympathy crept into his voice. The clock struck a half hour, then an hour—one less of the precious few remaining to the condemned boy. Eventually, I pieced Simón's story together.

Five months earlier Simón had left his bride and come to the United States, hoping to earn enough money to buy a farm in Mexico. While working on the railroad, he met an older man, José Mirando, who'd ridden with Pancho Villa. Mirando had recently been fired by John Miller, the section gang foreman, and was bitter. The railroad man was evil, Mirando said, and Simón could be certain that Miller would treat him as badly as he himself had been treated. The bandit kept at the lonely boy, cajoling, bullying, finally demanding that Simón help rob John Miller's house. Finally, the confused young man agreed. Mirando stood watch while Simón crept in and found a gun and some Liberty Bonds from the Great War. Hearing Miller's approaching footsteps, Mirando ordered Simón to shoot the foreman. Simón refused. When Miller spotted the boy and angrily berated him, Mirando yelled at Simón to kill the foreman, calling the lad a coward for standing such abuse.

Tears formed in Simón's eyes. "I didn't want to shoot Señor Miller, but Mirando kept urging me, taunting me. Finally he pulled out a gun and said he'd kill me if I didn't shoot the foreman. I looked away and pulled the trigger, hoping to miss, but the bullet killed him."

Emerging from the interview badly shaken, I asked the warden about the older man. "What happened to José Mirando?"

"Turned state's evidence and testified against the kid. Mirando's out now, free as a breeze. It's a real shame; Ruiz isn't a bad kid. He's religious; guess he thinks his saints will save him." Johnston searched my face, almost eagerly. "I don't suppose you'd care to see how it works."

I looked at him blankly.

"The hanging," he explained. "Maybe you'd like to see how we do it." He wagged his head slightly, mocking himself. "What an idea! You wouldn't like that at all."

"Oh, yes, I would!" I heard myself saying. "That boy was railroaded, anybody can see that. I want to see exactly what's going to happen to him. Show me."

On the ferry headed back to San Francisco, I seated myself by a window. No one seeing the prison from the outside could ever imagine the soul-wrenching bleakness of its interior. I knew the penitentiary was built like a medieval fortress. The slamming iron gates of the inner stockade still rang in my ears and somewhere behind them a boy waited to die. Warden Johnston said it was hopeless, but I wasn't going to accept that. This was Simón's big chance and, I sensed, mine as well. Slowly I began to write. The style I chose was methodical, deliberately laconic. I wanted my readers to be drawn in, slowly, perhaps unwittingly, hooked by the horror of what was to happen. It didn't matter that the boy was a Mexican national; he could be anyone's son.

All the "props" are in readiness. The rope, the scales, the trap door, the three iron balls, suspended from taut cords and concealed beneath the gallows floor—each has been thoroughly examined and deemed efficient. *And the Mexican boy who is to be the principal actor in tomorrow's tragedy? He, too, is ready—and awaits his fate with stoicism, a calmness that surpasses anything in the traditions of San Francisco's death row. . . .*

My story ran the next morning on the front page of the *News Call* under the banner headline: BOY HANGS TO-MORROW UNLESS GOVERNOR INTERVENES. Hastily sketched out on the ferry, it tugged at the city's heartstrings. I was good at that.

When Governor Stephens responded with a stay of execution, Mr. Older was jubilant. "Great story! Good work, Alma." But his compliments meant little compared to the proud hugs from Sam Reed, my husband of just six months. Sam had bootleg champagne waiting for me when I got home that night. A celebration.

"It's only a two-week stay," I reminded him. "Simón has already been sentenced. What can anyone do now?"

Sam's arms tightened about me. "The governor got most of those calls and wires from women—newly enfranchised voters. Give them a cause and they'll fight for it."

His words stayed with me long after our private party was over. I lay quietly, my head on his shoulder, listening to his even breathing as I turned the idea over and over in my mind. Sam was right; women voters were an untapped resource. How could I use them? The next day Central at the telephone office was kept busy directing incoming and outgoing calls. The lines were cracking, burning up with women calling each other to talk about Simón. "That poor boy!" "Could be anybody's child." "What can we do to save him?" The telephone company was hard put to keep up with them all.

Governor William D. Stephens is convinced that the women of California are opposed to the hanging of Simón Ruiz,

I wrote a few days later.

It was I who'd activated the twelve club leaders, representing some sixty thousand women, to converge on the executive office in Sacramento. My own plea had been the most eloquent of all. I couldn't quite write that into my story but I did hint a little.

My clubbies and I were good, no doubt about it, just not good enough. The issue, now called "boy hanging," quickly divided the state. The deputy sheriff of San Bernardino County, where Miller had been shot, countered our efforts by urging that the sentence be carried out immediately. Hundreds, professing to fear a massive crime wave, agreed. Their letters and wires poured into the governor's office. The best I could wrest was another reprieve. Two more weeks that Governor Stephens swore would be the last granted.

The boy's life was at stake, not to mention the biggest story of my life. Words alone were not going to save

Simón. I sat down at the typewriter and drafted a bill. If passed, the hanging age would be raised from fourteen to eighteen. That would do it! I was proud of myself, but where would I find the legislator willing to sponsor such a bill? None of the men I approached would touch it; each rejected the idea as fit only for bleeding hearts.

That evening before dinner, I turned absently to my girlhood friend, Theoline Whitney. "What am I going to do?"

"Really, Alma"—Theoline looked up from the salad she was tossing—"there's just one thing you can do."

I looked at her in surprise. Lately Theoline had taken to dropping by our apartment in the evenings. Sometimes she brought a casserole that she'd put together herself. Today it was a basket of vegetables from her parents' farm south of the city. Theoline's small, shapely figure looked demurely efficient as she bustled about tucking squash and tomatoes into our icebox.

"And just what is that one thing?" I asked, trying not to sound sarcastic. Theoline meant well but sometimes I wondered if she read anything in the newspaper other than reviews of her own singing recitals.

She tossed her curly head in a suggestion of impatience. "Go to a woman legislator, that's what."

"A woman . . . there's only one, Anna Saylor. She represents San Francisco."

"That's right. I voted for her, didn't you?"

"Of course, she was the first woman to run for office. If she takes this bill on, she'll be the last. It's political suicide."

"Or a chance to make history," Theoline countered. "If anyone can persuade her, it's you, Alma."

I hesitated, weighing Saylor's chances. I'd followed the assemblywoman's career dubiously. Several times, while covering her campaign, I'd half expected the middle-aged matron to wave a plate of twice-done potatoes at her audiences. Now she'd be taking on a *real* hot potato. What were a housewife's chances against Sacramento's political machine?

Fremont Older handed me the first edition himself. Its headline read: ASSEMBLYWOMAN WILL PRESENT BILL TO STOP HANGING BOYS. The whole news staff crowded around, excited and admiring. They were proud of me; even the toughest of the old hands admitted that I'd done good for "a skirt." I had the best boss in the world. Mr. Older not only backed my cause with stirring editorials, but agreed to send me to Sacramento for a month to lobby for the bill. "You'd go anyway," he said. "I might as well have you there as our correspondent."

If only Sam were as encouraging. My husband's interest in the issue had waned almost immediately. He'd grown resentful of my evenings in the library digging into the legal system or on the telephone rallying clubwomen. "Enough is enough, Alma." I was torn, adoring

Sam, hating the idea of being separated. But what chance had Simón without me? The battle would soon be over, I told myself. Then I'd make it up to Sam for all those hours of loneliness.

Theoline was an unexpected ally. "You love all this, don't you, Alma? You thrive on it." We'd met for a quick snack around the corner from the ferry building. I had my small bag beside me, poised to take the overnight steamer to Sacramento. "You want to help the boy, but it's more than that, isn't it? You thrive on being in the thick of things."

I nodded. Theoline and I had been friends since kindergarten. She understood me well. "You will look in on Sam, won't you?" I asked. "See that he's getting enough to eat? Don't let him be lonely."

"I won't. I promise." The paddleboat hooted. I grabbed my bag, fumbled for change. "I'll take care of it," she offered, picking up the bill. "I'll take care of everything."

Anna Saylor was waiting on the wharf in Sacramento early the next morning. "Wait till you see the papers!" she announced grimly. "The capitol's dead set against us. We need all the help we can get."

I established a command post at the Capitol Hotel, where clubwomen quickly set a telephone chain in motion. The enemy was formidable. Angry headlines threatened crime waves if children under eighteen were

exempted from death. They deplored our bill, demanding instead that the present law be strengthened. Bible-
banging clergyman were our strongest adversaries. "An
eye for an eye," they roared.

The Assembly fight was bitter but my own lobbyists
gathered strength. The bill was returned to committee.
This time, it came back with a recommendation for passage. On March 24, 1921, the Saylor bill was approved in
the House. Now for the Senate.

I'd been wiring Sam nightly with progress reports. His
infrequent answers were terse, asking only: WHEN ARE
YOU COMING HOME? Now, at last, I had promising
news to share and decided to indulge in the extravagance
of a long-distance call. The phone rang again and again. I
imagined it echoing in our small apartment. Where could
he be? I missed Sam terribly, missed our Sundays in bed
lazing over the newspaper, our Saturdays at the cinema
watching Charlie Chaplin. Memories of our lovemaking
filled me with longing.

For now, however, I had to concentrate on the job at
hand. Appalled at our victory, the *Sacramento Union* warned:
"Women lobbyists are exacting promises from senators to
vote for the bill."

We were, too, but not enough of them. I was growing
desperate. The senators' resistance was steely, seemingly
ingrained. Simón's precarious existence, the passage of
the amendment that could save him, had taken over my

life. Every waking moment was centered on his cause. Sometimes I wondered if my meeting with the boy wasn't somehow predestined, that it was my life's purpose to save not only Simón, but also hundreds, perhaps thousands, of others who had no one to speak for them. Now, for the first time, confronted with the seemingly impregnable resistance of the Senate, I began to have doubts. My pleas, my careful planning, the desperately hard work, the precious hours away from Sam—was it all for nothing?

The Senate was deadlocked, one vote all we needed. Where to get it? I studied the opposing senators. One vote, one man: John Inman, said to have an eye for the ladies . . .

"A bite to eat?" I suggested, smiling up at his florid face. I took his arm, feeling confident. "Surely you don't believe state-sanctioned murder is God's work—not for children."

"Not for anyone," he surprised me by answering. "I'm against capital punishment."

"You are?" my heart quickened. "But you've spoken out against our bill."

"I'll vote against it, too." Inman shook his head emphatically, dashing my hopes. "Belief is one thing, political agenda another. Sorry, little lady, this here's politics you're playing with, not some kind of sorority tea party. I've already promised my vote—swapped it for other promises."

Silently we walked back to the courthouse. Nothing more to say. I listened as roll was taken. Twenty in favor, Inman's the twentieth "no" vote. It remained only for the Senate's president to break the tie. Everyone knew how he felt. I could bear it no longer. That poor boy waiting in his cell. My eyes filled as I hurried outside. Sitting on the capitol steps, face buried in my hands, I scarcely heard the passing footsteps, wasn't aware they had stopped.

I didn't look up until I felt the hand on my shoulder. John Inman. I glared up at him, struggling to control my sobs. "You—you're supposed to be a man of honor—a statesman! Now you've traded a boy's life for a few votes in some crummy backroom deal." I reached frantically for a handkerchief, blotted at my nose and eyes. "Stop staring at me! Go look at yourself in the mirror—if you dare!"

He said nothing for what seemed a very long time. Then his hand tightened on my shoulder. I shrugged it off. After a moment, Inman turned and reentered the courthouse. It wasn't long before my curiosity overcame me; I followed him inside. Standing in the doorway of the Senate chamber, I saw that he'd taken his usual seat and was shuffling through some papers in his briefcase. As I watched, he rose to his feet. Looking straight at me, he called out loud and clear: "I demand a reconsideration."

The boy hanging bill, *my* boy hanging bill, passed twenty-one to twenty, the deciding vote cast by Inman.

What followed was pandemonium. Flashbulbs going off, women hugging one another, fairly shrieking their surprised delight, men back-slapping one another jubilantly or shaking their fists in rage.

"What happened?" I asked Inman when I was finally able to corner him. "Why did you change your vote?"

One cool gray eye closed in a wink. "Let's just say, I never could bear to see a lady cry." Three listening reporters hurriedly jotted down the quote. I could see a legend being born before my eyes. It wouldn't hurt my reputation at all. In fact, I rather liked it. The press had Inman cornered now, the party turned away.

Would I ever learn what had caused his abrupt change of heart? Shady maneuvering of some sort, surely. I was certain there was a story hidden somewhere, but for once I wouldn't pursue it. Heart pounding, I phoned the news about Simón to the *News Call*. I wanted to tell Sam, too, started to call, the coins ready, the receiver in my hand, but changed my mind. If I hurried, there was just time to catch the *Delta Duchess*.

It seemed as I rushed aboard that many of the passengers had already heard the trial's outcome. Word spread throughout the steamer. People were nodding and pointing in my direction. Some rushed to shake my hand, others glared angrily. Once my bag was stowed, I sought a secluded spot on deck. The water was smooth and flowing, lush foliage so close in places that it skimmed the boat's railing. I smelled the scent of the river, dampness, mud, tule. Inside a jazz band played, couples had begun to Charleston. Soon Sacramento faded from view. Sam and I would have to make this trip together some day soon.

My mind raced ahead. I would arrive at our door early the next morning with the newspaper. We'd read the headlines together. I couldn't wait to see his face.

Well, I did see his face—and Theoline's as well. Their faces and a lot more.

How long ago had that been? Two years? It seemed much longer. As I emerged from the jungle, Don Eduardo's *casa* loomed before me, white walls sparkling in the sunlight, sprays of bougainvillea blazing in all directions. Another world, another life. I recalled the pain, the anger, and the bitterness. It all seemed far away, almost as though it had happened to someone else.

13

A Perfect Martini

SAGE
Palo Alto, the present

It was nearly ten when I finished sorting my notes. I'd worked all evening at my desk in Palo Alto, jazz favorites floating softly from the next room, teacup at my elbow. Alma Reed's San Francisco years had been easy to track with so many of her "sob sister" stories on file at the *News Call*. Robberies, murders, trials. She'd covered them all: chasing fire wagons, buttonholing prosecutors and defendants, interviewing convicted killers on death row.

The latter made Alma famous—or infamous, depending on one's viewpoint. Not everybody approved then; not everyone approves now. Simón Ruiz was an illegal immigrant goaded to murder, condemned to death. Many had said, "Good riddance, too many of them here already." Some would still say that. Yet, more than eighty years later, the young reporter's "boy-hanging law" remained on the books.

Once again I picked up Alma's picture, studied the faded paper under the light, struck as always by the spirit and confidence in her wide eyes. She was so young, so much life ahead of her. *What do you want from me, Alma?* I ran my fingers lightly, regretfully, over the picture. *Not everyone can just go adventuring. Life deals some tough cards. Even Simón didn't get everything he wanted. Once the bill was passed, his life assured, don't you think he longed most of all for freedom? It didn't come for twenty years. Most of us have to wait, that's the way it is. Some wait forever. . . .*

I was closing down the computer when the phone rang. Who but the hospital would call so late? I wondered, glancing at my watch. Had something happened to Mark? I grabbed the phone, throat tense as I answered.

"Sage, is that you?" a relaxed, warm-timbered voice asked. "Dave here. David Winslow."

"David! What a surprise. When I lost your card, I thought I'd lost touch with you forever."

"You never e-mailed. . . . I thought you wanted to lose me."

"Are you serious! After all you did for Mark?"

"How is he?"

"Not very well," I told him. "He's in a convalescent hospital. The cancer has traveled to his spine. The terrible pain is gone, but he's paralyzed now from the waist down. The doctors doubt he'll ever walk again."

"I'm sorry to hear that. How are you holding up?"

How was I? Depressed? Exhausted? Sometimes even angry. That would never do. "Fine, just fine," the stock reply. Changing the subject, I asked, "How about you, David? Are you calling from Yucatán?"

"San Francisco—I just got into town."

An unexpected wave of pleasure swept over me as I asked, "What's brought you here?"

"I'm presenting a paper at a drug conference."

"Impressive! I wish I could hear you."

"That's what I hoped you'd say. Take a break. Come up tomorrow."

"Tomorrow won't work." I said, placing Alma's picture facedown on the desk. "Mark's specialist is coming. He wants to try a new kind of therapy."

"You sound like you could use a break afterward—and I'll just be in town for the day." He paused for a moment. "Why not meet for drinks at my hotel—the St. Francis— tomorrow when you get through at the hospital? Say around fivish?"

I picked up Alma's picture again, imagined a smile.

The next day, weaving through San Francisco traffic to the historic hotel, I felt surprisingly lighthearted despite the disappointing events of the past few hours. I hadn't really expected the new wonder doctor to change anything, but at least Mark was holding his own. I was grateful for that. As for myself, how long since I'd gone anywhere just for fun? Where was the harm in it?

The St. Francis's Compass Rose Room was tailor-made, a bar haunted by the ghost of every lover I'd ever had or wished I'd had, plus a bunch of other beautiful people, the kind one longs for at doubtful dinner parties. How long ago had *that* been? Lovers, even dinner parties, belonged to a past life. Long past. Another woman, another time. But this is now, a harmless moment just for me. And what better place to meet a new old friend?

My silver Moroccan bracelets clinked softly as I climbed the sweeping stairway. For once the scent in the air was expensive perfume, not medicine. Feeling like a schoolgirl playing hooky, I paused in the doorway, my highest heels sinking into the Oriental carpet. The interior of the bar was dark and mysterious, orchids trailing in all directions. An ornate gilt mirror reflected my image: a slender, silver-haired woman in a smoke-gray pantsuit. I touched the lapel like a talisman, enjoying the feel of velvet against my skin.

As I scanned the softly lit room, a tall man in a tie and blazer moved toward me. I hesitated, uncertain, then recognized the wry, lopsided smile. How good to see him. We hugged, kissed lightly, stepped back, and, each surveying the other, "You look great" was said almost in unison. Then laughter, only slightly forced.

"What you did in Yucatán saved Mark's life," I said looking up at him. "How can I ever—What can I say?"

"Don't say anything. We were lucky, that's all."

David led me back to a leafy corner. The nook, partially enclosed by an antique screen, was piled with pillows fashioned from old Chinese robes. He seated me at a cocktail table. Carved jade dragons twined about its pedestal. I relaxed against the pillows and stroked a dragon.

"Tell me about why you're here, the paper, what you do," I said to him.

David helped himself to a Brazil nut from a painted china dish. "My team is researching a virus that might feed into a cancer cure. It involves collecting specimens from various cultures. Last year it was Hungarian gypsies, this year the Maya. The descendants of the people who built those 'lost' cities are alive and well, you know."

Was there help here for Mark? My pulse quickened. "Have you discovered anything?"

He shook his head, as though reading my thoughts. "I'm afraid the cure, if any, is a long way off. So far all we've found are interesting links to other cultures—that's what I talked about today, findings that reinforce the anthropologists' land bridge theory. Indian samples identical to those we've found in northern Japan." David nodded to a server, a sleek creature in Chinese lounging pajamas. "I've already ordered a Scotch over—what about you?"

I smiled. How long since I'd felt pampered? "Bartenders here have a knack for turning juniper berries into pure silk—the best I've ever tasted."

"Now how did I know you were a martini kind of lady?"

Soon the server returned with a lacquer tray bearing our drinks. David lifted his in a toast. "To friendship?"

"To your research," I countered.

"What about *your* research? Where are you with that Alma Reed biography?"

"It's fascinating, but . . ." I attempted a game smile, barely held back a sigh. "The most important part of my research—the Felipe part—has to be done in Yucatán. . . . I can't leave Mark now."

My hand tightened on the glass, a classic triangle atop a tall stem. "Let's talk about something fun. Where do you live when you're not in Yucatán?"

"Georgetown . . . My wife died two years ago." He paused, looking down at his drink. "*Your* life is much more interesting. I know; I Googled you. The articles you've written told me lots of things," David's voice cut into my thoughts. "Clues about who you are."

I felt a tinge of pleasure at the thought of this attractive, perhaps important man taking the trouble to locate me. How long had it been since anything like that had happened? I glanced surreptitiously at my watch. Mark would be expecting me to call.

"The article you wrote about Yucatán is compelling," David continued. "I felt you in every line. The *way* you write—the things you see that others might not notice. I like the style, elegant but with a little sass tossed in—like you, I think."

I touched his fingers lightly. "Thank you."

He sat looking at my hand a moment. "Why aren't you and Mark married?"

I sat up with a start. "We're as good as married, what difference does a piece of paper make?"

"That sounds like a kid's line."

We both laughed. "I married years ago—a kid then for certain. It didn't work. I'm older now—at least chronologically. I like things the way they are."

"Ah—the independent woman." Before he could say more a man in a well-cut dark suit appeared at our table. A cashmere suit, I noted; alligator shoes, too. The man smiled broadly, extending his hand toward David. "Dr. Winslow, forgive me for intruding," he nodded politely at me. "I just wanted to say how impressed I was by your paper. Your conclusions regarding the early Maya are most provocative."

"Glad you enjoyed it," David said, rather curtly, I thought.

The man's well-manicured fingers offered a card from a silver case. "I'm Julian Roebuck, Roebuck Pharma. I'll call you, if I may, in Washington. There's something of mutual interest I'd like to discuss with you."

"Thank you," David said, seeming to dismiss him.

"Now there's a *real* drug lord." He nodded toward Roebuck's retreating back. "Those biotech companies are always trolling for government scientists. They offer big bucks, *very* big bucks sometimes, in hopes of luring us onto their own research teams."

"Are you biting?" I asked.

"Roebuck Pharma has one great attraction. It's in Silicon Valley. Maybe I'd get to see you once in awhile—oh, I know, just friends."

My pleasure at the idea surprised me. I felt almost guilty asking: "Might you consider his offer?"

David was silent a moment. "I can't say that I haven't been tempted by those guys from time to time—particularly now—but the fact is, my life is complicated."

"You're involved with someone," I said, and wished I hadn't.

"Several someones," he smiled. "I run the family farm in southeastern Pennsylvania. My parents live in the little town close by. My daughters go to college near there. . . . "

"You're a gentleman farmer then," I said, trying to assimilate this new side of David.

"Part-time. The farm's near enough to commute on weekends, but with these long assignments, I'm more of an absentee landlord—most of the land is rented out."

"But you can't rent out your family." I liked him better all the time.

"I wouldn't want to. I'm looking forward to getting back to them." He was silent for a few moments, sipping his drink. "But we were talking about you: a woman dedicated to a terminally ill man who is not her husband, a woman who says she likes things as they are."

I looked up from my drink. David's eyes were on mine, waiting. "Mark and I have been close friends, companions, lovers—whatever one calls it—for twelve years. He wanted to marry almost from the start. I didn't. The space felt good, our separate homes, somewhat separate lives. Then five years ago he was diagnosed. It's been downhill ever since."

"You didn't have to stay, you had no obligation," David reminded me.

"Of course I did! I *do*." My drink splashed as I set it down. "He counts on me." I was silent again, wondering how to explain to David, to anyone. I could tell him about the awful years leading up to Mark's collapse, the physical, practical, and moral responsibilities, the fear for his life, the ever increasing constriction of my own. I could tell him about the seventy-mile commute every day from my home to the convalescent hospital, the hours spent there reading, chatting, the effort to be cheerful, always cheerful, the constant fear for his life, my own growing fatigue. There were lots of things I might have told him but would not.

"The marriage talk has come up again recently," I found myself confiding. "Mark wants to so badly and it would make things easier for me, dealing with doctors and administrators. But I've decided against it. His sons might misunderstand, might think it . . . self-serving. No one knows how much time remains for Mark. We all have to work together to keep him as comfortable and happy as possible."

David put his hand on mine. "I think you're a very special lady."

"Thank you." I smiled, leaving my hand where it was. "I think the best thing about brief encounters is that everyone gets to keep their illusions."

"Let's have another drink on that."

Yes, I thought. Another drink, then dinner followed by a nightcap in David's cozy room somewhere in this vast hotel. It would be so easy not to drive home tonight. David was an interesting man, an exciting man, fun to be with. I felt genuinely happy for the first time in . . . how long? A violinist had begun to play. Our little alcove with its orchids and painted screens seemed like another world. Who would ever know? I sipped my martini, feeling the electricity of lovers and other strangers coming together in this subtly wicked place. And then I thought of Mark waiting, with little left to live for but my phone call.

I stood up.

"You're not leaving now?" David asked, rising too. His arms moved around me, his lips on mine. Nice lips, warm and firm. I knew I'd remember the moment for a long time, perhaps always.

"Thank you," I said, at last, pulling away. "Thank you for a perfect martini."

I turned away, didn't look back. Hurrying down the stairs, I thought gratefully of the Alma notes waiting on my desk. Vicarious living had one advantage. It kept you out of trouble.

14

The *Cenote* Gives Up Its Secrets

ALMA
Chichen Itza, 1923

"My time here is almost up," I quietly reminded Don Eduardo the next morning at breakfast.

Frowning, he put down his coffee cup. "As though I could forget." The archaeologist sat for a time watching me. What was he searching for?

"Meet me at the *cenote*," he said at last. "Come at day's end. We'll be alone. Perhaps . . . perhaps I'll have something of interest to tell you."

"You said a 'scoop,'" I reminded him.

"That remains to be seen." He rose from the breakfast table, nodding absently to the other stragglers intent on their own conversations, and walked away.

It was a busy morning: notes to check, last-minute photographs to take. I was all over the site and yet found time dragging. At noon, I was the first into the dining room, waiting for Don Eduardo's arrival. He came in late, and sat down between Dr. Morley and Earl. Was Don Eduardo avoiding me? That was surely a first. Now it was I who searched *his* face. He nodded, smiled blandly, and resumed his conversation.

The afternoon passed more slowly than the morning. I packed, then repacked. Finally, I pulled on my digging clothes, so worn now, picked up my pith helmet, and walked out into the tangled garden. The team's activities were winding down. Some big gun archaeologists had arrived earlier in the week. They were top-level scientists from Boston and Washington, curious about Chichen Itza, so long off limits, and eager to hear the survey team's conclusions firsthand. In the last few days they'd been all over the site, examining finds, asking questions, but now the excitement was dissipating. The talk was all about next year, who would make up the second expedition? The working day was essentially over, some archaeologists were already heading back to the hacienda, where a party would mark the conclusion of the Chichen Itza expedition.

"It's quitting time, Alma." Dr. Morley had spied me heading toward the *cenote,* notebook in hand. "The mariachis will be tuning up. What do you bet His Excellency is already waiting? You don't want to disappoint him."

"I'll be along shortly," I assured Morley. Despite my efforts to distance myself, Felipe's attentions must be very obvious if that absent-minded professor had noticed something between us. "Don't wait for me." I turned away and hurried down a narrow path, hoping no one would follow.

Don Eduardo sat on a small granite platform, the remains of a temple. He rested against a crumbling limestone slab, legs stretched stiffly before him. Below was the large pool of limpid green water. Numerous visits to the *cenote* had not dimmed my initial sense of malevolence. To me, the so-called sacred well was a gaping wound in the heart of the surrounding forest.

An iguana crawled from beneath a pile of rocks and blinked vacantly at me as I seated myself beside the archaeologist. Opening my leather pack, I took out a notebook and pencil. "What have you got for me?" I asked with more confidence than I felt.

"Patience, my girl," he chided. "What I have to say is a confession. Try not to judge me too harshly. You must listen to the whole thing in order to understand how it could have happened. The story is mine; only I know all of it."

I took out the pearl-handled pocketknife that my father had given me long ago and began to sharpen my pencil. With a buildup like that the man might have a real story to tell.

Don Eduardo moved his boot to deflect a trail of ants headed our way. "You have to know that when I first came here all I heard were legends about the *cenote*. After a time it seemed that my dreams were haunted by the sacrificial victims. They were mostly girls, you know. Girls cried more; the rain god preferred that."

Supported by the ledge, I listened to Don Eduardo's soft voice. Perhaps it hypnotized me. Slowly, as the late-afternoon sun slipped behind the jungle foliage, a brilliant flash of purple and gold, his words came alive. *A nubile Mayan beauty emerged from the small sanctuary crowning El Castillo. Dressed in white and wearing a bridal wreath of scarlet tulipanes, she was escorted from the chamber by black-masked priests. The beating of the death drums and the plaintive note of high-pitched flutes announced her descent down the great stairway. Below her in the courtyard grim-faced nobles and priests waited. Trembling, the helpless victim joined them in a march along the sacred path to the pool's edge. The baleful music reached a frenzied pitch as the young girl was lifted to the granite platform.* The platform where I now sat. Gradually I became aware that Don Eduardo was silent; his faded eyes watched me speculatively. I returned his stare, challenging. Was there more?

"You can't imagine how lonely it can get here at night," he said at last. "I had little to do but read the legends collected by early priests, read and dream. I determined to learn Maya. Then, as time passed, I became a confidant of the H'Menens."

I shook my head doubtfully. Where was he going with this? "The H'Menens?"

"Mayan wise men," he explained. "After many trials, they inducted me into a secret brotherhood and eventually trusted me enough to confirm the *cenote* legend. The sacrificial ceremony had been performed for centuries in times of crisis. They even pointed out the part of the *cenote* beneath which Chac had his palace."

"His palace! Oh, come on!" I slapped my notebook down on a rock.

Don Eduardo smiled indulgently. "I understand your skepticism, my dear. I, too, assumed the H'Menens were merely colorful raconteurs, but as I studied the history of the area as well as its legends, the story made perfect sense. Marriage to Chac in the depths of the well might bring water to a parched land. The maiden's brief life was a preparation for sacrifice, the *cenote* her gateway to immortal bliss. Imagine the priests and nobles crowded around the *cenote*'s rim, arms raised in supplication, then a shriek pierces the forest as the young woman is hurled headlong into this yawning water pit."

I turned away, shuddering, but Don Eduardo took my arm and forced me to meet his eyes. "You feel it, too?" he asked eagerly. "It's real for you as well."

"Surprisingly real," I said, my throat constricted with emotion. I'd stopped writing, was aware again of the fetid jungle smells, the perspiration soaking my blouse. "It's a very compelling legend."

"I thought I'd made myself clear. This is *not* a legend. I assure you, every bit of it is true."

"How can you know that?"

"Because I, too, have descended into the well."

My hand flew to my mouth. In the beautiful little pool in which I'd submerged myself a few days before, fantasies had claimed my imagination. Surely there could be no connection to the gaping pit before me. "*This* well?" I glanced down, horrified. "What are you saying!"

Don Eduardo wiped his brow. He looked very old at that moment. I had a desire to take his hand, but was fearful of distracting him from the story. He sighed softly, recalling: "There wasn't much to do here in the old days. My wife hated Yucatán from the start. Jane tried but could never feel as I did, and still do, about this place. She was desperately homesick for Boston. We fought constantly. Finally the day came when Jane gave it up and returned home with our young daughter. 'Just for a visit.' She never came back.

"With nothing but time on my hands I began to collect rare manuscripts—you've seen some of them. One day I came across a copy of a letter sent by the mayor of Valladolid to the king of Spain in 1579. Old people had told him stories from their youth. The intimacy of their descriptions had the ring of truth. The mayor had believed them. The more I thought about it, the more I began to wonder, and then there was something else . . ."

I stopped writing, looked up from my notebook. "What else?"

"If the nobles were willing to make the supreme sacrifice of human life—if that part was true—then what else might they have sacrificed?"

I shook my head. "I don't follow."

"Gold, of course, and jewels. Surely they, too, must exist. I determined to find out."

Studying the white-bearded man, I was reminded of Hunac Ceel. The Mayan hero and the visionary archaeologist sounded like kindred spirits, each plunging into the sacred well in search of fame and fortune. "What did you do?" I asked him, notebook in hand.

"I went from one dredging expert to another. They all said the same thing: 'If you want to commit suicide, find an easier way.' I'd about given up when a chance encounter changed my luck. I met Nicholas Pappas, a Greek sponge diver, and persuaded him to come back with me to Yucatán. The two of us found a primitive pontoon boat and added an air pump. Nicholas set about teaching a gang of Mayan workmen how to manage the pump. My life would depend on it. The copper helmet I wore weighed more than thirty pounds and had plate-glass goggles. There were lead necklaces nearly as heavy as the helmet, and canvas shoes with thick, wrought-iron soles."

I shook my head, unable to imagine the frail man

beside me undertaking such a daring adventure. "You were incredibly brave."

He smiled ruefully. "I was determined. With the speaking tube, air hose, and lifeline adjusted, Nicholas helped me to waddle to a ladder leading down into the water."

I shivered despite the heat. "It sounds terrifying."

"It *was* terrifying. No one had ever returned from the well."

"Except for Hunac Ceel," I reminded him.

"Except for the legendary Hunac," Don Eduardo conceded. "That's why I'm telling you this story. You, too, are an adventurer and, I think, a bit of an opportunist. You, Alma, are the right person at last, the one who will finally understand." He moved to a kneeling position and peered over the edge as though reliving the experience. "As I stepped onto the ladder, each of my Mayan helpers came forward to shake my hand. Their solemn faces told me they thought it a last farewell. Releasing my hold, I sank like lead into the water," he said, gesturing toward the well.

Looking across the *cenote*, I judged it to be at least two hundred feet across. The limestone wall dropped about seventy feet from the tree-fringed rim to the surface of the pool. Following my glance, he explained, "Beneath the water—some thirty feet of it—is a mud bed. I felt like I, too, was a sacrificial victim as I descended down, down, down into that ooze. Those early dives were nearly fatal. One ruptured my ear drum.

"During the first ten feet of descent, light rays changed from yellow to green and then to purplish black. After that I was in total darkness. Sharp pains shot through my ears. When I gulped and opened the air valves in my helmet, a sound like *pht! pht!* came from each ear. The pressure lessened and I lowered myself farther. This happened again and again before I reached the bottom. Curiously, I felt increasingly weightless the farther down I went. When at last I landed on a stone column fallen from the shrine above, I felt no weight at all. I was more like a bubble than a man burdened by heavy weights.

"My submarine flashlight was useless in the gruel-like water and mud. All was in darkness. For weeks, I made daily descents. Once, floating up to the surface without warning, I struck the bottom of the boat with a loud thud that terrified my helpers. They ran in all directions screaming, certain that Chac was rising in righteous anger at the invasion of his domain. I brought up load after load of mud to be examined. It netted nothing more than the sediment of centuries of jungle decay."

I flung a stone into the dark green water and watched it sink. "How long did this go on?"

"Years," he shrugged.

"You must have found something! What kept you going back into that dreadful pool again and again?"

He smiled expansively, aware I'm sure that I was hanging on every word. "In late 1903, two balls turned up in the mud. I pounded them, felt them, smelled them. Then I tore one open and touched a match to its center. As a long spiral of sweet-scented smoke curled upward, I remembered the words of the H'Menens: 'In ancient times our fathers burned sacred resin, and, by its fragrant smoke, prayers were wafted to the god whose home is in the sun.'

"I shouted and danced like a child, realizing that the two small balls were copal, which the Maya used as incense. It was the scent of victory. I was close. A few days later, I found the skeletons of three women. Soon after, some gold disks were uncovered, then jade—huge pieces of carved jade—pendants, necklaces—gold bracelets, precious ornaments beyond belief."

I sat speechless. It was an amazing story, surely too amazing to be true. "Why have you never told anyone?" I asked at last. "That was twenty years ago."

"If word had gotten out, the site would have been overrun by bandits, officials, anybody, everybody. I believed—I still believe—that the land was mine, the risk was mine. The treasure, too, was mine, to do with as I pleased.

I caught my breath. "And what did you do with it?"

"I sent it out of the country piece by piece in a diplomatic pouch to my benefactors at the Peabody Museum."

"Do you mean," my voice dropped to a whisper, "that you just packed all those precious things off to Boston? Didn't you think that might be stealing?"

"My dear girl, I'd hardly call it stealing. I simply sent the treasure away for safekeeping."

"But Chac, Kukulkan—the gods—" I blurted out, feeling foolish.

"Surely you don't believe those foolish stories!"

"*What* stories?" Silly as it seemed, I felt a tingle of dread creep over me.

"The Mayan workmen were badly frightened," Don Eduardo admitted. "They believed the well to be cursed. Their headman had warned them that anyone who took treasure from the *cenote* would lose the thing he loved most in the world."

I looked down at the dark water below. "Weren't *you* frightened?"

"Dear girl, that's only superstition. Besides, I'm an old man. I have nothing left to lose."

"Why did the workmen never tell anyone?"

"Who knows? Perhaps they felt that anyone who revealed my story would also be cursed."

15

The Palace of the Governor

I t's safe to say that everyone enjoyed the farewell
party at Don Eduardo's hacienda—everyone but
me. I was wildly excited by the *don*'s disclosure, but also
uneasy.

Sylvanus Morley's team was all present. They had
reason to be proud and were. His big guns were also assembled, each of them, I noted, wearing a newly acquired
guayabera shirt. Even big, bombastic Marshall Saville,
head the Museum of the American Indian—a prestigious
outfit if there ever was one—had forsaken his suit and tie.
Across from him sat the president of the Carnegie Institution, portly, pompous Dr. John C. Merriam. His organi-
zation had sponsored the dig. I wouldn't have been there
without his okay. The hint of a scandal was the last thing

he'd want. But the man that worried me most was the Peabody rep, the hawklike H. G. Spinden.

I could scarcely guess what lay ahead for Don Eduardo and for me, but tonight Morley's archaeologists were jubilant, Felipe's dignitaries sanguine. The expedition had proved successful; Yucatán's archaeological future beckoned bright with promise. Felipe was there, of course, wifeless as usual. At first I tried to avoid him, but he was constantly at my side, claiming too many dances. To refuse our host in his own country was unthinkable.

Don Eduardo smiled frequently, his manner toward the other archaeologists for the first time almost affable. More than once I caught Ann and Earl exchanging puzzled glances. I speculated that the archaeologist's disclosure to me might have removed a burden that he'd carried for years. I hoped so. During the course of the evening, he and Felipe made a joint announcement. There were two archaeological sites to the north, Uxmal and Loltun, that our party must see before leaving Yucatán. Don Eduardo and the governor would accompany us on the two-day excursion as our *directores generales*. Though this would make our return home a bit more complex, everyone seemed in agreement that the side trip was an unexpected bonus.

Again and again that night I wondered why everything had to have a price tag. Lady Luck had gifted me with the story of a lifetime, but at what threat to Don Eduardo's reputation? Fortune had also brought Felipe into my life, the embodiment of everything I admired. Yet if I gave in to this married man, the outcome could only be a backstreet melodrama. I had no illusions regarding the constancy of Latin lovers. Why shouldn't his libido be kindled by a bright and stylish foreigner, particularly one who shared his ideals? Even if Felipe's feelings went deeper than a passing fancy, even if he truly loved me, where could it lead? Divorce was unthinkable in this Latin land.

The next day I refused Felipe's invitation to ride in his car back to Mérida, pleading that I had much to discuss with Don Eduardo. It was true.

"Your confidence was an honor," I began as soon as the *don* and I stepped into the *fortinga* reserved for us. "I'm deeply touched, but I'm a reporter, you know. My duty is to the *Times*."

"You think I'm not aware of that?" He eased himself back against the lumpy cushions. "I deliberated a long time before telling you."

He wants acknowledgment, craves it, I realized in that instant. Well, why not! The old boy deserved it. Who's to say that Don Eduardo was not the most daring and innovative archaeologist of all time? Nevertheless, I still felt a responsibility to warn him. "You are aware of the story's possible repercussions?"

He smiled expansively, arms locked behind his head. "There will be talk. Some may resent me for keeping my discoveries secret for so long. But what is that compared to the public knowledge that such treasures exist? Now people everywhere will know and appreciate Yucatán's heritage. Evidence of one of the greatest civilizations in the world has been hidden far too long."

"I'm concerned about that, too," I persisted. "Apparently the Peabody wants it that way. Why else would they have conspired with you all these years? Why haven't *they* made your findings public? Suppose they refuse to let me look at your treasure? I can't write about something that I haven't seen myself."

Don Eduardo stroked his short, white beard. His brows furrowed. Apparently this possibility hadn't occurred to him. "Very well, then," he conceded. "If I must put my 'confession' in writing, I shall. Give me your notebook, your pencil." Tearing out a page, he wrote quickly, a few brief paragraphs, then signed his name with a flourish. "They can hardly ignore this."

I took the paper gratefully, scanning it carefully before slipping the small sheet into my purse. I breathed a sigh of relief: One problem dealt with—for the time being at least. What about the other?

That evening in Mérida, Felipe was our host at a gala banquet in the Gran Hotel. Just as I entered the dining room, an orchestra started playing. Splendidly dressed mariachis sang. What were the words? *Alma, mi Alma.* They were singing my name! What was that all about? I felt the color rush to my cheeks. A little dazzled by all the crystal and china, I searched the place cards. Felipe must be mad! He'd put me on his right. Everyone in the room seemed to be staring at us. Most particularly Morley and his high horse cronies: Spinden, Saville, and Merriman. What must the archaeological community think? Felipe was causing a minor scandal, but what could I do about it?

Nothing, I realized, glad that I'd worn my blue satin dress.

"Alma, mi Alma" played again and again. My name, it could hardly be a coincidence. Turning to Felipe, leaning close enough to smell the sandalwood soap on his skin, I smiled, confiding, "I've never had a song written for me before."

For a second, he looked blank, then gently took my hand. "Yes, of course, it *is* your song, your song in every sense, but *alma* also means 'soul.' 'Alma, mi Alma' is a Yucatecan favorite. I hoped you'd like it."

I sat back, staring at him speechless with embarrassment. What an egotist he must think me.

The governor's big cat eyes searched mine. "You deserve a song written just for you," he murmured gently.

I turned away, not trusting myself to answer or even look at him.

The rest of the evening was agony. When the banquet finally ended, our party separated to return to our rooms, where we quickly changed our clothes and packed a few necessary items for our trip to Uxmal. Within minutes we'd hastily reassembled in the hotel foyer. It had been decided that we would travel by night to avoid the heat. Once again we were back in our *fortingas*, this time en route to the depot where we boarded a train. The banquet orchestra trailed behind us. As usual, nothing happened in Yucatán without a musical accompaniment.

"Alma, mi Alma" played again as I boarded, Felipe at my side. I pulled away and hurried down the aisle. The others were gathering in the club car, but I fled to my compartment and slammed the bolt, daring Felipe to follow me. No one knocked.

I turned this way and that on the berth, the sheets crisp against my thin silk gown. What would it be like to lay here beside Felipe, listening to the pounding rhythm of the rails, the mournful whistle drifting out into the hot tropic night? Sleep, when it finally came, was anything but restful. Felipe haunted my dreams.

The train had pulled to a stop when I awakened in the morning. Rolling over, I opened the window curtain. Outside was the village of Muna, round, thatched huts circling a tiny park. The villagers gave us a quick breakfast of coffee, tortillas, and mangos. More *fortingas*, even worse for wear but brightly polished, waited to take us the remaining ten miles to Uxmal. I stayed close to Don

Eduardo for the outing, but this time there was no escaping Felipe, who maneuvered the three of us into the same car.

The road was a washboard. I feared I'd be jolted out of my bones; the noise was deafening, conversation almost impossible.

"It is rough," Felipe shouted his apology, "but still an improvement. Until recently, Uxmal was navigable only by *volan*."

I shuddered, thinking of the two-wheeled carts I'd seen careening precariously along the roads of Yucatán. I knew Empress Carlota had made this same trip some sixty years earlier. She'd have been wearing a corset and hoopskirt. Imagine.

Uxmal, once reached, was worth the price. Lofty pyramids and gracefully terraced buildings towered above us, the enigmatic remains of an architectural masterpiece centuries in the making. Temples, courtyards, and plazas dazzled in all directions. Their massive carved facades, geometric in shape, made me giddy. Everywhere I looked I saw tangles of turtles, undulating serpents, thrusting snouts, crossed bones and skulls.

Flanked by Felipe and Don Eduardo, I approached the tallest structure, an immense pyramid. "We call it the Temple of the Magician," Felipe told me. His hand rested lightly on my arm. I felt both drowsy and alert. The otherness of him, of his exotic world, apparent as never before.

Felipe was mysterious and frightening and wonderful.

I looked up at the huge bulk of gently rounded stone. The sharply rising stairway, much taller than Kukulkan's pyramid, looked too steep to climb.

"It isn't as bad as it appears," Don Eduardo reassured me.

I'd forgotten he was there.

"Around the other side, there's an iron chain that was installed for Empress Carlota's state visit. We can go up that way."

Clinging to the heavy chain, I silently blessed Carlota. It was a precipitous climb, the stone staircase some hundred feet high. I noted self-consciously that Felipe wasn't resorting to the chain. Heart pounding furiously, I finally reached the top step and sank down. Below lay a massive complex of temples, walls, and causeways only partially wrested from the jungle's jealous grasp. It was all about god or gods, I decided. Placating gods and constantly reminding people of their dependency upon them. But where were those gods now without someone to worship them?

On all sides were cryptic nameless mounds, overgrown with lush foliage waiting to reveal their long-concealed marvels. "What's that spectacular building?" I pointed to the south.

"The Palace of the Governor," Felipe said. "Shall I show it to you?"

The descent from the Temple of the Magicians was even scarier than the ascent. I did it backward, very slowly, one hand, one foot always on a step, never looking down.

"This must be what they mean by 'one step at a time,'" I gasped, when both trembling legs finally touched the ground.

"Your method is very efficient," Felipe said, taking my arm. "I will call it the jaguar crawl."

I smiled at him. Perhaps I hadn't looked as foolish as I'd felt. "Was this really a governor's palace?" I asked as we approached the next building, the most massive on the site.

"That's what the Spaniards called it," Felipe replied. "The city was deserted when they got here, as great a puzzle to the conquistadors as it is to us today. Maybe they thought, If it's that grand, it must have belonged to the governor." He grinned at me in a way that seemed endearingly boyish.

"Personally, I think it has to do with astronomy," Don Eduardo said. "Uxmal means 'place of the eternal moon.' I believe these buildings reflect the configuration of the heavens."

I glanced up from my hurried note-taking to look around. "But how could they do that without telescopes?"

"My dear, it wasn't only telescopes that they lacked." he smiled at my naïveté. "We're talking about Stone Age people. They had no cutting tools. This whole structure, this whole city, was built stone on stone with no wheels or draft animals."

I looked in wonder at the building. Its facade, a stone frieze, resembled nothing more than a length of sheer lace. Exquisite, massive, grand, yet curiously without heart. "What kind of people were these?" I asked.

"*¿Quien sabe?*" Don Eduardo shrugged. That too familiar answer.

As Felipe and I continued up the stairs, the archaeologist drifted off to join Morley's group back at the pyramid. "There are legends," Felipe ventured. "Some find truth in myth—I, for one."

Weary of climbing, I sank down on a parapet. Leaning back against one of the many snout-nosed masks of Chac, I looked up at Felipe. I loved his mouth, hated his wife—whoever she was. Hated myself more for having such thoughts. He was a married man with children. What was the matter with me?!

"Tell me a story," I suggested, "a myth that will explain everything."

Smiling, Felipe sat down beside me. I felt so content at his nearness that, at first, I scarcely listened. What was he saying? Something about the magician. I forced myself to concentrate, my eyes heavy lidded as I watched him.

"Tradition has it that the magician, the pyramid's builder, was a wise ruler who set in motion a government that thrived for hundreds of years. Part of its success was due to the Triple Alliance with Chichen Itza and Maya-pan, which he founded. That was all well and good until a love triangle emerged."

"Oh, dear," I sighed. These Mayan legends struck too close to home.

"Princess Sac-Nicte of Mayapan was beautiful," Felipe continued, unperturbed. "Canek, the young king of Chichen Itza, handsome. When they met by chance, it was love at first sight. Unfortunately, there was one major drawback. The lovely Sac-Nicte, daughter of Hunac Ceel, was already engaged to the king of Uxmal."

"Was that the same Hunac Ceel who dove into the sacred well?"

"The very same; I see you've been doing research." He nodded approvingly. "Sac-Nicte pleaded with her father, but such an ambitious man had little sympathy for romantic preference. As the daughter of a king, hers was a marriage of state. The agreement had been made, a slight to the king of Uxmal unthinkable. When Hunac Ceel brought his daughter to Uxmal for the nuptials, people flocked here, bearing lavish gifts from all corners of the Triple Alliance.

"Princess Sac-Nicte walked through the three days of ritual as though in a trance. On the third day, King Canek arrived with an army from Chichen Itza. The lovers disappeared, leaving the three armies to fight it out among themselves. The combined forces of Uxmal and Mayapan destroyed Chichen Itza. Oblivious to it all, Sac-Nicte and Canek settled into married life in what is now Guatemala."

The epic romance reminded me of Helen of Troy; fine for the lovers, but what about everyone else? Still, such a legend made as much sense as anything. Why were these magnificent cities abandoned? Why were they built in the first place? So much beauty everywhere, so much forgotten history whispering: See how time passes? What is the point of it all?

I leaned back, languidly turning my head. Just beyond Felipe on the parapet was a stone monolith. I stared curiously. It was very large, very . . . I gasped involuntarily, realizing now what I'd been looking at.

"Yes," he nodded, "it's a phallus. There are many here—a whole grove of them down the way. Some erect, others fallen, a petrified forest of fertility. There's a temple, too, the Temple of the Phalli, where they were used as drain spouts."

I suppressed a laugh, imagining the effect in the rainy season. But, of course, that was the whole idea. It was easy to understand the rain god's omnipresence. His mask was everywhere in Uxmal, protruding from friezes, filling in corners, and clinging to spaces above doorways. The Chac features—sneering, half-open mouth exposing jutting fangs, horns, globular eyes, and snoutlike nose—were designed to be awesome. And they were. Uxmal had been abandoned for nearly a thousand years, but here, in a land still desperately dependent on rain, the spirit of Chac felt very much alive.

These haunted ruins with their tragic legends of love and war, their hints of lust and desperation, would remain etched in my mind forever. I'd carry them in my heart as I would the memory of Felipe, framed against the Governor's Palace.

16

Into the Abyss

Despite the blistering heat, I got cold chills every time I thought of our final destination—the caves of Loltun. All my life I'd managed to avoid caverns; the very thought of them terrified me. Now, here I was in this strange land expected to descend into one. It didn't help that the rest of the party was so excited.

Felipe was discussing last-minute logistics with Don Eduardo as I boarded the train. Slipping past him, I sat down across from Ann and Earl, carefully packing away my assorted gear so that the seat beside me would be empty. This time I didn't care what anyone thought; I was frightened and wanted Felipe beside me. Unfortunately, it was Don Eduardo who slowly lowered himself onto the seat. Later, when Felipe came looking for me, the car had filled. I saw his disappointment. Once again I reminded myself that my imminent departure was the best possible thing for us both, yet I dreaded our farewell. How sad that Yucatán would be lost to me as well. I could never chance a return.

Slowly the train wound its way through the low, scrubby hills of the Puuc country, at last reaching a village with the unpronounceable name of Oxkutzcab. My tongue twisted the Maya syllables, stumbling miserably. "Ohsh-kootz-cahb."

The whole town waited to greet us—to greet Felipe. Mariachis, of course, exuberant men with soulful voices and dented instruments. Cheering schoolchildren freed for a morning. Smiling women patting tortillas or pouring mango juice. Masses of purple, blue, and gold flowers everywhere, their heavy sweetness sucking the air. More speeches, every man in town wanting to say something, mostly about Felipe. It was clear they adored him. I looked around at the rest of our party. Ann and Earl watched intently, nodding from time to time, but Sylvanus Morley's face was cool and impassive. "A man of the people," he'd described Felipe on the boat. I remembered the sneer. What should have been an accolade remained to him a matter for contempt. I was so proud of Felipe, why couldn't everyone see how wonderful he was? I wanted to smack Dr. Morley.

When the mariachis started up again, we climbed onto *plataformas,* splintery wood-bedded trucks that had been standing by to take us on the final leg of the expedition. We were on our way. The ruts in the road were craters. Pitching, snorting *plataformas* didn't discriminate. They careened into each of them, somehow lumbering out. Yesterday's unpaved road seemed like a highway, yesterday's battered *fortingas* limousines. Just when I thought my teeth would shake loose, our *plataforma* lurched to a stop before a rustic hut.

A small group of men dressed alike in white shirts and trousers stiff with starch waited outside. They were *chicleros,* Felipe told us, climbers who collected *chicle,* or sap, for chewing gum. He thought the men very brave. Not only did they have to worry about poisonous snakes and jaguars, but sometimes a *chiclero,* high above the ground, slashed too deeply into the trunk of the tall sapodilla tree—a fatal miscalculation that sent him hurtling to the jungle floor with the falling treetop.

Felipe warmly embraced their leader, Pedro, and introduced him as an old *compañero* from the revolution. I studied the stocky Maya, trying to imagine this genial man with his broad smile and warm handshake fighting beside Felipe. Pedro proudly fingered a small box camera hanging from a chain around his neck. Felipe turned to us, explaining that he'd issued cameras to the *chicleros* so that they could photograph ruins concealed by jungle. Each picture of an undiscovered site meant fifty pesos to the finder. "It's enough to feed their families for a month,"

Felipe said, "but I hope the experience will mean more than money. I want it to awaken pride in their history."

The *chicleros* leaped eagerly onto the *plataformas*, indifferent to the bouncing, heaving motion almost unbearable to the rest of us. "This is a special treat for them," Felipe explained. "Today they serve as the expedition's special assistants."

"You'll never forget Loltun," Don Eduardo yelled to me over the din of the trucks. "The caves are awe-inspiring, like an enormous tomb."

Hardly encouraging.

An hour later as we approached the cave's deeply shadowed mouth we found it obscured by heavy boulders and snaky jungle vines. I remembered that the ancient Maya regarded caves as entrances to the underworld and wondered about our guides. Was this a descent into hell for them or an opportunity to slip into sacred space? Hot air flowed toward us from inside, damp and earthy. As we groped and toed our way down the stone stairs to the rough, uneven floor of the cavern, I could dimly make out a vast, deep chamber beyond. With each step, I fought the desire to flee the almost palpable darkness and run back outside to the sun's dazzling safety. Something ran across my boot; I reached out for Felipe but he was too far ahead.

In single file, our party inched cautiously forward along a narrow ledge. Pedro and two companions lit the way with torches while another group of *chicleros* carrying ropes and tackle formed a rear guard. From time to time somebody tapped one of the many monolithic columns along the passage. It gave out an eerie hum: "Loltuuuuuuuuuuuuun."

The flickering torches penetrated only a small part of the gloom. I had a sense that we'd left our own world behind and entered a new one, where night and day were one and boundaries no longer existed. Mingled voices speaking Maya, Spanish, and English echoed through the darkness. I thought of lost souls moaning and wondered why I hadn't waited for the others outside. Now I'd come too far to find my way back alone.

The *chicleros* guided us through long corridors that snaked their way between endless grottoes until we finally emerged into a high-domed gallery filled with hundreds of stalactites and stalagmites. Each of us viewed them differently. One of the group looked at a stalactite and saw the Virgin of Guadalupe. It reminded me of thrusting fingers, the devil's fingers.

Don Eduardo pointed out his personal selection as the "prize exhibit in Loltun's subterranean museum." I studied the pearly white stalagmite, the "white flower" for which the caverns were named. Its cylindrical pedestal had a fluted base. The column's rounded crown resembled the tightly closed petals of a snow-white blossom. Despite the gloom, I had to admit that this caprice of nature was exquisite.

The spectacle of Loltun, its magnitude—Don Eduardo said the caves extended for miles beneath Yucatán's limestone crust—captured my imagination. He'd told me that the caves had twice sheltered the Maya, first in ancient times and later as a fortress and refuge during the Caste War, an ill-fated rebellion against the hacendados some eighty years earlier. Looking about, I saw traces of the ancient people who'd once lived in the cavern and tried to imagine the lives of those cave dwellers. How horrible it must have been to be confined to this black abyss. Once, stumbling against a *metate*, or corn grinder, I realized that I was walking through what must have been someone's living room. Felipe handed me a pottery shard he'd found on the floor. Don Eduardo called our attention to a band of hieroglyphics carved on a smooth section of vertical wall. Moss had grown over the inscriptions, but they were still visible. Dr. Morley conjectured that some resembled the Egyptian formula for mummification.

The archaeologists began to argue. I tried to focus on their words, on anything but the flickering shadows about me. The air stirred as though a sudden wind had come up. I heard a weird moaning sound and then all the torches went out at once, plunging us into total darkness.

"*¡Estamos perdidos!*" someone howled. "We are lost!" I heard scuffling all around me. Don Eduardo's slightly nasal voice, pleading for calmness, was barely audible. All about me people screamed. Some of the Maya were shouting. The blackness was heart-stopping. "Like a tomb," Don Eduardo had said. I forced myself to move forward only to trip over a stalagmite. The wall, when I stumbled against it, was cold and slimy. Terror swept over me; I struggled not to whimper.

An arm moved across my shoulders, unexpected and utterly wonderful. Felipe's voice boomed out beside me, Mayan words, a commanding tone I'd never heard. The sound echoed resoundingly through the cavern. Felipe's message, whatever it was, brought immediate action. The wailing ceased. Guides silently came forward to relight their torches from matches that he supplied. I marveled at the silent speed with which Felipe's orders were carried out.

"Tell me what you said that made them so obedient," I urged as we began to slowly retrace our steps to the entrance.

Felipe laughed. "I don't think you'd want to know."

"What caused the torches to go out?" Dr. Morley asked.

"Air blowing through some opening overhead," Felipe suggested. "Or perhaps Chac sneezed."

Nervous laughter.

I smiled, breathed a happy sigh. In an instant Felipe had changed everything. Instead of being frightened of the cave, I felt myself embracing it. The velvety blackness beyond our flickering lights had taken on an unexpected radiance that comforted me.

Felipe took my arm and we began our ascent from the abyss.

A Final Farewell

When the soft knock came, I knew it was Felipe. The compartment door bolted behind him, his arms enfolded me, the embrace almost a physical attack. "I've waited so long to hold you," he murmured, lips buried in my hair. The train's whistle sounded a warning far away.

Felipe eased the silk nightgown down over my shoulders, my hips. He stepped back against the door to look at me. I felt the warmth in his eyes. The train swayed as I walked toward him. My fingers traced his broad cheekbones, his mouth. The tiny compartment felt so safe, our own little world, as I removed his shirt and trousers. Our hearts beating, the rails clicking. The berth was narrow. Our knees, our elbows, sometimes our heads, bumped.

We whispered together, laughed, held each other closer, hands gently exploring. It had never been this way with Sam; I never imagined that it could be. As the train threaded its way through the jungle, beams of moonlight caressed us through the open window. The spangled sky spun faster, stars streaming behind us.

It seemed then that we had so much time, but how soon the first rays of morning illuminated the outskirts of Mérida. I nudged Felipe gently away. "Someone might see us."

"I would be proud to be seen with you. I want everyone to know."

"That's madness. Go, please. I need to—to collect myself. How can I ever face the others?"

He smiled gently, "Did your mama say that people can tell just by looking?"

I laughed in spite of myself. "As a matter of fact, she did. This morning she'd be right, too. It must be obvious that neither of us has slept a wink."

"Are you sorry?" he asked, searching my face.

Tears stung my eyes as I looked back at him. "I'll remember last night for the rest of my life."

"There will be other nights," he promised. "A lifetime of them."

"Oh, Felipe, don't be foolish!" I turned away, struggling against the tears. His hand caressed the nape of my neck, stroked my tangled hair. "Please," I gasped, "please go now." It took all my effort to pull away, but once free, I reached frantically for his forgotten clothes and shoved them at him. With a half-smile, he stepped into his trousers.

"Very well," he relented, buttoning his guayabera shirt, "but I will see you later at the Gran."

"No!" I pushed him away in earnest now. "No, this is our good-bye." I looked anxiously back at the window as I struggled to dress myself. "Holy Mother!" The train was coming into the station. I yanked the curtain closed. "Get out, please! I've got to dress."

I opened the door and shoved him into the narrow passageway; my eyes followed his progress down the long, swaying aisle. At the far end, Ann's door opened. I saw Felipe nod politely as he passed.

As our assembled group stood on the station platform, Felipe kept his distance, but his eyes caressed me with new familiarity. Surely everyone must notice. I felt happier than I'd ever been in my life. I was also miserable. I couldn't breathe. I wondered if I was going to faint. All around us archaeologists discussed plans for the final departure. We would breakfast at the hotel, complete our packing, and then return to the station for the train ride to Progreso. Our boat would leave at sunset.

Ann studied me, concern lighting her wide brown eyes. "Are you all right, Alma? You look feverish."

"Yes, of course, I'm fine." I turned away, ostensibly to see if my bags had been loaded with the rest. She and Earl squeezed into the *fortinga* beside me and kept up a steady stream of chatter all the way to the Gran. My head buzzed. From time to time I nodded absently in answer to some question but had no idea what they were saying. My thoughts circled like crazy birds. Arriving at the hotel, the others turned toward the dining room. I begged off, deciding to have coffee sent up.

Ann followed me to the circular stairway. "May I do anything to help? Pack maybe? Mine's almost done."

Was she all that desperate for gossip? I wondered. But as my eyes met Ann's, I was surprised by the worry apparent there. So, she was not giving up on the fallen woman. Perhaps, instead, I was to become a social work project.

I forced a smile, "No—no thanks. Enjoy your breakfast with the others. I'm fine, really, I just need a little time to get organized. I've only a few things left to pack."

In reality, my room was a shambles. Felipe's banquet had left me so undone that when we left for Uxmal I'd simply thrown a few necessary items into a bag and abandoned everything else where it lay. Well and good, I reasoned now, surveying the chaos around me. There'd be something besides Felipe to think about.

I placed Don Eduardo's signed confession and my notebook carefully in the handbag that I would carry with me. I picked up the blue satin gown I'd worn to the banquet and folded it away in my trunk. That gala event, only two nights ago, how far away it seemed. How innocent.

I could hear maids clattering in the hallway with breakfast trays of steaming chocolate and *churros,* knocking on doors and waking guests with a gentle *Buenos dias.* How normal it all sounded, as though everything were just the same.

I'd packed my digging clothes when someone knocked. My coffee, I thought, eagerly flinging open the door. Instead it was Felipe.

"You shouldn't have come—"

He smothered my words with his mouth, but I pulled free.

"The train leaves in an hour. I've got to pack."

He laughed lightly. "Oh, my little *peregrina,* don't worry about packing. Just take a few things for the boat and leave the rest here. When you return, they will be waiting for you—just where will be my little surprise."

My fingers sought to silence his lips, but he continued to talk, his arms encircling me. "I know that you must return to the *Times* to handle the *cenote* matter. That's your job and you must do it." When I looked at him in astonishment, he explained. "Don Eduardo confided in me yesterday—it was his obligation to Yucatán, he said, that I know before the entire world finds out. It will be a big story, bigger than you realize. You have a jaguar by the tail. But surely a month will suffice—travel time, time at your paper, time at the Peabody—then back here to Mérida, back to me."

"No, Felipe. *¡No es posible!*" I pulled away from him. "I shall never return to Mérida. What we've done is wrong." I sobbed, face hidden in my hands. Forcing myself to go on, I tearfully explained, "Everyone thinks that I'm a widow, because I told them that." I paused, took a deep breath, and continued, "I'm really divorced." When he didn't reply, I looked up, expecting surprise, even anger, but saw only an indulgent smile.

I shook my head. "Apparently you've made it your business to discover that as well. I shouldn't be surprised. Well, no matter, I *want* you to know everything about me. I've come so far from the Church, I'm not sure what I believe anymore, but there's one thing I *know*. You made a promise to your wife just like my husband made one to me. Sam broke his promise, now I've helped you to break yours. What does that make me?" I turned away, angry with both of us.

"Don't you imagine that I've thought of all this?" he asked, holding me at arm's length. "I have, many times. I knew from the beginning that you were an honorable woman. That is one of the things I love about you. It's as much a part of my *peregrina* as her vivacity, her curiosity, or"—his hand cupped my chin, raising my head—"her shattering, ruinous blue eyes."

Felipe's own eyes were morose. I'd never seen him look so tired. "Don't you think I tried to stay away from you in the beginning?" he asked. "I did, by all the saints, I did. I let whole days go by without driving out to Chichen Itza, but the sound of your voice echoed in my ears. There is no one like you. You are always so excited about the world, about life—and especially about the Yucatán. When we talk, it's playful and open, always fresh and vital. Imagine a life together—not only the work we can share, the changes we can bring to the lives of the people, but the parties, the midnight drinks, even the arguments."

"Stop!" I cried, my hands covering my ears. "I can't listen to you anymore."

But Felipe wouldn't stop. He took my hands, holding me by the wrists, forcing me to face him when I tried to turn away. "You've never asked about my wife, but I will tell you. She is a Maya, a good woman, but we have not lived together as man and wife for many years."

"But I'm sure—"

He stopped me. "You are sure that I have had others, but you are wrong. *There have been no other women.* If I have a mistress, it is Yucatán. All of my life my thoughts, my energy, my very soul has been devoted to this land. Now you can be part of that. Think of what we can accomplish together."

"No!" I cried, backing away from him. "Don't talk that way, don't even imagine that we have a future together."

"Why not?" he challenged. "The life that we can have, the good that we can do, is far more important than some rule set up long, long ago. I am thirty-eight, half a life-time, surely, and you are—how old?"

"I'm—" I hesitated. Usually I said twenty-three. "I'm twenty-seven," I whispered.

He took my hand. "Very young, but not a child. My own sons are young men, my daughter already married."

I was startled by his children's ages. Somehow I'd pic-tured them as young. But it made no difference. He was their father; it was up to him to set an example for them.

"Now it is our turn," he said, as though reading my thoughts.

I shook my head wearily. "It's no use, there's nothing more to say. This is our good-bye. What we say later at the train will be for others." Felipe's eyes glistened as he stepped back to avoid the closing door.

I moved through the official leave-taking as though in a trance. Ann and Earl stayed with me, gentle, tactful buffers shielding me from the pressures of departure. As if by magic, my bags were lined up and checked in, my papers ready. Earl found a comfortable corner seat on the train for me. Ann must have sensed that all I wanted was to be alone and ran interference. I don't remember board-ing the Ward Line steamer. I recall only the white shores of Yucatán fading from view. Palms caught in a sudden breeze swayed forward, waving good-bye.

If You're Going to Kill Me

SAGE

San Francisco, the present time

I wanted everything to be perfect for Mark's sixtieth birthday. Perfect as it could be. The convalescent hospital's so-called rec room was filled with flowers and balloons. Mark held court in his Armani jeans and red turtleneck, his smile so warm one could almost forget that his throne was a wheelchair.

Mark's sons, Kevin and Lance, had flown in with their trendy wives and noisy children. Their appearance made the day for their fragile patriarch, as I'd known it would. I kept busy dispensing slices of Mark's favorite lemon cream cake and glasses of champagne to a steady stream of former law partners and clients, neighbors, and many long-time friends.

From time to time I looked over at Mark and saw him laughing at some recaptured memory of a legal triumph or a boyhood prank. Each well-wisher turned up another fragmented detail of his life, many long buried. I felt like the team leader of an archaeology crew.

More than a decade separated me from Mark but that had seemed negligible until his illness. I had always liked older men, preferred them in fact; but now that *I* was older, there seemed less to learn from them. Perhaps less that I wanted to learn. How would it feel to be sixty? I pushed the idea away. Time was already going by too fast. All day I'd struggled not to think about the Alma Reed book, the advance I'd promised to repay. Best not to think beyond the party. "More champagne?" I looked up and smiled at Kevin, who stood before me, flute in hand. The liquid sparkled in the late-afternoon sunshine, frothing as I poured.

"Good stuff," he commented. "You went all the way with this party."

"It's a big milestone." *Perhaps his last.*

As though reading my thoughts, Kevin set his glass down, came around the serving table to hug me. "You've been wonderful, Sage. Dad is lucky to have you. *We're* lucky to have you."

Sure you are! Sainting me makes it so much easier on you, so much simpler to stay away, to leave the daily grind to me. When had they ever been here when I really needed them? "Thank you," I murmured.

Lance joined us, was standing at my side. "How much time do they give him?"

"A few months, possibly a year." The words echoed in my ears, a death sentence. "We're not accepting that," I continued in a firmer voice. "Mark's gone as far as he can go with science; he's had chemo and radiation. Now we're trying alternatives—diet, mind-set. Yesterday a faith healer came. Mark liked her; she reminded him of his mother."

"I saw the books in his room." Lance looked dubious. "There are so many quacks around. How do you know what to believe? Or who?"

"Is it wise to get his hopes up?" Kevin asked.

"What else does he have?" I challenged them.

By evening, the last guests had left. Kevin and Lance and their families crowded into a limo, heading off to the airport. Soon they'd be back in Portland and Denver. "Only a phone call away," each had assured me. Watching their limo disappear from view, I felt more alone than ever.

A nurse wheeled Mark back to his room, helped me to settle him into bed. Jolly cards jammed every available dresser space, flowers banked the room. It had already taken me three round trips with the wheelchair to bring in Mark's presents—candy, puzzles, and many, many books.

He sank back wearily. "It was a big day," I acknowledged, tousling his hair.

"But a good one. Thank you."

"Would you like me to read to you?" I searched among the piled presents. "Look, here's *1491*. You've been wanting to read it." I flipped to the index, running my finger down the *m*'s. "Lots here about the Maya." I turned to a promising page. "Oh! Mark, see this, it's a reference to Sylvanus Morley, *Alma's* Sylvanus."

"What about him?" Mark pulled himself up a little straighter, smiling at my enthusiasm.

"He was attempting to address that inevitable question: Why did the Maya abandon their cities? It says here that Morley's theory—just a hunch at the time—is still the most popular hypothesis.

" 'The Maya collapsed because they overshot the carrying capacity of their environment. They exhausted their resource base, began to die of starvation and thirst, and then fled their cities *en masse*, leaving them as silent warnings of the perils of ecological hubris.' "

"Hubris, is it?" Mark laughed wryly. "How fitting, how universal, how *now*. They thought they could do it all and live forever. So, where are they?" There was a look of sadness in his eyes, an expression I'd rarely seen. "When I was twenty I was sure I'd be the greatest trial lawyer in the world. That wasn't all, either; it was more than just being the next Clarence Darrow. I was going to be a great social reformer and write books that won big prizes about saving the universe. On the side, I'd be heavyweight champion of the world, and when Hollywood got around to making a movie about my life, they wouldn't have to scearch for someone to play me. I'd be perfect."

"Of course you would," I assured Mark, taking his hand.

"I'm not kidding, Sage. I really believed I could do all that, fully expected to do it. What happened, anyway? It's a mystery, like where did the Maya go? I keep wondering, where did I go?"

"You built a thriving practice and a fine family just like they built splendid cities. Nothing can ever change those achievements," I assured him. Mark nodded, not too convincingly. I saw that he was growing sleepy and put the book down, dimmed the lights. When I looked back, Mark's eyes were closed, his breathing even. I kissed him lightly and turned toward the door.

"It goes awfully fast, Sage," his voice cut through the darkened room, stopped me. "One minute you think you have it all and the next you know you never will. Things happen that you don't expect. You can't control them; they control you."

Driving back to Palo Alto, I pondered Mark's questions. What was I to make of it, I wondered, turning into my apartment's parking garage. Mark had accepted all that happened to him with strength and equanimity. I loved his humor and his cheerfulness. The dissatisfaction that he'd expressed this evening was out of character, yet how well it mirrored my own frustrations. I, too, was approaching a milestone birthday. What would I have to show for fifty years? At twenty I'd fully expected to write the great American novel. Now I doubted that I would write *any* novel. Biography, too, was a respected medium, I reminded myself. I'd made a fair start at that, but my current work was stalled.

Once inside my apartment, I turned on the computer. Not surprisingly, there was an e-mail from David waiting. Since our meeting at the Compass Rose Room, we'd exchanged messages two or three times a week. Jokes and quips mostly. What was the harm in that? Nothing unless you counted that idiotic surge of pleasure I invariably received at the sight of his codename on my screen: jaguarpaw@aol.com.

I kicked off my heels but before I could open the message, Mews was literally in my face. A hungry cat can't be ignored. Reluctantly, I got up and hurried out to the kitchen. Back again, I settled into my chair and clicked eagerly on the mouse. "Okay, David," I said aloud, "let's see something funny. I could really use a laugh tonight."

David's message was not funny.

My heart thumped with excitement as I read: "Have met someone who knew Alma Reed. He's very old. Additionally, I've gone through *La Prensa*'s files. Great stuff about Felipe. You won't believe what they did to him. You've got to get down here. Three days in Mérida can wrap it up for you."

Three days. But it wouldn't be three, it would be five, what with the going and coming. A whole continent to be crossed and then recrossed. So much time away from Mark when he needed me most. How much time did he have? But what was it that he'd said? *One minute you think you have it all and the next you know you never will.* How much time did *I* have? Would there ever be another chance like this one?

M ark was smiling when I entered his hospital room the following morning. The old Mark. "Sorry about last night. Guess I got a little carried away." He grinned. "Never could stand a crying drunk, but I guess that was me. One glass of champagne too many."

I doubted that he'd had any, but searching his eyes today, clear and calm, I decided to blame overexcitement. Too many people, too many memories crowding down on him. I placed two mugs of coffee on the table beside him and sat down.

"What's up?" he asked, reaching for his mug. "You've got something on your mind."

I looked down a moment. "You know me so well," I acknowledged. "It's my book."

"I thought that was settled. You're returning the cash advance to the publisher." He set his coffee down carefully. "Is there a problem? You should have told me. I'll be glad, happy, to pay them the money for you."

I shook my head. "It isn't the money; they want the book. I've been thinking about it, trying to decide what to do. Most of the research is finished, even some of the writing. I'm so close. It's just the Felipe part that I don't have."

Mark's expression changed, his face suddenly hard. "No, Sage. I don't want you to go back to Yucatán."

"It would be for just a few days—five days. I was thinking that . . . perhaps in a month or two . . . after you've had a chance to try out the new diet that we read about in Sri Nicholas's book. There're saying such wonderful things about it. I'm sure it's the breakthrough we've been waiting for. Then maybe—"

"*No,* not then or anytime. I need you here."

"But Mark, I've just heard about this old man who actually knew Alma Reed. I need to interview him *now.* He won't live much longer."

"Exactly my point."

I sank back in the chair, guilt and frustration washing over me in angry waves. What could I say to him? What was there to say?

As it turned out, I didn't have to say anything. I watched the play of expression on Mark's face. He was way ahead of me

"I asked you to marry me once again," he reminded me. "It was just a few days ago, right here in this room. Remember? Yesterday at the birthday party the idea kept coming back, I couldn't get the thought out of my head.

How wonderful it would have been if that gathering had been celebrating us."

I gasped. "I thought we'd settled the marriage thing once and for all . . . your sons. You know what they'd think."

"I don't give a damn what they think! I want you to be my wife. It means everything to me. *You* are everything to me."

Silently, I watched him. Somewhere behind me I felt an iron door slowly closing. He had it all worked out.

Mark, too, was silent, considering. I knew that glint, the sense of weighing something, knew it well. Mark's lawyer look. "I'll tell you what, Sage, let's set the wedding date right away. Say, a month from today?" He fingered the calendar at his bedside. "April twenty-first. In the meantime, go ahead and take that trip to Yucatán. Go now."

"Now?" I echoed the word.

"My Mexican gardener had a saying that I've never forgotten: *Si me vas a matar mañana que maten de una vez.*"

Our eyes met. "And what does that mean?"

Mark's smile was wry as he crossed his arms behind his head, leaning back against soft pillows. " 'If you're going to kill me tomorrow, then kill me today.' " He winked at me and just for an instant I glimpsed the old Mark. "If you think you have to go, why put it off?" he shrugged. "Get the trip over with; get it over with once and for all. When you come back, I'll be here waiting for you."

Making Headlines

ALMA

Dearest Felipe had been right, I did have a jaguar by the tail. For a time its challenge numbed the sorrow of parting.

The luminaries who'd visited the archaeological expedition during the past two weeks were returning with us to New York. They were a lordly lot. The grandiloquent Marshall Saville, head of the Museum of the American Indian. Dr. John C. Merriam, president of the Carnegie Institute—where would I be without his okay? But the man who continued to worry me most was H. G. Spinden, the Peabody rep. Surely he'd been aware of the smuggling going on right under his nose. Why had he allowed it? Had he, in fact, encouraged it? Whatever his motivations, Spinden was in for an unpleasant surprise.

An invitation from Merriam to join them at dinner our first night out to sea gave me an opportunity to study these esteemed archaeologists, a closed corporation if there ever was one. Tonight all were jovial. Their faces radiated satisfaction, shone with anticipation of reunions with admiring, possibly envious colleagues. Flushed with food and wine, they toasted one another, laughed louder than usual. Watching them closely, I wondered how each would react to the bomb I was about to drop. Dr. Spinden would, of course, be furious, but what about his colleagues?

"Did you get your story, little lady?" Spinden asked, leaning forward to fill my wineglass.

"You bet I did." Smiling sweetly, I raised the glass and nodded at him.

Soon I excused myself, returning to my stuffy little stateroom. The portable typewriter that had been my companion throughout the journey was waiting there for me, its keys hot and sticky. The *thunk* of the carriage return echoed in my head as I worked the story over. Over and over. One Lucky Strike followed another, smoldering forgotten in the tray.

As the hours passed, second thoughts assailed me. The entire story was based on Don Eduardo's word. What if he'd lied? Or even exaggerated? It was I who would bear the brunt of it, not only with Spinden and the other archaeologists, but also with Mr. Ochs. The very thought of it made me ill. As I leaned back, eyes closed, a picture formed in my head. Don Eduardo sitting at the *cenote*'s edge. His eyes, his voice, so intent. The old archaeologist had spoken the truth. I knew he had. I relaxed, ready now, eager, to stake my reputation on his words.

When the ship docked the next morning in Havana, my story was complete. A taxi drove me through the sultry streets to the cable office, where I filed a detailed exposé. It would reach Mr. Ochs in minutes. While Ann and the others toured Havana, I remained in the office, anxiously awaiting his reply. It didn't take long.

STORY UNBELIEVABLE. CORROBORATION ESSENTIAL. GET QUOTES FROM TEAM. THEN SEND NEWS RELEASE IMMEDIATELY. THE FULL STORY MUST FOLLOW EXAMINATION OF PEABODY TREASURE.

I was disappointed that Mr. Ochs wasn't just going to run with the story as I'd written it—based entirely on Don Eduardo's confession—but not surprised. It seemed only natural that he would want some kind of acknowledgment from the other archaeologists.

Returning to the ship, I went directly to Dr. Merriam's cabin and tapped softly at the door. The archaeologist's smile faded fast as I presented the situation. He glared at me, his face angry and disbelieving, as the story unfolded. At last the man could stand it no longer. "How dare you!" he exploded. "A vast treasure stolen by an esteemed archaeologist, then deliberately hidden by one of the most distinguished museums in the world. The idea is preposterous!"

"Edward Thompson gave me his word," I reminded him. "Why would he lie?"

"Why, indeed! It's *you* who are lying, a cub reporter trying to make a name for herself with some cooked up, impossible story. Do you imagine that you can make fools of us? Don't even think about it, you silly girl. We'll fight you tooth and nail. When we get through with you, whatever reputation you have will be ruined forever. No paper will dare to hire you. I promise you, Alma Reed, this is the last story you will ever write."

Through clenched teeth, I answered, "I have Edward Thompson's confession in writing. Would you care to read it?"

Merriam's bushy brows came together as he scanned the single sheet I held before him. My hands trembled, fearing that he'd tear the paper from my grasp. Instead he shouted: "Get Saville and Spinden in here. Get them *now*!"

"Very well, sir," I replied, "but remember the ship leaves Havana in just four hours."

I paused to control the quiver in my voice. "I intend to cable my paper before we leave. This is the greatest archaeological story of our age. Surely you agree that an official comment must be included."

The short story I eventually wrote took two hours to hammer out. The stopgap compromise, datelined Havana, March 1, 1923, and destined for page one of the *Times,* initially read:

What is conceded to be the most important find of archaeological objects ever made in America was revealed yesterday at Mérida by Edward H. Thompson, owner of the hacienda at Chichen Itza, Yucatán, where the famous Mayan ruins are located. The discovery, which had been kept secret, includes priceless turquoise masks, jade carvings, gold ornaments, and numerous other objects that throw new light on the ancient Mayan civilization. The objects, now privately held in the Peabody Museum in Boston, were found in the sacred *cenote* near the ruins.

Among the most important individual objects discovered is a sacrificial knife with an ebony handle in the form of two twined serpents biting the flint blade. Fragments of textiles of unknown weaves, solidified masses of copal embalming human hearts, and beautiful jade ornaments are among the treasures. The gold ornaments include breast shields, pendants, bells, earrings, and other rings.

At the conclusion of their trip, Dr. J. C. Merriam, president of the Carnegie Institution and Professor Marshall H. Saville, head of the Museum of the American Indian, pronounced this discovery to be the most important source of information unraveling the story of the Mayas now available to science.

That was the best I could wring from Merriam and Saville. Spinden, red-faced and glaring, merely repeated again and again: "Young lady, do you realize who you are speaking to? Do you understand just whom you are accusing?" To the others, he professed to know nothing about a treasure stashed in his museum. "The whole idea is a vicious lie," he insisted. Merriam and Saville appeared to believe him, but did they? *Did they really?*

I was bitterly disappointed. The press release left so much unsaid. What were readers to think? What would Mr. Ochs think? For the time being there was nothing more that I could do.

The voyage to New York grew increasingly strained. Not surprisingly, there were no more dinner invitations from the big boys. But that wasn't the worst. Several times I came upon small, animated groups of archaeologists only to have them abruptly break off their conversations at the sight of me. Torn by longing for Felipe, and excluded from the easy camaraderie I'd come to take for granted, I felt lonely and isolated.

"They're treating me like some kind of traitor," I complained to Ann.

"Well, you have unleashed a dragon—no doubt about it." She glanced up from her morning tea. I saw—or thought I saw—excitement in Ann's eyes. "Earl thinks that nothing will ever be quite the same again. Artifacts have been taken from sites everywhere in the world. It's been common practice until now."

"Some might say *stolen* from sites everywhere in the world."

"That's a bit strong! Most scientists would consider it 'removal for safekeeping.' What's different here is the secrecy. Sneaking things out without saying anything and then *hiding* them—the disclosure will be an embarrassment to the archaeological community, particularly if the treasure is as vast as you claim."

"*I* claim! It's Don Eduardo's story."

Ann nodded thoughtfully. "Poor man, his career will be ruined."

"He didn't seem to think so. The *don* bought his property fair and square. He owns the *cenote*—some would say he owned its contents as well. But," I reluctantly continued, "the treasure has been kept a secret from Mexico all these years. It's been a twenty-year conspiracy between him and the Peabody."

What a relief when the Statue of Liberty came into view. Mr. Ochs had reserved a room for me at the Algonquin. Perhaps I'd see a few celebrities, even make some connections. As it turned out, there was no time to relax and soak up atmosphere. A message waited when I checked in: Mr. Ochs wanted me in his office immediately. Within minutes I was back out on Forty-fourth Street, hailing a cab.

"Some story you've got!" he greeted me, then added, "Those fancy diggers have been calling and cabling for days. I hope to hell you can prove it!"

I pulled Don Eduardo's now very wrinkled confession from my bag and handed it to him.

He read the paper carefully, then placed it on his desk, smoothing out the folds. "Thompson *wrote* this? Really wrote it?"

"He certainly did!" I assured him. "I watched him write it."

Mr. Ochs picked up the phone. "Get me the Peabody. I want to speak with the director right now."

My heart pounded as the minutes ticked by.

From the publisher's half of the conversation I could tell that someone on the other end was trying to stall him. I felt certain that Dr. Spinden had already warned them.

Mr. Ochs grasped the receiver while his left hand drummed impatiently on the polished desk. "I've had it!" he growled at last. "You're bluffing," he told the director. "You know it, I know it. Let's not waste any more time. My reporter, a photographer, and a representative of the Mexican government will be at your place tomorrow morning. The world is going to know the whole story whether you like it or not."

20

My Next Assignment

The Peabody Museum was formidable, substance and tradition built into every red brick. Climbing the steps to the front entrance reminded me of the ascent to Kukulkan's pyramid. At the top, Dr. Spinden, the high priest, stood ready to tear out my thumping heart. The set of those thin, white lips suggested that he'd relish the job. I straightened my shoulders. He wasn't going to sacrifice *my* story on the altar of his sacred traditions.

I introduced my companions, Ricardo Alvarez, the Mexican consul, and the *Times* photographer, Herb Schwartz. Arms tightly folded across his chest, Spinden acknowledged them with an imperious nod, then shifted his cool, quizzical glance back to me. As if he didn't know what we wanted! I looked right back at him. "We've come to examine the treasure."

"Let me see Thompson's letter."

"You know its contents well," I reminded him.

"I want to see it again." His bulky body filled the doorway.

Angrily, I snatched the "confession" from my purse and handed it to him. We stood on the steps, cold wind whipping about us, as he studied the single sheet, face impermeable. I wondered if Dr. Spinden played poker. He'd be good; but this time, he was obliged to fold.

The museum director handed the paper back to me with just two fingers, as though it were smeared with something disgusting. "You may wait inside," he said at last, opening the large door for us.

The three of us sat in the anteroom, listening to distant footsteps echo down long halls, catching occasional muted voices. The stuffy air smelled of dust. Didn't anyone ever come here? An hour passed. "I'll find a telephone," I said, raising my voice. "Mr. Ochs said to call the police if I needed to."

"That won't be necessary." Dr. Spinden, faced flushed with anger, appeared in the doorway. "Come with me."

As we followed him down a long hallway, I caught fleeting glimpses of rooms off to the side. The Peabody looked more like a storehouse than a museum. American Indian artifacts, stacks of baskets, a few pots. I would have loved to explore but there was no opportunity to linger. Dr. Spinden marched us briskly to a freight elevator at the rear of the building.

My heart raced. I felt like Don Eduardo descending into the depths of the *cenote*. Wasn't this also a forgotten tomb?

We got out on the basement level. Were the artifacts for which the archaeologist had risked so much actually gathering dust in this cellar? Dr. Spinden led us down another long hall to a door that he opened with a key, one of many bulging from his chain. We stepped inside. Bare bulbs flashed on. My eyes blinked in wonder at floor-to-ceiling shelves crammed with artifacts. Everywhere I looked I saw gold breastplates, jade pectorals, turquoise pendants, jeweled statues, amber bracelets. I relaxed into a sigh. Here was my vindication—treasure beyond belief.

Herb's hands trembled as he set up his tripod. The Mexican consul whipped out a notebook and moved slowly, adoringly, from artifact to artifact, recording each in careful detail. I pointed out what I thought were the most significant items for Herb to photograph. It all seemed to be there, exactly as I'd been told, except . . . I turned to Dr. Spinden, remembering the drawing I'd discovered on the *don*'s desk, the sketch that first convinced me of a dark mystery waiting to be revealed. "Don Eduardo told me about a sacrificial knife. Where is it?"

Dr. Spinden reached into a pasteboard box. "This?" Casually, he handed me an exquisite stiletto of polished obsidian carved in the form of twined serpents biting a flint blade.

I held the knife carefully, testing the edge with one finger, reliving that sultry afternoon in Chichen Itza when the *don* had told me of his incredible luck. The archaeologist made the discovery in three sections—one scoop of mud bringing up the blade. There was a piece missing near the point. The next scoop produced the handle. Days later, he had uncovered the final tiny piece hidden in another foot of ooze.

Riding back to New York on the train, I sketched out the story. It was good. The best I'd ever written. It pleased me to think of Felipe reading it, thousands of miles away.

My lover wrote every day: amusing anecdotes from his past, happenings in Mérida, dreams of the future. They were delivered to me at the *New York Times*—creating quite a stir. Every night, I sat by the window of my room at the Algonquin, poring over his words. New York suffered one rainstorm after another, steady drizzle mirroring my depression. Cars honked and screeched outside as I recalled the warm timbre of Felipe's voice, the melodies of his mariachis.

As if my longing weren't sorrow enough, I heard disturbing news from Yucatán. Wire services had lost no time picking up my front-page story. The Mexican government was in arms, a lawsuit under way for recovery of the treasure. Anger against Don Eduardo was mounting. In Mérida, headlines denounced the archaeologist as a thief, a traitor, the worst kind of villain. Many cried out that imprisonment was too good for him.

I'd not allowed myself to answer Felipe's letters, but now, alarmed by the turn of events, I sent him a hasty cable pleading for leniency for Don Eduardo.

Felipe responded immediately with a cable of his own:

YOUR DON WILL NEVER BE IMPRISONED, I PROMISE, BUT
THE GOVERNMENT MUST HAVE A STRICT ACCOUNT-
ING. SURELY, YOU KNOW THIS, MY LITTLE PEREGRINA.
WHEN ARE YOU COMING BACK?

The political furor over the treasure accelerated until it reached international proportions. Every country would now be on the alert to guard its heritage more vigilantly. The treasure had been officially evaluated at more than two million dollars. What was going through Don Eduardo's mind? I wondered. Did he regret telling me his story or was he enjoying the melodrama after so many years in the shadows?

Mr. Ochs kept me busy. The sacred well was by no means my only Yucatán story. I wrote numerous articles about Chichen Itza, Uxmal, and, last of all, Loltun. As unseasonable winds howled down the concrete canyons of New York, I thought of jungle nights filled with the scent of flowers, the symphony of chirping insects. Longing with all my heart for Felipe, I burned his letters one by one. It is over, I told myself. I had to make certain that it was over.

The morning my Loltun article appeared, I was clearing out the desk temporarily assigned to me when Mr. Ochs emerged from his office. He nodded curtly for me to come in. The big man was about to give me my walking papers, I knew it. I'd done the job he'd hired me for. I'd also pointedly ignored his reference to an available soc position. The society editor was a harridan whose bible was the social registerite. Her opinion of me, a California upstart, was clear. I had no business interviewing the Astors and Rockefellers, much less the Van Rensselaers. I'd be stuck forever writing up third-rate weddings. No, thanks!

I said a little prayer to St. Anthony, my favorite from childhood, and stepped into Mr. Ochs's walnut-paneled sanctum. Perhaps there'd be a small bonus that would tide me over till I found another position.

"Glad to see you cut your hair," the publisher greeted me before I'd even shut the door. "It'll be cooler for Mexico."

"Mexico!"

"We're sending you back."

"Oh, no, I can't! The Yucatán assignment's finished. I've milked it dry."

"Done a fine job too. That's why I want you back there. Hear you speak Spanish like a native. Say something now."

"*No voy a Mexico. Yo no quiero volver a Yucatán.*"

"Sounds good. What the hell does it mean?"

"I'm not going to Mexico. I don't want to go back to Yucatán."

"Skip Yucatán for now. Wait and see what the next team of diggers turns up. I want you in Mexico City. Find out what Obregón's up to. Not sure I trust that guy. People are knocking one another off pretty fast down there. See if you can make sense of it."

"I appreciate your confidence, Mr. Ochs, but what about a change of venue? Like Turkey? I've been reading a lot about it. Let me go to Istanbul. I'd like to interview Kemal Pasha. I'm sure I could bring back something big, maybe—"

"Turkey's already assigned," he said, cutting me off. "You're our girl in Mexico. Take it or leave it."

Gulping a deep breath, I met his narrow gray eyes straight on. "What about a staff position here?"

"You turned your nose up at the soc opening."

"I'm a city room reporter, Mr. Ochs."

"No dice. Sorry, we've got our quota of skirts on city side."

"I'm sorry, too, Mr. Ochs. I'm a good reporter. I covered the Fatty Arbuckle trial, you know."

"I made it my business to know. I know about the Ruiz kid you got off as well. I saw to it that the Mexican embassy heard all about that too. You'll be a real heroine in Mexico City. Come on, Alma. . . . Perhaps I can add a little sweetener. What about thirty-five dollars a week? That'd go a long way in Mexico."

Indeed, it would go a long way anywhere. I hesitated.

"What about a six-month assignment? I'd want you in the capital first . . . until their government shakes down. After that you'd travel around, write some color stuff—on an expense account, of course."

I hesitated. How tempting . . .

"Just six months, Alma; after that, we'll talk again. Who knows what might be available then. . . ." If it were anyone but Mr. Ochs I'd have called it wheedling. "After Mexico, I'll send you back to Frisco through the Panama Canal."

"Could I do that now . . . go home first?"

"Hell no, you can't do it now! I want you on the boat to Veracruz day after tomorrow. But you can *call* home . . . on me."

The connection was surprisingly good, Mama's voice clear most of the time. "Yesterday I saw Dorothy Parker," I told her. "She was at the next table."

"Dorothy who? Someone from home, honey?"

"Dorothy Parker! She's only the most famous woman writer in the country."

Mama wasn't impressed. Instead, she asked, "When are you coming home?"

"That's why I called, Mama. I won't be home for a while. Mr. Ochs is sending me back to Mexico."

"Alma! That's bad news. I miss you. Everybody does."

An unexpected wave of nostalgia swept—no, crashed—over me. The house on Buchanan Street with its odor of corned beef and cabbage imbedded in the walls. I was aware of a pause on the other end of the line. *Now what?*

"Alma, I saw Sam the other day, Sam and Theoline. They're married. She's in the family way."

"Really." I took a breath, digesting that one. "How far along?"

"About six months, I'd say."

I felt a surge of the old anger, but how quickly it subsided. If it hadn't been for Sam's affair, I'd have never gone to Yucatán, never have gotten my big story, never have met Felipe. How strange life was.

She let it go, changing the subject. "I don't like this Mexico business. The papers are full of rumors. That President Obregón seems to be getting rid of his competition right and left."

"Mama! Where are you getting all this?"

"From your old boss, Fremont Older. I went to see him. He told me a lot more than you do in your letters. That governor, the one in Yucatán . . ."

"What about him?"

"He isn't very popular with the rich people. Mr. Older doesn't think he'll be in power long."

"Don't believe everything you hear." I smiled to myself. Mama was Mama, always worrying about something. "Felipe is a wonderful man. He's doing amazing things for his state, for the people of Yucatán."

"Felipe, is it?"

"He was very helpful to the archaeologists on the team, the ones I went to Yucatán with," I explained. "I couldn't keep calling him Your Excellency all the time."

"Is he married?"

"Yes, Mother," I admitted, holding back a sigh. I knew what was coming.

"Now be careful, Alma. I've heard about Latin men. They only want one thing, and they'll say anything to get it."

"Mama! I'm a grown woman."

"And I'm still your mother."

"This connection isn't very good. It's crackling. I can't hear you," I lied. "I'd better hang up."

"I can hear *you*. About that man—"

"It doesn't matter, Mama. Mexico City's a long way from Yucatán."

"Oh, honey, I wish you'd come home. I'm lonely. It's just Isabel and Prescott at home. Isabel has a fella, they're engaged, and Prescott's got a paper route. He wants to be a sports reporter. It's awfully quiet around here."

"Mr. Ochs says it's only for six months. Then I'm coming back to San Francisco. I'll stay with you at the house. I *want* to come home."

"Alma? Are you all right?"

"Yes, Mama. I'm fine. I'm really fine." And for the moment, I was.

Hardly had I gotten back to my desk when the phone rang. It was Ann calling from Boston. "You're in trouble!" she exclaimed. "I'm coming down tomorrow. Where can we meet?" We agreed on the Press Club. Whatever the bombshell she was about to explode, I was pleased and excited at the prospect of showing her my world.

"I'm glad you're still speaking to me," I said as the waiter seated us. "I've been wondering how the archaeology crowd would react to all the publicity."

"They're furious—with themselves, with one another, and particularly with you. They feel betrayed. All hell has broken loose. It looks like Dr. Spinden will be dismissed, but that's not why I came. I'm worried about *you*. They've discovered that you're not really a doctor, that you knew nothing about archaeology when you went on the expedition. They're going to tell Adolph Ochs." Ann opened her black beaded purse and took out an envelope, which she slipped under my napkin. "Earl and I wanted you to have this . . . a small nest egg until you can find some kind of work."

I didn't know whether to laugh or cry. "Ann," I said at last, reaching across the table to take her hand. "Mr. Ochs already knows. He was a reporter long before he became an editor. He made it his business to investigate everything about me when I sent that first cable from Havana."

"And it doesn't matter to him?" she asked, eyes wide with astonishment.

"Not really, not as long as my stories check out. Actually," I said, handing her back the envelope, "he's given me a promotion."

We sat back, relaxed, smiling across the table. How smart and sure we felt in our city suits, mine a Chanel knockoff that I'd found on Seventh Avenue, Ann's probably the real thing.

She looked about at the other diners, newspaper people for the most part mixed with a few PR guys and magazine editors. Most appeared to be arguing the morning's headlines. The red rose on Ann's black cloche bobbed ever so slightly as she studied them. A scientist at work in a new setting. Her curious eyes roved the room. "It's another world here," she said at last. "The mysteries that we archaeologists try so hard to solve have been cold for a thousand years. Your life, this life, is all happening now." Her dimples flashed in a mischievous smile. "Earl and I think the stir you've caused is rather amusing. Dr. Spinden and even Sylvanus are both so high and mighty."

I leaned forward, the room was noisy. "Do you think Sylvanus knew?"

"No!" Ann's eyes were indignant. "No one from the team knew. It took us all by surprise. Dr. Spinden must have been aware; how could he not have been? But he never let on to the rest of us."

"No matter what happens to Don Eduardo, they'll have to take him seriously," I said. "No one's going to write him off as a doddering amateur now."

"What about you, Alma?" Ann abruptly changed the subject. "You seem to fit right in here." She nodded toward the other diners. "Are you staying on in New York?"

I pulled a pack of cigarettes from my bag. In an instant a waiter was at my side with a light. "I'd like to, but for now I'm going back to Mexico."

Ann clapped her gloved hands together with excitement. "To be with Felipe!"

"Absolutely not," I said, picking up my menu. "That's over. Over."

Ann eyed me from beneath the brim of her hat. "Don't expect me to believe that malarkey." The red cabbage rose bobbed, emphasizing each word. "Perhaps some rules are meant to be broken. The governor frightens some people, but any sane person must realize that the old ways have to change. This is the twentieth century, for heaven's sake. You and the governor could build a life together that other people just dream about. Earl and I have talked a lot about it. Perhaps older people, our parents, for instance, wouldn't agree, but what do *they* know? We think you two are made for each other."

"Perhaps. . . . Felipe thinks so . . . but a backstreet affair is all it could ever be." I emphatically set down my coffee cup. "That isn't enough for me. I won't settle for being a mistress, not even of a great man. I want a life of my own and, one way or another, I intend to have it."

21

A Pair of Risk-Takers

SAGE

Again and again, I wondered where had it all gone wrong for Felipe Carrillo Puerto. Was Alma Reed in some way to blame? My time in Mérida would be brief. I resolved to make every minute count.

The flight seemed to take forever. I longed to see David and yet felt nervous, almost frightened, at the prospect. What would I say? How should I act? Then I saw his tall, rangy form waiting just outside customs and didn't have to worry anymore. David held me tightly for a moment; it felt wonderful. With one arm around me, the other holding my bag, he maneuvered us through the crowd to a car he'd parked in front of the terminal.

We drove directly to the ranch where Jorge Lopez lived with his son. It seemed as if no time at all had passed since our last meeting. We chatted easily, picking up where we'd left off. At first the narrow country road seemed to go nowhere; David stopped several times to consult his directions. We crossed a narrow bridge and then the highway forked. He turned off to the right. The road was no longer paved. Bouncing from rut to rut, we progressed slowly for possibly an hour. "You're wonderful to take time to do this," I told him. "I could have taken a taxi."

"Would I miss the interview of the century?! Are you kidding?" he laughed, his eyes on the narrow overgrown track ahead.

Finally, in the distance, we spotted a dilapidated adobe farmhouse, roof covered by broken tiles, yard a tangled jungle. Pulling up the narrow drive, we spotted some twenty people sitting in rockers watching us from the veranda.

I stepped out of the car, walking ahead of David down the stone path. It had been swept clean. In our honor? I assumed so, and was touched by their attempt to create order out of chaos. As we approached, the onlookers rose. The Lopez family, smiling stair steps, toddler to octagenarian. A white-haired gentleman came forward. "I am Pedro Lopez," he said, bowing before me. "*Recepción a mi casa.*" Now the whole family was smiling, crowding toward us. Would we like coffee? *¿Agua? ¿Cerveza?* Tequila? The smallest girl toddled toward us, in her hands a large bouquet of golden flowers. They were for me.

Señor Lopez led us to a small patio behind the house where an old man sat dozing in the late-afternoon sun. He looked well cared for in his starched white shirt and trousers, his thin hair neatly combed. "*Mi padre,*" Señor Lopez said proudly. "*El es noventa seis años de viejo*"—ninety-six years old. Gently, he roused his snoring father. "*Este Señora Sandborn y Señor Winslow,*" he introduced us. "*Mi padre, Don Jorge.*"

The old man gazed up at us, his soulful dark eyes clouded by cataracts. The sweet smile revealed one tooth. Señora Lopez bustled toward us, carrying a pitcher of dark beer and a platter of homemade cheese.

I sat down opposite Don Jorge. David stood behind me, leaning forward from time to time against my high-backed cane chair. I took out my notebook and pen. "Your father," I leaned toward him, speaking slowly, carefully, "*su padre,* he *sabe* Felipe Carrillo Puerto?"

"*Sí, sí, es verdad.*" The old gentleman scratched absently about the ears of a small pig that had strayed onto the patio and was now nuzzling his bare foot. "His Excellency *un hombre grande. Mi padre grande, tambien. Ellos ambos muertos.*"

"Yes," I nodded, taking his thin, almost clawlike hand in mine, "your father and the governor are both dead, *muy triste, pero ¿como?* How did they die?"

Two hens, feisty and curious, joined our gathering, attracted seemingly by the red nail polish peeking through my sandals. Don Jorge withdrew his hand from mine and reached into his pocket for some grain.

"*Padre él tiene gusto de animales*—he likes the animals," Señor Lopez explained. "They are his *solo amigos* now." He paused, obviously searching his English for words to explain further. "Everyone my father knew, his *compadres,* are now dead."

I nodded sympathetically, but leaned forward again. "*Don Jorge—¿como muertos, Felipe Carrillo Puerto y su padre? ¿Como?* How did they die?"

"*¿Como muertos?*" he repeated incredulously as though surprised by the question. "*Todos saben ese.*"

"Everybody knows?" David repeated.

"*Sí, por supuesto. Por supuesto,* of course." Don Jorge stood up, scattering the chickens. "Boom! Boom!" he shouted, holding his arm out before him like a rifle. "Boom! Boom!" he cried again. The pig squealed excitedly.

"Someone shot them!" I exclaimed in surprise. "But who? Who killed the governor and your father?"

"*¿Quien tiro ellos?*" David asked, leaning forward, lightly touching the man on his shoulder.

Don Jorge looked at his own outstretched arm in puzzlement, as though wondering why he was standing in that fashion. David and Señor Lopez settled him carefully back into the chair, tucking a small tattered blanket about his legs. The old man's eyes had grown cloudier. His face puzzled, he pointed a trembling finger at me. "*¿Quien?*" He murmured softly and then his eyes closed, his body slumped sideways.

"Is he all right?" I gasped.

"*Sí,* he is just tired," Señor Lopez said, steadying the old man gently. "It is time for *mi padre's* siesta."

I rose to my feet, "But surely *you* can tell us. Who shot the governor? Who shot your grandfather?"

Señor Lopez looked at me in surprise. "Everyone knows that! Juan Ricárdez Broca. *¡Que cabrón! Un hombre mal. Señora,* you can read it all for yourself *en los archivos.*"

Juan Ricárdez Broca . . . At last I had a name. . . . Broca, an evil man responsible for a shooting. Señor Lopez had called him a bastard. Perhaps I'd finally found the key for which I'd been searching.

In the next two days I settled quickly into a routine. Early each morning, Spanish dictionary in hand, I went to *La Prensa.* The archives were located in the newspaper's basement—stifling hot, badly lit. Late in the afternoon I'd pull myself away, drenched with perspiration, covered with the dust of decades. My eyes were tired, my hands grimy from ancient newsprint, but I was happier than I'd been in years. Here was the kind of story that every writer dreams about. Love and glory, sex and betrayal. There was even a Mayan curse. I couldn't believe my luck.

In the evenings David showed me the city: a street dance one evening, a concert the next. There was always so much to talk about at dinner. My Felipe research was unfolding, leading me deeper and deeper down a trail of unbelievable duplicity. "Maybe I'm an archaeologist, too,"

I confided to David. "The treasure I seek is the truth." The one thing we didn't discuss was my approaching marriage. I didn't want to talk about it, didn't want to think about it. Here I was actually having fun while Mark lay confined to a bed, the last months—hours—of his life draining away. Was that right? Was it fair? The answer was always no. It didn't matter, I told myself. This was my time, such a short time.

"You could say this is where it all began," David commented the second evening, as he guided me into a crowded cantina.

I looked about. We were in a colonial building, adobe walls, grilled windows, faded photographs on the walls. I looked again at the photos. "Is this the bar where we met?" I asked him, remembering that urgent and yet laconically mysterious night. "What do you mean 'where it all began'?"

"I meant the biography that you're writing. It was here in El Troubador that I told you about Alma. Remember?"

"Of course." I relaxed. "My quest did begin with a song and the fragment of a legend." I smiled, thinking of all I'd accomplished in the past two days. Could I have done it without David? Not so easily, not so well.

"You'd make a great reporter," I told him. "You've got the soul of a snoop."

He smiled that lopsided grin. "What is a scientist other than a glorified snoop? Sniffing out leads is what we do. Following them to their conclusion is the name of the game."

I smiled back. "That old man you found got me started. I've been running ever since. Don Jorge's father was Felipe's aide, loyal to the end, *with* him at the end, but their family view is biased. How could it not be? I still have more checking to do before I know the whole story—if that's even possible."

David leaned back, still smiling softly. "I loved the way Don Jorge called the governor *un hombre grande*. The way Mexicans roll their *r*'s! I gather the entire state admires him. Everywhere I look I see streets, schools, office buildings, named Felipe Carrillo Puerto. There's even a town, over near the coast."

"He's popular now," I conceded, "but back when Yucatán was an oligarchy, they called Felipe a Marxist. Those were fighting words, perhaps killing words."

David signaled for another round of margaritas. "I notice you call him Felipe, as if he were a friend."

"He is a friend; I'm getting to know him," I admitted. "Alma, too; I've come to *really* know her."

David sat silently studying me. "You and Alma are a lot alike," he said at last. "Besides the obvious—both writers, travelers—I see you as two sensuous, passionate women, the kind who throw themselves into things . . . a pair of risk-takers."

"Don't count on it," I shook my head, pushed back a wave that had fallen forward. "Alma's life was boldly written—lots of flourishes and exclamation marks. Mine's copy-book hand, round and regular, hardly a letter out of line."

"You sell yourself short." He laid his hand on mine. "Far too short."

I felt a shiver of excitement, but moved my hand, picked up my margarita.

David and I took a *calesa* across Parque Santa Lucía to my hotel. Relaxing against the old cushions, I caught the rhythm of horses' hooves on ancient paving stones. In the distance a small white chapel shimmered in the moonlight. I thought of Mark and our impending wedding. It would, I knew, make him very happy.

"You're quiet," David said. "What are you thinking about?"

"My research," I told him, struggling to shift gears. "One more day will pull it together. *La Prensa*'s archives are a treasure trove, but the pictures . . ."

"Pretty graphic?"

"Indescribable. Don Jorge wasn't kidding; a firing squad shot Felipe. That guy, Colonel Broca, was a savage. He wanted to be governor and wasn't about to let Felipe or anyone else stand in his way. It was a bloodbath."

Our *calesa* had pulled up in front of the Gran. The driver was at my side, gallantly extending his hand. I placed a quick kiss on David's cheek and climbed out, hurrying through the hotel's massive doors.

David had booked the Gran for me when he discovered that Alma Reed had stayed there. I'd loved the place on sight, relished the idea of my heroine sweeping down those same broad mahogany stairs from the dining room or riding in the tiny birdcage elevator. This evening I looked around my room with special pleasure. There was no way of knowing if it was the same one Alma had occupied, but it must be similar. I touched the gold swag drapes on the high windows and wondered: Am I really like her?

A soft ring cut into my reverie. I picked up the antique phone. It was Mark. "You're late," he said impatiently. "I called twice."

"Oh, I am sorry," I consoled him. "They eat later here than at home." I'd planned to tell Mark about the dinner with David, the help he'd been to me, but decided against it. Instead I reminded him: "My work will be finished tomorrow. I'll be home late the day after."

There was a pause on the other end of the line. "Sage," he said at last. "Kevin and Lance are flying in tomorrow. You were right; they do need a little time to get used to the idea of our marriage."

I had expected family resistance from the start. Suppressing a sigh, I answered: "It's not the marriage that bothers them—it's the money. I don't want it, Mark. I mean it; you must explain that."

"It's *my* money, Sage. You've been the center piece of my life for twelve years. Can't you imagine how important it is for me to know that you'll be taken care of?"

"Your money doesn't matter to me, truly. I knew they'd be upset. We shouldn't—"

"We should and are going to," he answered. "You've been in my will for more than ten years. The boys need to understand that. I've set up a trust that includes all of you. Until they get that into their heads, things may get awkward. God knows, I've handled enough wills in my day. People often say things they regret later. Best that it's all settled before you come back. Take a few days—three days. Get out of the city. Go to that island you like. Lie in the sun, look over your notes."

Mark would say no more. "Be a good girl," he murmured after our good-byes.

I didn't envy Mark the next three days. It couldn't be easy. Kevin and Lance had spent very little time with their father in the last few years, but they were well aware of his financial assets. They'd been anticipating a comfortable estate divided just two ways. Now they'd be angry, perhaps fearful. But, for me, three extra days was a kind of reprieve. Perhaps I *would* go to Isla Mujeres. Best not to linger in Mérida once my work was complete; David was far too tempting.

Slipping out of my denim wraparound and underclothes, I stepped into the shower. It had been a long, hot day. How delicious the water felt. A few minutes later, soothed and pampered, I put on a light silk robe and moved out onto the balcony. Music and laughter drifted up from the café below. I leaned over the railing, enjoying the ambience. It was a true tropical night, warm, balmy, the scent of jasmine filling the air. In a far corner I could make out a man in white sitting alone at a small table. He looked a bit like David but it was too dark to tell.

Throughout the next day I felt a mixture of relief and sadness as the evening approached. Hard as I'd worked, these past three days in Mérida had been an idyll. Too pleasant, best that it be over soon. This evening would be my last with David. That afternoon, returning home from *La Prensa,* I spied a dress that made me think of Alma; flapper lines, flirty short skirt. My red sandals matched the opulent roses embroidered into the black fabric. I walked away, then turned back and entered the store.

Later, in my bedroom, turning this way and that before the ornately carved mirror, I admired the effect. A young girl might wear such a dress, but it also looked good on me. A college boy might not notice but his professor would. I wanted to look good for David. Was that so wrong? Of course, it was! What kind of thoughts were these for a woman about to be married? But then, it was hardly a conventional marriage. Would the Mayan girls have enjoyed an evening out before their plunge into the well? Some of them surely, the ones like me.

Seated in a pool of moonlight surrounded by fragrant flowers, we dined long and lavishly in the white-arched courtyard of Porticos, the city's best-kept secret. Dinner over, I felt reluctant to leave and sensed that David didn't want to, either. "Have the Kahlúa sundae with coconut ice cream," he urged. "It's their signature." Then we had an espresso. Had to have that.

Putting down his cup, David reached into the pocket of his white jacket. "I have a surprise for you," he said, pulling out a video tape. "It's an old movie about Felipe and Alma. I saw a reference on the Internet and scoured the town looking for it."

He handed me a tape; on the cover a garish couple kissed fervently. *La Peregrina.* "Oh, David, that's fabulous!" I exclaimed. "Let's go back to the hotel and watch it now."

I rose, picking up my rebozo. Carefully, David placed the lacy covering about my shoulders. I was so aware of his fingers that I almost stumbled.

We walked the few blocks to the Gran, sometimes stopping briefly to look into the shop windows—hammocks, embroidery, painted dishes. David took my hand but I allowed my fingers to slip away. We passed a small neighborhood theater where he bought popcorn from the vendor outside. "No movie is complete without it."

Inside the grand old Gran, I glanced about the comfortable lobby, with its lush palm trees and elaborate grillwork. "There's an alcove with a big TV behind that archway," I told him. "It'll be perfect for us." As I led the way to a little sitting room off the main corridor, David whispered something to a passing waiter. We'd hardly settled into large comfortable chairs before the waiter arrived with a silver tray. Deftly he arranged a champagne bucket and glasses on a small table between us. "Doesn't everyone drink champagne with their popcorn when they watch a home movie?"

"Home movie." The words had such a pleasant, reassuring ring to them. "Of course," I agreed, clinking his glass.

The film began on the small screen. Trumpets sounded, an elaborate fanfare; credits, many credits. It looked old, 1960s, maybe; the actors unfamiliar. The story started with a train chugging through the jungle; Alma Reed sat with another woman chatting in English. She was eager to interview "the savior of Yucatán." The train arrived in Mérida; Felipe was there to greet her. "From now on I will speak no more English," Alma announced. "My conversation will be only in *Español*."

The action that followed was so flamboyant that I scarcely needed a translator, though at times David filled in. In a scene that I couldn't believe, Felipe told his wife that he loved another. The poor woman, instead of smacking him, burst into song.

"What's that all about?" I asked David, incredulous.

"Felipe's wife loves him so much that she wants only his happiness. If he cares more for another, then he must leave."

"Felipe's kneeling at her feet!" I exclaimed. "What's he saying?"

" 'You are my saint.' "

I laughed. "The wife is so unselfish she tells him to just go for it?"

"So it would appear." David stood behind my chair, his hands on my shoulders. "The lady is a most unselfish partner, thinking only of her loved one's happiness." He moved his hand down my arm.

David shouldn't be touching me. I shouldn't be letting him touch me. I leaned away.

The movie, a stereotypical melodrama, was a disappointment, shedding no new light whatsoever on the real Alma or Felipe, but I did enjoy the music. "La Peregrina." As the theme climbed to a crescendo and more credits flitted across the screen, I rose to my feet, stretching. David stood before me now, eyes sad as they searched my face. How drab life was going to be without this kind, funny, most attractive man. We would say our good-byes here. It would be easier. I leaned forward to kiss him lightly.

At that moment the entrance to our nook filled with laughing women. "Are you finished with your movie?"

one asked in English, while thumbing through a collection of videos on the shelf.

"Quite through," I assured her.

"Ooh, look, they've got *Titanic* in English." As the others crowded around the table, David took my hand and led me out into the corridor. We could talk there, but no. Two men stood at a small table, poring over a newspaper and exclaiming angrily in Spanish.

Wordlessly, we stepped into the tiny elevator. I caught the faint scent of his shaving lotion as we stood quietly, listening to the birdcage's creaks and groans. The brass door opened. My heels clicked on the marble floor as I walked the short distance to my bedroom door, David behind me. I opened my purse but the key slipped from my fingers. We bumped heads reaching for it.

David turned the key in the lock and pushed the door open. I backed inside. He stood watching me from the doorway. "I'm sorry the movie was such a bummer."

I shrugged, wondering what to say about the world we had somehow built for ourselves over a few dinners. A world that was coming to an end. Right now. We stared silently at each other. And then we were too close to look and it was all touch and feel. The door closed and we were lying across the satin-covered bed. *This is what I want. This is what I've been missing.*

David drew my face to his. It was nothing like our first kiss at the Compass Rose Room. Back then he'd kissed me as if he knew me. Now it was as though he had just discovered there was a lot to learn. At last he drew back, searching my face. "Oh, Sage, what a time we're going to have."

22

Forgetting Felipe

ALMA

Mr. Ochs booked me on the most direct route to Mexico City but that still meant sailing past the Yucatán Peninsula. I resolved to stay in my cabin, but couldn't. The sight drew me like a magnet. As I stood at the rail, the shoreline beckoned, water sapphire blue, sand like fine talcum. A row of pastel buildings, peach, yellow, and green, shimmered in the distance. Felipe near, yet so far away.

As the ship slipped into Progreso, my relief mingled with sadness at the announcement that only disembarking passengers would be allowed off. Better not to set as much as a toe on this alluring land. I leaned against the rail and watched bale after bale of henequen loaded with quiet efficiency. The ship's stay in port would be brief.

Departing travelers radiated nervous excitement. "Who has the trunk?" "Did I pack my pills?" Where's the baby?!" Soon they were gone and new voyagers swarmed up the gangplank, eager, anxious, impatient. Tonight there would be different companions at the dining table, sitting in seats occupied only hours before by people they would never know. In my present gloom, I saw the chanced intimacy, the missed connections as a metaphor for life.

The ship's horn sounded, the landing rope tossed to waiting hands on deck. We backed away from the dock, Progreso slowly fading from view. I turned away, heading toward my cabin. Another loud blast stopped me, then the sound of mariachis in the distance. Looking back, I spotted a launch filled with flowers headed toward us. A man stood in the bow waving frantically. As the launch approached, I recognized Jorge, the young aid who had first taken me to Felipe's office. "Señora Reed! Señora Reed!" he called eagerly. My cheeks burned at the curious glances of other passengers clustered about the railing. The boat came alongside, a ladder was lowered, and Jorge, clutching a huge bouquet of red roses, clambered onboard. Excitement lit his large dark eyes.

With a bow he handed me the flowers. "His Excellency hopes that you will forgive him for not coming himself." Jorge bowed again, seemingly oblivious to the inquisitive onlookers crowding around us.

"Why didn't he?" I hated myself for asking.

Jorge drew closer, his voice lowered. "Our underground picked up rumors . . . hacendados threatening trouble. Only a few rabble rousers, nothing serious," he hastily added, "but His Excellency thought it prudent to remain in Mérida till things calm down. He begs you to join him there now, to return with me."

Longing swept over me in waves. I held my breath, struggled for control. "No," I said firmly, handing the roses back to Jorge. "Tell His Excellency that I shall *never* return to Mérida."

Jorge's exuberant smile faded. He looked from the flowers to me.

I smiled apologetically. "I can't. It's useless to discuss further."

The ship's horn sounded an impatient message. Jorge looked stricken. "His Excellency will be very disappointed."

My throat tightened. "I know."

The horn blasted again. Jorge turned reluctantly and climbed back down to his launch. Garlands of flowers festooned the small craft, their brightness bobbed mockingly in the light breeze.

"You've turned down a good man."

I looked up, startled. The ship's captain, Angus Blackadder, was standing at my side. I admired the short, stocky Scot, liked his weathered face offset by a sweeping handlebar mustache.

"It's no secret, you know." Blackadder took a deep puff from his pipe. "The whole of Yucatán—the whole of Mexico is talking. Everything the governor does is common knowledge."

I dabbed at my eyes. "That's what I hoped to avoid. The last thing I want to do is hurt him politically."

"You haven't, at least not yet. There's nothing the Méridians relish more than a good romance."

I studied the captain's keen blue eyes, wondering at all he'd seen and heard. "You've worked these waters for years," I said at last. "You know this country. What do you think would happen if I went back?"

"North Americans aren't popular around here. Your International Harvester sets the price on henequen—slave wages for our workers. But who can fight a company backed by Washington?" He absently stroked his black mustache. "But you're a different story, a heroine. Word's gotten around about how you saved that boy in the States. And now the *cenote* business has everyone talking. It's quite a thing you did. Who could blame the great Felipe Carrillo Puerto for losing his head? But if you were to return to him"—Blackadder shrugged—"that's anybody's guess. This is a Catholic country. The man's married; he has four children. If you've been around Mexico, you know what that means."

"Only too well. " I looked into his eyes, narrow from squinting across endless horizons, and hesitated. "Tell me," I asked at last, "tell me what *you* think?"

"I think it's time the governor had some happiness. He deserves it. The man's not had an easy life, for all the good he's done others. He was still a boy when he married. The woman he chose then . . ."

I thought of my own experience with Sam. "Who knows what they wanted in the beginning? Marriage is a minefield."

"The governor's case is a bit different."

"Really? I think not. For him, it's easy. He's Latin. If his wife no longer suits him, he can take a mistress. No one will think less of him."

"Ah, lassie, you judge too harshly. A man like Felipe requires more than a mistress. He needs a partner, one who understands the world."

I shook my head. I'd been over that ground many times, dreaming of what our life might be. Felipe and I shared the same thoughts, the same visions. *The same heart-beats.* "It's impossible," I told Blackadder. "Felipe's an idealist, but also a politician. He made a choice to negate the European part of himself. Consciously or otherwise, a Mayan wife was part of that. He'll make the same kind of choice when he puts me behind him."

"Perhaps," the captain puffed on his pipe. "Perhaps not." We stood for a time in silence as the coastline receded to a thin green line, then disappeared. Finally, Blackadder spoke again. "You know about the governor's reforms in Yucatán, but what about the Yaquis?"

"Yaquis?" I shivered, recalling the barbarous tales my father had told of prospecting days along the Arizona-Mexico border.

"They were a wild bunch," the captain agreed, "fiercely independent, but their tribal life worked well for centuries . . . until Díaz decided to 'civilize' them."

I listened as Blackadder told me of the times he'd transported Yaqui prisoners from Veracruz to Progreso on the orders of the old dictator Díaz. He described the scenes on the dock when husbands and wives, children and parents, were separated, then forced like cattle into the cargo holds of waiting ships for transport to the henequen plantations. "If hacienda life was bad for the native Maya, imagine how terrible it must have been for those freeborn Indians from Sonora. Your man changed all that. He returned them to their homelands, more often than not at his own expense."

"He's *not* my man," I told the captain. "Still, it's quite a story. Felipe never told me." I stood silent for a time. "I already know how good he is. Perhaps he's the best man in the world . . . certainly the best for me." Straightening my shoulders, I reminded Blackadder, reminded myself: "I've a life of my own to live. It's waiting for me in Mexico City."

And, it seemed, Mexico City *was* waiting for me. A word from the publisher of the *New York Times* had set a glorious city in motion. The Simón Ruiz story had struck a chord in the public mind. Officials, glittering with braid and medals, waited at the train station to sweep me into a large, open touring car. I was paraded down the Paseo de la Reforma, a thoroughfare lined with broad, leafy trees and magnificent statues. I thought it the most beautiful street I'd ever seen. "Paris couldn't be more gorgeous," I speculated aloud to the official beside me. "No, it could not," he agreed. "This boulevard was designed by Empress Carlota to rival her beloved Paris." All around us, the Reforma was thronged with cheering people, many tossing bright flowers at our car while confetti floated down like pink snowflakes. For these glorious moments, *I* was the empress.

At the Hotel Regis in El Centro, the manager escorted me to an elegant suite filled with even more flowers. That wasn't all. The bathroom was crammed with birdcages. In the capital, I learned, a bird in a cage was a tribute surpassing flowers. There would be many birdcages in the weeks ahead. It was a touching gesture, flattering, too, I supposed, but something of a nuisance. I released the wild birds late at night from my balcony and paid the hotel maid to find homes for the tame ones.

The local youngbloods, sons of the old, landed gentry, eagerly escorted me to balls and receptions. The generals, part of a newer aristocracy, besieged me as well. Busy as I was filing my own stories to the *New York Times*, hardly a day passed that I didn't give an interview to some periodical or attend a party in my honor. The story of Simón Ruiz was told and retold.

Nothing I ever saw before or after equaled the excitement of that postrevolutionary epoch. Joy charged the atmosphere; hope was the air we breathed. War was over, old inequities swept away. In their place were an exuberant idealism and the expectancy that hard-working, honest people would be rewarded no matter who they were. It was a golden time, a time without precedent. I felt as if I were watching a gigantic century plant—the vigorous agave so symbolic of Mexico—burst into bloom, infusing the world with radiance. I thought it splendidly mystical, for the last vestiges of the fight for independence from Spain had ended just one hundred years earlier.

With a certain irony I addressed myself to a search for the burial place of Cortés. A group of men who counted their descent from the conquistadors professed to know its whereabouts. During a freedom celebration, years earlier, hatred of Mexico's conqueror took the form of a plot to steal his ashes. When the government refused to intervene, members of the "oldest families" averted the violation of Cortés's elaborate coffin. The remains were spirited away and interred. But where? Members of Mexico City's elitist Spanish Club hinted after a few drinks that they knew. What a story! If only I could ferret out the truth. I welcomed the challenge, hoping that it would prove an antidote to my pain and longing for Felipe.

One evening late in August I sallied forth to a grand ball certain that on this night I would crack the Cortés story. It was a gala affair hosted by President Obregón at the palace. I wore a red satin gown with an overlay of fringe that shimmied as I walked. My slippers, too, were red, as was the ostrich feather fastened to my gold head-band. Surely, I reasoned, one man among so many knew something. And surely such a man—if I could be alone with him—would offer at least a hint. But no man would leave me alone with another for even an instant. Two generals escorted me to the ball; four accompanied me back to the Regis. All insisted upon crowding into the small, ornately gilded elevator beside me. I breathed a sigh of relief when we reached the top, as did the attendant who wiped the sweat from his forehead.

Now they stood outside my door, each insisting that he and he alone be invited in for a nightcap. What did they take me for? Or was it a game? I chose to think it was and treated their appeals lightly.

"*Es muy tarde.*" I sighed, tilting my head to rest on folded hands beneath my cheek as on a pillow.

"Let me come in; you'll sleep so much better with a little of this," one offered, pulling an ornately engraved silver flask from his pocket.

"*No, gracias, es tarde.*" My back was to the door now as I pulled the key from my tiny beaded bag.

"Then tomorrow—a ride through Chapultepec Park."

"No, breakfast at Casa de Azulejos—you can sit where Pancho Villa sat."

"Disgusting!" another countered. "How dare you suggest that she sully herself in that way. I shall take her to the floating gardens, where she will sail like Cleopatra."

"Better than that, I shall take her for a ride on my private train."

"Mine is much grander. She shall go with me."

I looked from one to the other. Only a few years before they'd been poor farm boys pushing plows. Now they looked magnificent with their red sashes and gold epaulettes—like toy soldiers sprung to life. Incredibly, they all did have private trains. I'd seen them. Some of the generals were younger than I, yet had somehow managed to ally themselves with the winning side and emerge from the holocaust with fortunes beyond belief. Their life in the capital was dreamlike, so different from the real life that I had glimpsed with Felipe. *My darling, where are you now?*

"Señora Reed, you look *muy triste*—so sad. You must indeed be tired." One man took my hand and pressed it to his lips. "I shall ring you *mañana.*"

"And so shall I!"

"And I."

"*Yo tambien.*"

Each claimed my hand for a fleeting kiss and gazed soulfully into my eyes. The evening that had started out so full of promise now seemed endless. My mouth felt stretched from smiling.

"*Mañana,*" I said, pushing gently at their chests. Such handsome boys in their starched uniforms. Once again, I thought of toy soldiers. But all those medals . . . what had they done to earn them? Better not to know. I slipped the key quickly into the lock.

"*Buenas noches,*" I said, blowing them a conciliatory kiss before closing the door firmly behind me. I leaned against it for a minute, eyes closed, listening to their fading footsteps. The evening's effort to be alert and lively to those young men, to play my part in their comic opera, overwhelmed me.

"I've been waiting for you, little *peregrina.* It has been a long evening, but now you are here at last."

My eyes flew open. "Felipe!" I gasped as he rose from the chaise. "What are you doing here?"

As he walked toward me, my throat swelled, my eyes filled with angry, frustrated tears. "You've no right to follow me this way. I can't stand it, I really can't stand it! How can I get on with my life when you refuse to leave me alone?"

He merely smiled. Taking me in his arms, he stroked my hair gently, soothingly. "But I thought you loved me," he murmured softly into my ear. "I could have sworn you said that."

"What does loving you have to do with anything?" I wailed.

Felipe's smile broadened. "I should think it would have everything to do with it. I sent you flowers—you flung them away. I sent a boat—you refused to get in it. So now I have come all the way from Yucatán to ask you to marry me."

"Oh, so I'm to assume you've murdered your wife. I'm not amused." Struggling to control my sobs, I reached gratefully for his proffered handkerchief.

"My former wife is very well, thank you. I can't say that she sends you her regards, but she is alive and well, I assure you."

"Former wife! Divorce is against the law in Mexico."

He held me at arm's length, smiling at my teary face. "Alma, dear love, I have sworn to liberate my people socially as well as economically. Why be a governor if I cannot also be free?"

I shook my head in bewilderment. "What are you saying?"

"It is quite simple, *mi corazón*. I have caused the passage of an act legalizing divorce and I, myself, am the very first to make use of it. In three months' time, we can be married."

"Oh, my darling," I gasped, "what have you done?!"

23

The Good Life

The world fell away, leaving nothing but Felipe and me dancing together on a glittering stage. The gallants who'd attended me so ardently watched wistfully. Felipe was the man of the hour. At the grand balls, the receptions, and in the chic cafés, people whispered excitedly. Felipe Carrillo Puerto was a hero, a statesman, the friend and confidant of the president. How heady to be his treasured companion, to see the admiration in the eyes of men, the envy in the glances of women. It was delicious to talk, oh so seriously, to the English ambassador while, under the table, Felipe's hand caressed my leg.

We savored the Bohemian side of the city as well, drinking with Orozco, Rivera, and their like, artists who drew sketches on the walls and tablecloths of their favorite cafés as payment. It was fun to forsake European cuisine and wine in favor of tacos and *pulque,* to dance the *jarabe* and *sandunga* rather than the waltz or foxtrot.

Having liberated Mexico City with Zapata, Felipe knew all the neighborhood bars, which I enjoyed as much as the gilded bistros lining the Reforma. *Pulquerías,* they were called, named for the fiery liquor made from the maguey plant. The cantinas' names were whimsical: "Wise Men Who Never Never Study," "The Magnificent Jewess," "The Errors of Cupid," "No One Will Ever Know," and "Who Cares Anyway."

What a contrast to the galas at Chapultepec Palace, where we were the guests of President Obregón. One evening as the three of us stood together on the balcony following a ceremony, the cheers for Felipe were even greater than those directed toward Obregón. I saw the president's thoughtful gaze rest on Felipe. Perhaps, feeling my eyes, he shifted his attention to me and smiled.

"What a couple you make! When shall I expect a wedding invitation?"

"She has yet to say yes," Felipe admitted as we moved back from the parapet.

"The hell, you say!" the president exclaimed in surprise. "After all you've gone through—the new law, the divorce. Doesn't she realize . . ."

"Alma is afraid her presence may damage my career."

"That's impossible. You *are* Yucatán. Your people adore you. They will accept anything." He turned to me. "Catch the moment, Señora Reed. Seize it now. One never knows when, if ever, it will come again."

More than his words, Álvaro Obregón's eyes held me. Sharp, shiny, like black obsidian. At that instant, more than ever before, I felt *el presidente*'s power. Here was the man who had conspired to defeat the aging dictator Díaz. The dark horse in a revolutionary band that had once included Madero, Zapata, Villa, and Carranza. Obregón had lost an arm in the revolution but emerged the victor. In the end, it was a cleverly orchestrated duel. The others died violent deaths linked to the president. Only Villa survived, living now in uneasy exile on his ranch in Chihuahua.

President Obregón turned to Felipe and said something I didn't catch.

Felipe placed his hands on my shoulders, turning me gently to face him. "Alma, *mi corazón,* allow *el presidente* to announce our engagement to all of Mexico." He took my hands, kissed each tenderly, then pulled a velvet box from his pocket. "I've been carrying this with me for more than a week, waiting. There has to be a right time. Let it be now."

My fingers trembled slightly as I opened the box. The ring inside made me gasp. Diamonds flanked a large sapphire, sparkling blue yet with a hidden depth. I thought of the *cenote* where I'd dreamed of Kukulkan and realized that, for me, the god and the governor were one and the same.

"I've never seen anything so beautiful," I told him. My heart raced; this was happening too fast. I looked from one man to the other. Had they planned the moment to catch me unawares? Flattering, of course, but I felt uneasy.

"Will you wear it, for me?" Felipe took my left hand, caressing the ring finger. "Say you will."

A wave of panic swept over me as I thought of Kuku-lkan, a hero god ruined by a woman. What was I doing to Felipe? What was I doing to myself? It was too much. I couldn't think any longer, didn't want to think. My own longing was too great to deny.

I looked up at my beloved and nodded, unable to speak. Felipe's eyes shone as he slipped the ring onto my finger. It felt like a dream, the reality of decision floating somewhere above me.

Taking our hands in his, Obregón led us back across the black-and-white-tile floor to the marble balcony. In the distance, the lights of Mexico City gleamed, a forest of twinkling stars. Below us, hundreds, possibly thousands, of laughing, jostling people still crowded the courtyard. It was a festive throng, many carrying flowers and brightly colored balloons.

President Obregón raised his arm for silence. A speculative murmur rose, swelled to a roar. I felt my cheeks flame with excitement as he spoke the words: "It is my great pleasure to announce the engagement of our honored guest, Señora Alma Reed, a great friend and ally of

Mexico, to His Excellency, Felipe Carrillo Puerto, governor of Yucatán."

As if on cue, the band began to play again. To my immense relief, the crowd was with us. *Let it be like this in Yucatán,* I prayed. Cheering people streamed forward, tearing at their programs, shredding them into confetti. Others squeezed past the guards and pushed their way into the flower garden. Pulling at the tenderly cultivated roses, they tossed the blooms into the air. I glanced apprehensively at Obregón, but he merely smiled and waved to the people below, apparently charmed by their enthusiasm.

"What a popular couple you are," he smiled. "Both so beautiful, so dedicated . . . like Maxmilian and Carlota. Surely they must once have stood just where you are standing now."

A strange analogy, I thought. The idealistic young emperor, Maxmilian, foisted on Mexico by conniving European powers, had been shot by a firing squad. The aged Carlota was said to be a prisoner in a French asylum.

I searched his small, dark eyes, saw nothing but pleasure in the moment. "President Obregón, you are too kind," I said, pulling a fleecy stole about my shoulders against the chill.

From my dressing table, I could see Felipe's reflection. He lay on my bed, watching like a large jungle cat.

I was naked and loved it, loved the thought of that cat pouncing on me, devouring me.

"I don't care for long engagements. Do you?" he asked.

"You have something in mind? An alternative?" I raised the ivory-handled hairbrush, arching my back languorously.

"The Regis has been wonderful for us. . . . So convenient, suites right next door to one another. . . ." Felipe rose, crossed the room in an instant. His lips moved over my throat, whispering.

Wonderful didn't begin to describe it. Going out day after day, night after night, then returning to our private satin-sheeted world. We'd had a nightly choice: my room, peach and lavender, or his, a soft brown trimmed in green. I loved this sensuous, carefree life, wanted it to go on forever.

"But it will be very different in Mérida," he warned. "People are conservative there. Engaged couples rarely hold hands in public. They never . . ." he paused, leaned forward, and slipped his tongue into my mouth.

Later, I dozed for a time and when I awakened Felipe's fingers were running idly over my belly.

"What are you thinking?" I murmured sleepily.

"I was wondering how many children we will have."

"What about your 'family planning' program?" I asked him, instantly awake. "The personal freedom you preach? I heard your speeches and was impressed."

"That is for others. I want all the children that God grants us—and you care to receive."

"One might be lovely. But," I warned him, "I don't want a life like my mother's. I'll continue to write, of course, and I also want to help with your reforms." *Brave words. I wanted so much for them to be true.* "Oh, I hope the people will accept me," I breathed. "I'll try so hard."

"You will be splendid," Felipe said, cradling me in his arms. "The people will more than accept you," he assured me between little nibbling kisses. "They'll love you as I do. How could they not love you? You'll not only be a fine ambassador for your country, but a positive influence on mine."

"But when," I asked, turning, trapping his legs between my own, "when will this new life begin for us?"

"As I said, I don't care for long engagements. What would you say to a Christmas wedding?" he asked. "For the time being you will live in Mérida at the Gran. I will book a suite for you overlooking the garden. My divorce will be final in December."

"Three whole months, so long, and you really think that we can't . . ."

"We shall have to be very discreet."

"But for now . . ."

It was a long time before we slept. When I awakened we were making love again. The phone rang. We let it ring. Later, as I drowsed, it rang again. Listening sleepily to Felipe's voice, I slowly, unwillingly, became aware of the concerned tone. What I picked up from his side of the conversation didn't sound good, some kind of trouble. An uprising? I sat up, watching his face anxiously.

"What's happened?" I asked when he hung up.

Felipe shook his head. "Blanca Flor has always been trouble. Have you heard of it?"

"A large hacienda to the south, over the Campeche border. Didn't Empress Carlota stay there?"

He nodded. "Very fitting that she would. Blanca Flor is a bulwark of conservatism. The hacendados there would turn the clock back to the conquistadors if they could. Now the leaders of a counterrevolutionary band are holed up there trying to gain support."

"What's going to happen, Felipe?" Recognizing that our idyll was at an end, I sat up.

"I must return to Yucatán immediately."

I threw back the covers. "I'll have to pack."

"No." His hand caressed my cheek. "I must go alone. In a few days, I'll have things under control. When you receive my message that all is safe, come immediately. Come to me in Mérida. That's when our real life will begin."

24

The Nature of an Affair

SAGE

The sun invaded my room at the Gran, pools of molten light engulfing the bed where we lay. Reluctantly, I opened my eyes. The travel clock beside me read 10:15.

David was lying on his side, watching. "Good morning, sleepyhead. "I've been waiting for you to wake up." His arm slid around me. "We've got three days. Want to spend them on the coast, maybe lie on the beach?"

Three days with David. Didn't I deserve that much? *But what about David?* What did he deserve? I hadn't wanted to tell him about my approaching marriage, had thus far managed to avoid it, but last night had changed everything. How could I go on living a lie? All I wanted now was to enjoy the moment, but there was no way around it. I would have to tell David the truth.

I pulled the covers around my naked shoulders. "We can't go anywhere. I should have told you sooner, but I just couldn't seem to bring myself to talk about it. I felt guilty and ashamed, but we were having such a good time . . . I was afraid all that would change. Now I know it will."

David looked at me, puzzled. He took my face in his hands. "Nothing can be that bad. Tell me what's been bothering you."

I looked away, not wanting to meet his eyes. "Back in San Francisco, after your e-mail, Mark didn't want me to leave. He hated the idea of my coming down here. His condition makes him angry much of the time. Often he takes that frustration out on me—asking—ordering—me to do a thousand errands, yet nothing ever satisfies him. It's getting harder all the time. I'm always at his beck and call. Sometimes I get angry, too—not at him. I know it's not really Mark saying and doing those things. It's the terrible, relentless cancer that's changed him into a different person. Mark can't help it. He's hurt and frightened." I backed away from David, still holding the sheet like a shield before me. Taking a deep breath, I continued, "Just before I left to come down here, Mark asked me to marry him once again. He was so upset about my leaving that this time I agreed."

"What?!" David sat up beside me, his face flushed. "Those damn lawyers and their plea bargains! He finally got to you, didn't he?"

"I'm sorry, David." I looked hard into his eyes and watched the anger slowly melt. "Mark wants this marriage very much. He has so little time, it seemed a small thing."

David shook his head as though dazed by what he'd heard. "No, Sage, it's a very big thing. You've got to give me—give us—these next three days."

What could I say? I was so happy that he still wanted me after what I'd done, I couldn't think about anything else. Wasn't going to think.

"I'd planned to go to the coast today," I told David over breakfast, "but now—with you—I'd like to stay at an old plantation house from Alma's time, somewhere that she might have gone. I photographed a place like that on a press trip last year. It's not far from here," I told him, adding: "Hacienda del Valle is the prettiest hotel in Mexico."

David made a quick phone call. In less than an hour we were driving past thatched cottages and mango groves. An hour more and jungle surrounded us. We rounded a curve and looming before us was a high stone wall with an arched gateway. A sentry checked off our names as his ancestor might have done a hundred years earlier. Had Alma Reed once passed through these gates? It pleased me to think so. As we proceeded down the broad driveway toward a hacienda nearly as long as a football field, I tried to imagine the opulence of the del Valle world.

"It isn't much but they called it home," David joked, gesturing at the burnished gold mansion with its graceful columns encircled by morning glories. As we approached, the carved mahogany door swung open. Two Mayan bellmen, dressed as Spanish grandees, stepped out, and behind them a young woman in white, pleated skirt floating out behind her as she descended the stairs.

"I am Valencia de Garcia," she said, extending a slim well-manicured hand. "Allow me to welcome you to Hacienda del Valle." The bellmen bowed; one took our bags, the other our car. As Señorita de Garcia accompanied us back up the stairs to the registration desk, she explained that, as vice president in charge of marketing, she was doing an inspection tour of the property. Valencia was young and pretty. I liked the red scarf tied in a rakish, pirate manner over her brown curly hair. Large gold hoop earrings flashed as she spoke animatedly. The quintessential PR rep. I'd met many over the years, but there was something a bit different in the cool confidence of this one.

We chatted as David filled out the registration form, Valencia describing the hotel's amenities. I looked curiously at the well-appointed lobby, admiring a suit of armor and an antique chest. Both sixteenth century, she told me.

My eyes came to rest on an ornately framed painting. I moved closer to examine the work, a double portrait of an aristocratic pair in 1920s clothing. "What a striking couple!" I exclaimed. "Do you know who they were?"

"Indeed I do. Doña Alejandra and Don Ricardo del Valle. My great-grandmother was their only child."

"Then this hotel is your family home?"

"Not anymore." A wry smile played about Valencia's lips. "The house was abandoned in the 1940s. The land went to pay debts after nylon took over the rope market. Five years ago the Splendido chain bought the ruin. They've spent millions on the restoration. Their architects, bless them, rebuilt it from old photographs. What you see is as it was. Enjoy!" She gave us a mock curtsy and hurried off, clipboard in hand.

David and I clambered over half-excavated ruins, swam in the pool, explored lush gardens dotted with charming gazebos. After a perfect day we enjoyed blissful massages in our room. In the lush tropical foliage just outside the open window, two parakeets crooned to each other while strong hands slathered honey over our backs. "An ancient Mayan beauty treatment," one masseuse explained. I smiled at David, lying on the massage table beside mine, and wondered if we'd somehow slipped into heaven.

The moralist in me nagged: Could it be just sex—new skin, new smells? But I knew it was more. The sex part, so delicious, felt slight compared to the bright, shining image of myself reflected in David's eyes. A man who was all I wanted or admired called me "wonderful." I had begun to believe him. Was this a new beginning for me, a chance to be the woman I used to be before Mark's needs had drained me dry?

The masseuses quietly left. I turned and blew David a kiss.

That evening we enthusiastically described the day's adventures to Valencia, who greeted us in a room called the Chapel. It was, in reality, the bar.

"Did you visit the *cenote*?" she asked.

"*Cenote!*" I shivered, thinking of the sacred well at Chichen Itza. "No, we missed that. Was this one also used for sacrifices?"

A slight frown creased Valencia's smooth brow. "No, not that I've heard. Those are just myths. No one believes them. Anyway, our *cenote* is small and very beautiful. Guests sometimes swim there. You'll find it near the big bougainvillea tree, just beyond the ruins."

I studied Valencia, wondering about her background. So much wealth and privilege bestowing a graceful elegance taken for granted until the very end. "I can't imagine that your ancestors would like their family chapel turned into a bar," I said, nodding toward the far wall, where a large assortment of crucifixes served simply as decorations. In one corner of the room two small pews were arranged facing each other. In another, an altar held dishes of chips and salsa.

Valencia flashed a smile. "Perhaps they'd be amused. From what I'm told, the del Valle loved to party."

I pressed further. "There's a name that crops up often in Yucatán, Felipe Carrillo Puerto. I suppose you've heard of him?"

Valencia's smile froze. "Everyone has heard of him but he was not the hero you may imagine. My family fought beside Montejo, the conqueror of Yucatán. This land was granted to us by the king of Spain hundreds of years ago. Felipe Carrillo Puerto and the revolution he fought for changed that forever. . . . People don't understand. We took care of our workers. They loved us. Many of them stayed on even after their debt cards were burned—" Valencia broke off. In an instant the bright smile was back. "I'm sure you're not interested in a history lesson." She signaled to the bartender. "Please enjoy your drinks." Still smiling, she left us.

"I suppose some workers did hang on," David mused. "What did they know but henequen? Then along came nylon. . . ."

We didn't dwell on it. We had our own story.

The next day David and I visited the pink flamingo preserve. A motorboat took us first through a dense mangrove swamp. The waterway was narrow, branches intruding on either side. I thought of them as the outside world reaching in to pull us back and stayed close to David. Once we saw an alligator; he swam the other way. Gradually the water changed from muddy green to deep azure as the channel opened out onto a large lagoon. The boatman cut his engine and we drifted. Slowly, silently, we rounded a curve and there they were—hundreds, perhaps thousands, of flamingoes ranging from the palest pink to vermillion. Some soared upward, crimson against the blue, blue sky, but most swayed languorously in the shallow water.

"It's getting close to their nesting time." David slipped his tan arm around my shoulders. "Those guys are courting—like me."

I leaned against him, enjoying his scent, as I watched the incredible creatures strut and preen, bills touching, long graceful necks caressing.

"Some say they mate for life," he told me.

And how long were those lives? I wondered. That set me to thinking about Mark. The guilt again. *What was I doing here?!*

The next day we drove to Izamal, parked our car on the outskirts of town, and hired a *calesa* to take us to the village square. The walls we passed were a rich maize that shimmered to gold in the sunlight. It was midday and doors were closed. I imagined lovers slumbering behind vine-covered walls. Perhaps David imagined the same; his arm tightened around my shoulders. "Oh, I'm so in lust," I whispered into his ear.

Growling like a jaguar, he pulled me close.

The *calesa* continued down the cobbled street, coming

to a stop before a massive stone monastery that domi-nated the square. I'd visited St. Anthony de Padua on my press trip and recalled its size, second only to St. Peter's in Rome. But I also remembered a sense of melancholy.

As David helped me out of the *calesa* onto the cobbled street, I wondered what he would think. Before us stone stairs curved gracefully up to the monastery. At the top we stepped onto a grassy atrium surrounded by many sweeping arches. "Pretty impressive," he said, his hand in mine, "but it feels forlorn."

"Maybe that's because the monastery was built on the ruins of a Mayan temple to their god, Itzamna," I told him. "It seems like somebody always has to sacrifice something or someone around here."

We wandered into the church and admired a statue of Mary said to have wrought miracles. "Maybe it was really Itzamna who caused them," David suggested.

I looked at him, tall and rangy in his jeans, that crooked smile again, and prayed for a miracle. Something big enough to satisfy three people. Any god would do. *Ixchel, are you listening? Pick up the phone!*

Sitting on an ancient stone parapet overlooking the town, I studied what was left of the Mayan ruins. The once proud monastery that had supplanted them was today merely a monument. It reminded me of Valencia, displaced lady of the manor. Yucatán was an unforgiving land where heroes died violent deaths and vast fortunes were amassed only to be lost. These past three days were in themselves a miracle. How dared I ask for more?

When we got back to the hotel, David suggested a dip in the *cenote*. It was late afternoon and the grounds appeared deserted. We walked past the ruins to where the garden ended and the jungle began. The path was overgrown, not much used. We almost missed the small cavern, all but obscured by foliage. I pushed aside a thick branch and gasped at the unexpected beauty beyond. Inside the grotto, the small *cenote*, illuminated by shafts of sunlight, sparkled pure turquoise.

No one would come out here at this hour, we agreed. Wordlessly, we slipped out of our clothes. The pool was shallow, reaching just below my breasts. Sighing happily, I leaned against the mossy wall. The lush, moist jungle enfolded us. It smelled of growing things. I felt like the first woman in the world, perhaps the only woman. David the only man.

That night after dinner we sat out on the veranda of our bungalow. All around us tiny lights twinkled. "I love fireflies," I murmured. "We don't have them in California."

David took my hand. "There's a lightshow every night on the front porch of my farmhouse."

"Perhaps you'll think of me sometimes when you watch it."

"I don't want to think of you." David sat up sharply and turned to face me. "I want you there beside me, Sage. There's a lot I've wanted to say; this is as good a time as any. My project's about finished. Another month or so and I'll be out of here. I'm going to take a few weeks' leave and go home to my farm. I sure would love to have you there with me. Will you come?"

"That's impossible. I've already told you. In less than a month I'll be married."

"Aren't you the one who said 'What difference does a piece of paper make'?" he reminded me. "In this case, it would seem very little. The man's in a wheelchair. I understand that you won't leave him. I respect you for it, but that doesn't mean you have to make a martyr of yourself."

I pushed him away and rose to my feet. "Just before I came down here Mark joked that my taking this trip would kill him. Maybe it wasn't a joke." I was trembling. "Is that what you want?"

In an instant David was at my side, taking me in his arms, soothing me. "Sweetheart, sweetheart, calm down. Everything will be all right. We can still have a life. I'll come out to the coast. I can get a leave of absence from NIH and take a job consulting in Silicon Valley."

"You'd hate that."

"Not if it meant seeing you. Something can be arranged, some compromise; I know it can. In the meantime, come meet my family. I've a great place for you to write, a large screened porch overlooking a brook. You'll love it. All you have to do is come up with some excuse—"

"Excuse." The word hit me hard. It wasn't that an affair was so wrong; the act of sex scarcely seemed important when compared to other things. It was the subterfuge that such a liaison would require. I saw myself already, rushing from Mark's side to read David's e-mails, to receive his phone calls, my thoughts constantly straying to David; time, energy, feeling, drained from Mark when he needed me most. Worse yet were the thoughts that could creep unbidden into my consciousness, hopes and dreams of some fantasized future with David. That was where the true guilt lay.

I loved Mark, loved all that we'd shared together, and cherished what remained. He and I were partners; I wouldn't, couldn't, steal from the till.

My fingers caressed David's face, slowly, softly, as if to memorize it. "If I were a woman who could do that, you wouldn't love me."

"But I do love you," he said; his arms tightened around me.

"That's what I'm saying."

"This is it, then?" he asked, gesturing at the bungalow, the starlit sky above. "This is all we'll ever have?"

"It's a lot, don't you think?"

"More than I've ever had before," he said, squeezing my shoulder, "but I wanted it to last forever."

"We'll have the memory forever. Our hearts can come back. At least mine will." I looked away so David wouldn't see the tears, stared hard at the flickering fireflies. One thing I knew: the well of sacrifice was not a myth.

25

La Peregrina's Journey

ALMA

Mexico City, the intoxicating capital that I had loved, faded slowly before my eyes. Without Felipe it became a dismal twilight city, a place where sentences went unfinished, where people disappeared. Felipe wrote long letters, one each day, but where was the summons to join him? The days passed, one, two, three, a week, then two weeks and one more. What was going on in Yucatán? I combed the newspapers, but found nothing. Perhaps President Obregón could tell me, but for some reason I hesitated.

I felt frightened and alone, but kept busy. There were lots of stories to write, the ones I'd put on hold that last perfect month. I hurried to complete them. There was a visit to the pyramids of Teotihuacan. Then a tour of the crumbling ruins of Cortés's first palace in Cuernavaca. The rumor that his bones were secretly buried there kept circling back to me but the trail always dried up. The old Spanish families were proud of their heritage, fearful of the desecration that could easily follow disclosure of the brutal conquistador's remains. I longed to crack this story, but then Felipe's telegram came. I could wait no longer. Nothing would stand in the way of my joining him.

There was one last gala, a farewell dinner in my honor at Chapultepec Palace. President Obregón placed me at his right, a gallant host. "My generals will miss you," he said, refilling my goblet.

I took a sip of claret, eyed him over the gold-etched rim. "Your generals . . . I've wondered about them. There are so many. For a time, I thought that every man in Mexico City was a general."

The president laughed heartily. "I'm not surprised. After the revolution I invited five hundred of them, the most voracious of our fighters, the hungriest predators, to join me here in the capital."

"Five hundred!" I exclaimed in surprise. "What do they all do here?"

"As little as possible, but their posts all have prestigious titles." He leaned back in his padded armchair. "They came eagerly; no Mexican general can withstand a cannonball of fifty thousand pesos. It was a small price to pay, extremely economical. Leaving them in the provinces would have invited banditry on a far greater scale. And, sooner or later, one of them would have started another revolution."

I leaned back, too, studying my host. For all his smug affability, Obregón was a hard-eyed survivor. During the course of the evening, he'd bragged about owning a chickpea farm that employed more than fifteen hundred workers. He was proud, too, of a lucrative new government contract that would supply railroad ties to newly nationalized trains. Felipe, who'd discussed these acquisitions with me, suspected that Obregón's promised reforms were already forgotten. *El presidente* might call himself a revolutionary, but he was also a man determined to carve his own empire.

After dinner, as we danced, the president asked many questions about Felipe's accomplishments in Yucatán.

"I hope you'll come to see them for yourself," I suggested. "Perhaps you will be our guest."

"Ah, so, you've set a wedding date." White teeth flashed beneath his thick, dark mustache.

"At first, we thought Christmas," I told him. "But now I believe it will be New Year's Eve. We like the idea of a fresh beginning together."

"How delightful." President Obregón smiled. "Have you thought of having the ceremony in San Francisco?"

"San Francisco?" I looked at him in surprise.

"Surely your family must be eager to meet Felipe. What

a treat for them, for all of you, to celebrate the ceremony in that great city."

"But Felipe has so much to do in Yucatán. I hardly think . . ."

"Yes, yes, of course," Obregón agreed. "He does have much to do." He touched his lips to my fingers and bowed slightly as the song came to an end.

I've never forgotten the moment that followed. We were standing in the center of the ballroom beneath an immense cut-glass chandelier. The president was looking splendid with his gold medals gleaming in the light. We were laughing at a little joke when an aide appeared and whispered something in Obregón's ear. Did I imagine it, or did *el presidente*'s smile broaden for an instant?

"*¡Caramba!*" he exclaimed to the aide. "That is terrible. You must be mistaken," he insisted, his face now a mask of horrified surprise.

"What is it?" I asked, my reporter self aroused. "Can you tell me?"

Obregón took my hand. "My dear," he said, shaking his head sadly, "soon the whole world will know. Pancho Villa has been shot, gunned down in his car while returning home from a tryst. His body was found riddled with bullets."

I watched people all around me react to the news. Some looked stricken, others not so stricken. No one appeared as shocked as I would have expected. What had *el presidente* said to Felipe and me? *Life can change, sometimes end in an instant. What can any of us do but live each day to the fullest?* In a world so savage, I knew I must take his words to heart. The orchestra began to play again, a fast waltz. President Obregón held out his hand to me.

Felipe followed his wire with a formal invitation. He was hosting a world conference of journalists to outline his vision for Yucatán. His strategy impressed me, a clever ploy to downplay the insurrection at Blanca Flor while showcasing his own achievements. The event would benefit me as well. There'd be plenty of story material to justify my return to Yucatán. Remembering how adamant I'd been about not going back, I could imagine Mr. Ochs's surprise at this sudden change of venue.

The departure day was stormy. Heavy rain slashed at the window as the train headed eastward toward Veracruz. Usually I hated rain but this time the wild weather excited me as well. I felt almost delirious at the thought of seeing Felipe again. Being crammed into the train car with a bunch of other journalists also bound for the conference excited me too. This, too, was all part of my life. Everything that mattered was coming together for me at last. But to my surprise, the other correspondents treated me with polite deference—not at all what I was accustomed to from colleagues. Missing the old press trip camaraderie, I felt distanced. Even worse, they sometimes cut their conversations short when I approached.

Perhaps some politicians' wives got used to that sort of thing. I doubted I ever could.

I was glad when our special train finally reached Veracruz. From there a warship had been commandeered by the president to take us to Progreso. A generous gesture, I'd thought, once again revising my assessment of Obregón. Still, the man remained a question mark, someone to be watched.

The rain had increased during the journey east. Heavy waves lashed the wharf. Captain Rodriguez warned our party that serious storm warnings had been issued. He was reluctant to depart, but the contingent of correspondents was large and vocal. The conference was scheduled to begin the next night. We had deadlines to meet. The waves looked formidable, yet even more than the others, I was eager to be off. Felipe was waiting.

When Captain Rodriguez gave his grudging consent, I hurried up the gangplank all the while trying to keep an eye on the accumulation of bags and boxes I'd acquired in Mexico City. It took several sailors to carry them all. The amused expressions on the other writers' faces were hard to miss. I felt uncomfortable, but not for long. What the hell! Engaged women shop. I was marrying the governor of Yucatán, for heaven's sake.

The warship contained no private staterooms so the captain gallantly allowed me to use his. The other journalists eyed me with envy, but what could anyone say? I was the only woman onboard. Captain Rodriguez's quarters were Spartan: a bunk, a chair, maps on the wall, pictures of pretty ladies on the neatly arranged desk. Many pretty ladies. One for every port? At least. The three small windows were tightly sealed against tumultuous seas splashing well above them. Bracing myself against the wall, I watched the harbor recede from view. The ship pitched, prow aloft over the waves' crests, then buried itself deep in giant troughs, plunging and rising, her deck awash. A huge wave slammed the vessel. I heard a violent crash outside. It sounded like a tray of dishes. The ship listed badly.

Trying to ignore my queasiness, I slipped off my dark blue traveling suit and hung it in the tiny closet beside the dress I'd wear that night. No need to unpack anything else. I lay down on the bunk and pulled out my notebook with the notes from the previous day's interview with Plutarco Calles.

Calles was Mexico's number-two man, President Obregón's handpicked successor. He had spoken candidly, the exclusive interview a coup, yet the presidential protégé's cynicism left me uneasy. Mexico's future had been arranged by Obregón and would continue to be arranged by Obregón, Calles explained to me. He had been selected to succeed Obregón, but, after a six-year term, would have step down to allow Obregón to become president once again. I was shocked and frightened by this seeming replay of the old Díaz dictatorship. What might such a travesty of revolutionary justice mean for Felipe and his own idealistic goals? Whom could we trust in this treacherous world?

At six a bell rang. Cocktail time. The other journalists were gathering in the officers' wardroom. It would be so easy to just stay put. I wouldn't have to eat, wouldn't have to talk. But what if I missed something? I dragged myself off the bunk and slipped a pale peach gown over my head. It was satin and fit in all the right places with a hemline that flared saucily as I turned. I felt anything but saucy as I walked unsteadily down the passageway toward the sound of clinking glasses. "Tequila is a great remedy for seasickness," Captain Rodriguez was assuring the assembled journalists and a few pale-looking officers who assisted as hosts.

As the water roared and the wind shrieked, some writers tried the salt and lime remedy. You squeeze the lime, squirt the juice into a little salt deposit in the hollow between your thumb and first finger, quickly suck the mixture, then toss it down with a gulp of tequila. I'd tried it a few times with Felipe at La Opera, our favorite bar in Mexico City. Now, as I took a shot glass and tipped my head back, I remembered the bullet holes left by Pancho Villa in the bar's Art Nouveau ceiling. Live hard, die hard. The tequila burned my throat, taking my mind off other things.

The captain's cocktail gala was a forced affair followed by a dinner no one could enjoy. It wasn't that Rodrigez and his men hadn't tried. Obviously, they had. The tablecloth was snow white; the silver plate with the ship's monogram sparkled. The cook presented an ambitious menu. Chilled watercress soup, roast capon, chocolate mousse, and numerous assorted side dishes of fruits and vegetables. Rodriguez was solicitous: "I find hot pepper a great aid to seasickness." He handed me a silver tray with a bottle of pepper sauce on it and then a basket of tortillas wrapped in linen.

Surely no one regretted the end of the dinner when it finally came. I was grateful for the privacy of the captain's stateroom. On the other side of the thin walls I heard others being sick. Every passenger seemed to heave in rhythm with the sea. Grasping the edge of the bunk, I struggled out of my clothes and into a nightgown just before the ship gave a mighty lurch that knocked me across the bunk. I pulled at the adjustable railing on the side. It didn't come up very high but at least I was off my feet.

The pitch and toss of the sea made for an uneasy cradle but after a time I fell into a fitful slumber besieged by dreams. They were macabre. I fought to awaken but could not. Then I saw Felipe standing on a mountain, smiling confidently as I'd seen him many times. I waved, running forward, but he didn't see me. Before my eyes, the mountain transformed into a fiery volcano. Felipe saw me then and waved good-bye as the mountain collapsed, engulfing him in flames.

I sat straight up in bed, my heart pounding wildly. Fearful darkness surrounded me as I fumbled for the overhead lamp. What a relief when my trembling fingers found it. Light filled the room. There was my dinner dress, a crumpled heap on the floor where I'd left it, and my valise across the room. Struggling to expel the dreadful vision, I became aware of music in the distance. Slowly I picked out a melody, lilting, throbbing, yet strangely sad, as if yearning for a lost love. What was it? Who could be singing at this hour and in the midst of a storm?

Pulling myself out of bed, I braced against the bunk and slipped on a dressing gown. It was difficult to keep my footing; the ship lurched wildly. Once, I fell sprawling across the floor, but managed to pull myself up. At last, staggering, I reached the door and opened it to the surprise of my life.

Six mariachis, stationed just outside the door, sang soulfully. In order to remain standing, they'd tied themselves in place with ropes, yet still wove precariously back and forth. At the sight of me, the violinists and guitar players tipped their sombreros and smiled broadly, all the while bravely keeping time with the trombonist. Slowly, I began to pick out the words:

> Wanderer of the clear and divine eyes
> And cheeks aflame with the redness of the sky,
> Little woman of the red lips,
> And hair radiant as the sun,
> Traveler who left your own scenes—

When you leave my palm groves and my land,

Traveler of the enchanting face,

Don't forget—don't forget—my land,

Don't forget—don't forget—my love.

Forget his land, forget his love! Not likely. Studying the men's earnest faces, I realized that I'd seen each of them before. They'd first performed beneath my window in Mérida and later appeared at numerous official functions. I vividly recalled them on the station platform serenading my departing train in Yucatán.

"Your song is beautiful," I said when at last they finished. "I've never heard it before."

"This is the first time it has been performed in public," their leader told me.

I looked at him, puzzled. "I didn't see you board the ship. You weren't at the captain's dinner."

"No," the spokesman agreed. "His Excellency insisted that we conceal ourselves. His instructions were that we perform for you and you alone exactly at midnight."

Tears filled my eyes as he continued. "It is your song, Señora Reed. His Excellency commissioned it just for you. He said to tell you that it was time that you had a song of your very own."

"What's it called?" I asked, my voice husky.

" 'La Peregrina,' " his reply. "The wanderer."

26

Valencia's Advice

Felipe and I had promised ourselves to be good. It had seemed a simple vow to make in Mexico City, where everything was perfect, where we were never more than a caress apart. In Mérida, the celibacy proved more difficult. We had to be careful; someone was always watching, disapproval palpable. We longed to duck into a dark doorway for a quick kiss or, better yet, to closet ourselves in Felipe's office or my hotel suite. To make certain that we didn't forget our vows, Felipe hired a chaperone for me, Blanca Alvarez.

Blanca was a bit older than I, attractive, curious, intelligent, the daughter of a prominent family rumored to have been impoverished by the revolution. She was always at my side—even at the news conference. I hated it that Felipe and I were never alone, but realized there was no other way. Mérida had changed in ways his letters had omitted. The pending divorce and our subsequent engagement announcement had divided the city. Some Méridians, captivated by the romance, scattered flowers in my path, but others were outraged. I saw the epithet *puta* scrawled on Felipe's car. Once an old woman spat at me as I passed her on the street.

In Mexico City we'd talked the nights away, planning the future. I would be at Felipe's side, assisting him with his programs while establishing my own. I'd organize women's groups to champion social causes. I'd establish university programs where young men and women could study archaeology so that they, themselves, might excavate the treasures in their own land. I saw myself promoting the artists, poets, and musicians of Yucatán, yet knew that without the peoples' acceptance, nothing was possible.

On the ship returning to Mérida, the mariachis told me that Felipe had commissioned Luis Rosada de la Vega and Ricardo Palmerin, the most popular song-writing team in Mexico, to write the words and music for "La Peregrina." It didn't surprise me to discover that they were native Yucatecans. Surely the deep pathos that made the music stirring was an outpouring of their Mayan souls.

I watched Felipe in action and was proud that his reforms, unlike those in France or Russia, had been bloodless. The current conference that he sponsored was a showcase, the summary of his public life thus far. I knew it was only the beginning. One afternoon I, with the other journalists, accompanied Felipe to an *ejido,* or brotherhood ceremony, at the village of Suma five kilometers from Mérida. Ancestral land was to be returned to villagers who would farm it communally as their forebears had done in preconquest times. Felipe's plan was new and untried. Angry headlines in newspapers loyal to the hacendados denounced the action, while posters proclaimed Felipe a hero. The journalists' reaction was also sharply divided. Some angrily disapproved, others applauded Felipe's daring. Notepads were out. This was Felipe as the rest of the world saw him: a busy, urgent man doing important things. I thought briefly of my own privileged intimacy, my private knowledge of the governor, and reveled in it.

An orchestra greeted our arrival, brass instruments glittering in the sunlight. Some fifty or so of the town's leading citizens waited eagerly to escort us from the railroad station. My heart quickened at the sight of history unfolding. The man I loved was responsible. *But the land . . . the Maya owned it once . . . but who owned it yesterday? There must be angry* hacendados *out there somewhere. . . . Wasn't this all a little premature?*

Our procession of journalists passed under a cardboard arch adorned with Mayan symbols and fresh flowers. At the end of the unpaved street leading to the village plaza, the city leaders broke rank in front of a low wooden building. Holding his sombrero over his heart, the *presidente municipal* came forward to greet us. Some two hundred *campesinos,* attired in white shirts and trousers like their representative, crowded into the plaza around the table where Felipe was seated.

The women of the town pushed closer, watching eagerly. They were dressed in their finest *huipiles,* starchy white cotton embroidered with vibrant flowers at the throat and around the hem above a cascade of lacy petticoats. Babies stirred restlessly in their mothers' rebozos. Older children wiggled their way closer to watch Felipe sign the paper that would return land seized from Suma by conquistadors centuries before. Then the celebration began: feasting and fireworks. Speeches, too, of course, but they weren't so boring when it was Felipe doing the talking. My Spanish was better now. I could follow most of it quite well and was taking notes right along with the Latin reporters.

Observing the happy, hopeful townspeople, I found it hard to imagine their ancestors fighting and dying, yet Suma had been the scene of some of the bloodiest battles in the so-called Caste War. It was an uprising that had killed thousands but changed nothing. Now, at last and without bloodshed, Felipe was returning the Maya's birthright. At the conclusion of the ceremony, he admonished the villagers: "Use your freedom to become better citizens; never revenge yourselves on some individual who was himself a victim of the wretched order that is gone forever."

That was *my* man speaking. I looked about, saw other journalists scribbling furiously.

I telegraphed the story to the *Times* and *News Call*. It was my intention to remain in the background, asking questions, taking notes like any other journalist, but Felipe wouldn't allow it. Although both governor and conference director, he was also a man celebrating his engagement.

"How old is the governor?" I overheard people ask one another, speculating. "Forty?" "Really? He looks younger." During the course of the many festivities connected to the conference, I met the song writers, Palmerin and de la Vega, Felipe's long-time friends. "Our governor looks better than he did before the revolution," the composer told me. "I've never seen Felipe so happy," his poet partner, de la Vega, agreed. "You are good for him."

I looked from one to the other. Something about the two men invited confidence. "I hope you're right. I worry about how people will react to all the fuss Felipe makes over me. He's not exactly discreet. I'm always seated at his right. He dances only with me. Every band concert begins with your wonderful song, 'La Peregrina.' It's fabulous, like a fairy tale, but sometimes it frightens me. The people . . ."

"The people love it," Palmerin broke in. "Take my word, Mérida is a city of poets. There is nothing they like better here than a true romance."

"Unless it's a bit of juicy scandal," de la Vega confessed. "They adore you for giving them something new to gossip about."

Not everyone shared the composers' enthusiasm. Few hacendados attended the gala celebration that marked the conference's conclusion. It was a haughty slap in the face. I wondered what Felipe would say when we finally had a moment to talk. Forcing a confident half-smile, I scanned the room. The Municipal Palace looked glorious, banks of lilies and hibiscus everywhere, gala streamers, bright balloons. Guests stood in clusters drinking champagne or congregated about long tables covered with delicacies. Most ate and drank with the eagerness of guests unaccustomed to largesse. Then unexpectedly I spied a familiar face. Valencia del Valle.

The elegant young heiress who had, with her parents, entertained me so regally a few months back stood against a white marble column, surveying the party scene. When our eyes caught, she smiled and moved forward, swaying gracefully. We met in the center of the room. Valencia's gold bangles tinkled as she embraced me.

"Let's go out onto the terrace," she suggested after kissing me lightly on each cheek.

It seemed to me that every eye centered on us. Every ear heard the tap of our high-heeled slippers on the marble floor. Why had Valencia come? It appeared almost foolhardy in the face of such open rejection by the others of her class. I was relieved when we passed under the high, white arches of the foyer onto the broad veranda.

Valencia's eyes, once so mischievous and merry, regarded me appraisingly. "You've changed," she said after we'd seated ourselves on high-backed rattan chairs facing out onto the courtyard.

"Changed?" I repeated, taking the glass of champagne offered by a silent waiter. "Perhaps it's my hair. I had it bobbed in New York, but now I'm not sure what to do with it." I thought of the wispy strands in back that needed trimming. Earlier that afternoon I'd covered them with a red hibiscus.

"Try Chantel on Calle Madron." Valencia patted her own smooth coiffure. "Chantel was Lupe Alvarez's personal hairdresser, you know. Lupe brought her back from Paris, but now," Valencia frowned, "the family's lost so much land. Lupe's husband insisted that she cut back on her household accounts. Imagine, having to let your hairdresser go! But Chantel's a clever girl. She's opened her own little shop. Mama and I go to her whenever we're in town. Many of us have had to make sacrifices. This isn't the best of times." She paused, pulling her lavishly embroidered shawl about her. It was coral damask with thick silken fringe. No one would mistake Valencia del Valle for the Little Match Girl.

"Do you blame Felipe for that?"

"Of course."

"Surely you must see the great good he's doing. Felipe wants the best for everyone." I hesitated, at a loss for words, certain that Valencia would never agree, never even understand what I wanted so much to explain. "Very little land was redistributed—only absentee owners were affected at all. Overseers farm the land while hacendados live out their lives in France or Italy, spending Yucatán's profits far away."

"That kind of reasoning works only if you're not a land owner. Hacendados are people, not numbers in a political tract; we're real people, angry people. Your Felipe is stealing our land."

"No!" I gasped. "It isn't like that at all." I caught my breath, struggled for a lighter, softer tone, one that wouldn't carry to the small groups standing in the doorway pretending not to listen. "Surely it's only fair that the Maya who planted the henequen in the first place should share in the benefits. Did you know that Itzamna, the father of their gods, taught them its use—or so the story goes."

"That's sacrilege, pure sacrilege! You wear the cross. . . ." Valencia fingered the pendant that Felipe had placed about my throat only that very morning. "Lovely amber . . . How can you say such things? They're positively pagan. No wonder I never see you in church."

"But I do go sometimes," I said, gesturing to the waiter to refill Valencia's glass. "Felipe and I attend mass at the Santa Lucía Chapel. We're going to be married in the courtyard."

Valencia's dark eyes widened. "Do you know its history? That chapel was built for black slaves."

"I know it was, but now it's for everyone, just like Felipe's government is for everyone." When Valencia didn't answer, I found myself rattling on. "It's a darling little church and then there's Parque Santa Lucía across the street. We'll have the reception there with mariachis and Mayan dancers, you know those wonderfully graceful ones that dance with trays of champagne on their heads." I pulled myself together and looked Valencia straight in the eye. "I hope that you and your mother and Señor del Valle will be there."

Valencia looked back at me over the rim of her champagne flute for what seemed a very long time. Finally, she took a quick sip and set the glass down on the table beside us. "*Madre* says the governor has bought you a house."

For a moment I forgot the strain between us as I thought of Villa Aurora. That's what Felipe and I called our home-to-be. The governor's palace had seemed far too grandiose. Besides, it carried memories of cruel despots. We had talked of something new, something just for us. When I returned from Mexico City, Villa Aurora was waiting.

"Do you like it?" Felipe had asked, his eyes on mine, watching intently. "We don't have to live here. We can find another home if you don't like this."

"Like it? I love it! This house is a little jewel." And in truth it was. Golden-hued like a marigold, its thick walls were masters of surprise, the keepers of our secrets. Looking at the stark exterior, no one would guess what lay inside. I loved the glazed tile floors, the graceful staircase, the colonnaded courtyard ablaze with bougainvilleas. What a joy these past few days had been. Whenever there was a free moment, we were off combing the shops. Already there were Mayan statues for our garden, Spanish paintings, colonial tables, and hand-painted armoires.

Just yesterday Felipe had led me to a small alcove off the master bedroom. The day before it had been empty. Now there was a French antique dressing table and above it an exquisite beveled-glass mirror. When I exclaimed over its finely carved gold frame, Felipe told me that it dated from the sixteenth century. "I like to think of you sitting here, brushing your hair."

He didn't add, but I knew he was thinking, "when you grow it long again." At that moment, I would have promised him anything. It was fortunate, too—for our vowed celibacy—that Felipe's driver and Blanca, the chaperone, waited in the next room.

My wandering thoughts returned to the present, to Valencia's quizzical expression. I felt myself flush. It was almost as though the other woman read my mind. "It wasn't what I sought—this marriage," I found myself saying. "I left Yucatán and returned to my country, just as I told your mother I would."

"Yet you came back," Valencia reminded me.

"But Felipe had filed for divorce. It was the path he himself pursued. I had nothing to do with his decision. But once he chose that path, why shouldn't I come back?" The words echoed in the still air, defiant sounding even to me. "I love him. We love each other."

"Perhaps then you should persuade him to leave, to go to San Francisco."

"San Francisco!" My heart quickened as I thought of President Obregón's suggestion. *Where was this coming from?*

"Why look so surprised?" Valencia sounded strangely impatient. "You two could have a very full life there. Papa says the governor has friends in your country who admire him greatly."

"Yes," I nodded. "He corresponds with many, one in particular, the secretary of the navy. His name is Roosevelt, Franklin Roosevelt. There are others as well," I rattled on, strangely nervous. "It's really very gratifying that so many in my country appreciate Felipe's worth, but, of course, he also has many admirers in Yucatán."

"Really?" Valencia arched a delicate brow. "Where are they today?" She nodded toward the reception hall. "Look around you. Do you see any of the old families represented? Colonel Broca, for instance, the people who really matter?"

"You came," I reminded her. Once again the words echoed oddly. My heart thumped crazily.

"I came to see *you,* hoping to convince you . . . my father says the governor's course is foolhardy. Even *el presidente*—" she stopped suddenly.

"President Obregón is Felipe's friend, his ally," I said, more confidently than I felt.

"Yes, yes, of course. Everyone knows that, don't they, yet still . . ." Valencia flashed a charming smile. "The holidays will be here before you know it. *Mi madre* says you should go home to see your *madre.* She must miss you very much. You should go to see her soon. And, as for your intended, surely his place is with you. How delightful if you two could spend the holidays together."

"And we will," I assured her, rising to my feet. "We *will* spend the holidays together—right here in Mérida."

Everywhere I looked, blossoms seemed to explode: pink, purple, orange. In the distance a fountain splashed noisily. The courtyard was incredibly lush and beautiful, yet for the first time the radiance felt alien, somehow mocking. Would I ever be a part of this exotic land? Would—could—Yucatán ever accept me? I felt a sudden need to see Felipe that very moment. Brushing past the waiter who had returned with more champagne, I took Valencia's hand for an instant. "Thank you, thank you for coming. I know it must have been . . . awkward for you. Perhaps one day we can be friends. I'd like that, but for now, I must rejoin the party."

Turning quickly I almost ran back into the reception area. Felipe was just mounting the dais. His eyes swept the room, looking for me. I smiled, spreading my fingers in the semblance of a wave.

He nodded, his face brightening, such a handsome figure in his white pants and crisp guayabera shirt. The uniform of his people, but how well it suited Felipe. He looked carefree in that moment, a man in his prime. You could see that by the expression on his face, the wide, confident smile on his mouth as he looked just at me.

Day of the Dead

As October drew to a close, the excitement in Mérida mounted. Weird trinkets filled the shops. Everywhere I looked faces leered: terra-cotta skulls, bone-handled key rings etched in the likeness of demons, tiny plaster witch dolls. In public parks and buildings, people were putting up altars against white, shroudlike backdrops.

"The invitation is out to the dead," Blanca, my ever-present chaperone, explained. "Whatever the deceased relished in life is offered in death. During the Fiesta de los Muertos, we invite the spirits back to indulge in earthly pleasures."

Blanca's smile was disarming but the scene was macabre. I'd glimpsed plaster skeletons playing musical instruments, driving fire trucks, riding horses. There were nurse skeletons, cowboy skeletons, even bride skeletons. Perhaps those offerings, infused as they were with grotesque humor, could be laughed away. Maybe. The candy and beer bottles that rested beside them could not. Real things for live people. "It's so morbid. Who wants to be reminded of death?"

"Señora Reed, everyone dies . . . everyone." Blanca was still smiling. It occurred to me that she was always smiling, her small, even features frozen in genteel acquiescence.

I turned back to the altar, studied it dubiously. "Why don't you come home with me and see our family shrine?" Blanca suggested.

"You have one in your house!"

"There's not a home in Mérida without one. Come see ours. My mother has urged me to invite you to tea."

"I'd like that very much." I was curious about my pretty chaperone, who apparently had only three dresses, each well made and stylish but showing signs of wear. Blanca rotated them faithfully.

The following day when our *fortinga* pulled up in front of Blanca's home, I was surprised. We were on Paseo de Montejo, the less fashionable end, but still Montejo. Blanca Alvarez lived in a mansion. Or so it seemed. The grounds blended with those on either side, clipped lawns and well-tended roses; but inside, the marble foyer was dark and in need of paint. I squinted at a classical mural that dominated one wall. Diana, bow in her hands, hounds at her heels. It was beautifully done, perhaps museum quality, but did I smell mildew?

"The house has been divided into apartments. We live upstairs," she explained, nodding toward a sweeping staircase.

This one swept and swept, seemingly to infinity. We reached the top panting. Blanca and her parents had three tiny rooms on the fourth floor. I imagined my aristocratic companion sleeping on the sofa in the living room. Where else?

Señora Alvarez was silver-haired, plump but still soignée. A large carved tortoiseshell comb secured her smooth chignon. She gestured toward the rosewood tea table placed before a window. Family silver gleamed in the sunlight; a fountain splashed in the courtyard below. Not bad, really. Looking around the cluttered room, I spotted other salvaged treasures. Spanish paintings, carved mahogany chests and tables.

To my right was an altar decorated in much the same way as the public ones. Moving closer, I noticed many photographs of a young man, handsome, dashing, really, with his slim mustache and confident smile.

"That's Manuel, my son," Señora Alvarez explained. "He died in the revolution."

Ah, yes, the uniform, I noticed it now. Manuel had been a Federalista, fighting for the old government against revolutionaries like Felipe. I hesitated, uncertain what to say.

"Manuel died a hero's death," his mother said. "We are very proud of him."

"Of course you are."

"Perhaps you noticed the whiskey on the altar," Blanca pointed out, "Manuel enjoyed his whiskey. I suppose all soldiers do."

"And chocolates," Señora Alvarez said, "he had—how do you say?—the sweet teeth." She presided deftly at the tea table all the while making polite conversation in excellent, if stilted, English.

The specter of the revolution hung heavily over the small apartment. The Alvarez family had so obviously come out on the wrong side. What did they think of Felipe and his reforms? Elegant, cultivated ladies adept at putting guests at ease, they gave no clue.

Soon it was time to leave. "Felipe—my fiancé—is expecting me at a reception," I explained.

"But of course," Señora Alvarez agreed, rising from the table. She walked with us to the door. As I turned to say good-bye, the altar loomed large, Manuel's smiling face larger still.

I thanked her; we shook hands. Blanca and I were half way down the stairs when I turned around and looked up at Señora Alvarez watching us from the top. "Felipe's changes take time," I said, "but in the end they will benefit everyone. I know they will. I—I am very proud of him."

Señora Alvarez's voice echoed eerily down the circular stairwell. "Of course you are."

The Fiesta de los Muertos began that night. Call it Halloween, Thanksgiving, or Memorial Day. All three rolled into one doesn't begin to describe it. At home the very word "death" burns our lips. In Yucatán, they celebrate it with elaborate protocol. The fiesta's first night was reserved for spirits with no living relatives. Felipe pointed out the jugs of water and chunks of bread placed on street corners. The next night was set aside for the unfortunate souls who'd died violently. Once again food and drink had been left outside homes, large and small, but now the offerings were more elaborate. They were intended to placate malevolent spirits, to keep them content in another world.

On the third night, dead children were welcomed home to play. Felipe and I visited many of his constituents. In each home the elaborately constructed shrine was decorated with lighted candles, food, and treasured toys. I saw licorice witches and bread baked in the shape of skulls with grimacing faces made of raisins and candy coating. Even more unnerving were the candy skulls, about the size of apples, with names inscribed in colored sugar . . . Pedro, Maria, José. Candy is candy, I told myself, watching a group of children reach for the morbid sweets, but death is death.

On All Saints' Day the fiesta reached its crescendo: larger crowds, altars, altars, more altars everywhere, pyramids of skull bread. Parades of candy devils. Mariachi bands, wherever I turned, each vying raucously with the other. Just when I thought the whole city would explode before my eyes, a real explosion came. Standing at Felipe's side I watched the grand finale: a stream of fireworks cascading from the rooftops, a shower of jewels eerily illuminating shrines and banners strung on clotheslines crisscrossing the plaza.

Felipe's eyes shone, his hand squeezed mine. *Did I know this man?*

"You love it all, don't you?" I asked.

"Don't you?" He looked at me in surprise.

"I don't know," I hesitated. "The spectacle is marvelous, but the message behind it . . ."

"The message is very clear. Laugh at death, for it is a part of life."

"Not *our* life." I hugged him, for once not caring who might be watching. "What shall we do tomorrow?"

Felipe hesitated. "The fiesta's final day is a more private celebration, a family affair rather than a civic one."

"You'll want to be with your children."

"Can you understand why I must go alone this time?"

"Of course," I said and tried to mean it. Felipe's children had refused to meet me, as had his mother. I told myself again and again that it was only a matter of time before

I won them over. In the meantime, I'd love them sight unseen. His mother had given Felipe to me. His children were part of him. How long could they withstand the love I already felt for them? Felipe insisted that it would be soon, but I had my doubts. He brushed off my fears about the children, about the people. "This is our time, Alma," he'd reminded me more than once, admonishing me to "enjoy it."

I urged Blanca to take the day off. With Felipe away, what did I need with a chaperone? The past month had been so filled with activities that quiet time for myself would be pleasant. I'd get caught up with personal tasks, outline stories, write letters. Or so I thought. To my surprise, the hours dragged. Felipe and I, though never completely alone, spent much of every day together. Without him, the hours seemed endless. I'd grown dependent on his nearness. Surprisingly, I liked that new dependency. Soon there'd be no need for a chaperone, I mused contentedly.

When my hotel suite grew confining, I took to the streets, walked about the city, wading through drifts of confetti and wilting marigolds, listening to the tinny bands. I tried to imagine myself as Felipe's wife, preparing for next year's Fiesta de los Muertos. Would I make candy skulls for his children? Well, they were a little old for that. Maybe some day his grandchildren or our children. No, I doubted it. The Day of the Dead aspect of Mexican culture felt too monstrous to ever embrace, but perhaps I'd attempt the bread. It was sweet, surprisingly good. . . .

Who was I kidding? I'd never baked in my life.

The streets, grown quiet now, were forlorn, the plaza nearly deserted. At the east end was the cathedral with its lofty towers. The full machismo glory of the conquistadors reflected in the soaring structure, a fortress with narrow slits for weapons; but when I went inside, the dark interior had a stark stripped-down look. Clearly its medieval defenses hadn't saved the cathedral from being sacked by revolutionaries.

In the back of the basilica, hundreds of candles glowed before the Virgin's shrine. It looked as though centuries of offerings had been piled before a brown-skinned saint in her white lace dress. I saw medals and wedding rings, crutches and chalices, tiaras and tools. Had they been placed there as pleas or in thanksgiving?

Impulsively, I knelt before the saint, crossing myself awkwardly. How long had it been since I'd done that? "Bless me, Virgin, for I have sinned." Well, I hadn't sinned *recently,* but that was only because . . . oh, what did that matter?! *Please someone up there help me to understand this strange new world. Help me to be the wife Felipe deserves. And, Felipe, kind and good Felipe, keep him safe.*

As darkness fell, I went eagerly to Panteón General, the city's largest cemetery, certain that, despite the crowds, Felipe and I would at last have some time alone together.

We'd rationalized the previous night that celebrants would be too absorbed in their own family dramas to pay attention to anyone else's. Even if a few did notice us, did it really matter? Surely they were getting used to me now, were coming to accept our approaching marriage.

At least I prayed they were.

Inside the cemetery, candles cast flickering shadows across cool, gray tombstones where mourners kept watch. Most sat quietly, some sipping from bottles of Negra Leon. Families gathered about the graves, their arms filled with flowers. Vendors wheeled in tortillas, beer, and the ubiquitous candy skulls.

Moving from grave to grave, I worried about intruding on their grief yet passed unnoticed. Where was Felipe? I wondered, turning this way and that. I'd expected him to be waiting, watching for me as he'd promised. Then, at last, I spied a familiar face. Just ahead of me was Don Eduardo. I stopped in my tracks. What could I say to him? What would he say to me? Sure enough, he'd seen me, was shouldering his way through the crowd in my direction. I braced myself for an awkward encounter.

To my surprise, the archaeologist swept me into his arms in a warm *abrazo*. "Alma, *mi* Alma, you are lovely as ever!"

Gratefully, I hugged him back. "I wasn't sure you'd even speak to me."

"I knew the risks when I told you my little secret."

"*Little* secret? You've set the world on its ear. Everyone has an opinion. Most particularly, the Mexican government. I heard you were in the capital defending a lawsuit."

"Indeed, I have been." He nodded. "There's been a continuance. I'm taking advantage of the time to spend the holiday with my wife. Her parents are buried here." He gestured toward a nearby tomb, where Doña Celestina knelt before an elaborate bower of marigolds.

I smiled and waved, but Doña Celestina glared angrily and looked away.

Don Eduardo dismissed his wife's reaction with a shrug of his narrow shoulders. "Don't be concerned. She's more angry with me for telling you. Actually, Celestina always felt that the treasure should have remained in Yucatán."

"A view shared by many."

"Your fiancé, as well?"

"Felipe remains your good friend, but thinks the Peabody should return the treasure to the Mayan people."

Don Eduardo smiled. "Not likely."

"Nevermind the treasure. What about you? Aren't you concerned about the lawsuit?"

"I shall win it," he assured me, his demeanor confident as his words.

"I hope so, for your sake." I touched his arm lightly. "I've had misgivings from the very beginning. I'm concerned for your reputation."

Don Eduardo laughed. "My diving and digging days are long gone. Whatever the decision, isn't it better to end with a bang rather than a whimper?"

"Perhaps," I conceded. "At least now the world knows just how brave you are, the risks you took . . . even if they can't agree as to whether what you did was right."

"Right or wrong, Alma—between the two of us, we've put Yucatán on the map."

"Yes, Felipe's happy about that—the tourists who will come—but I worry about the cost to you. What if you should lose?"

Don Eduardo shrugged. "There's little at stake." His tone was matter of fact as he explained, "I've no fortune to attach. I've spent everything I ever had on diving equipment. There's nothing left but the hacienda. No one can ever take that from us and nothing else really matters. The old house, my library, that's all I care about. I'll end my days there puttering about and reading. Not a bad life, really."

"¡Hola!" Felipe had come up behind us. He slipped an arm about my waist and leaned forward to shake the archaeologist's hand.

Don Eduardo smiled at us. "I hope you and Alma will visit me often."

"Yes!" we responded almost in unison.

As we said good-bye to Don Eduardo, the old archaeologist hugged me close. "Watch your back, *mi querida*," he whispered, his rough mustache scratching my ear. "You're the one who should worry—not me."

Before I could question him, a family carrying huge armfuls of marigolds and lilies came between us. More people had come into the cemetery, were pushing in all directions. A vendor jostled me, a cluster of balloons with skull faces floating eerily above him.

When I caught sight of Don Eduardo again, Celestina was pulling him toward her family tomb.

"Would you like to leave, perhaps go for a drive?" Felipe suggested.

When I nodded eagerly, he guided me through the pushing, shoving crowd. Breathless, we paused just outside the cemetery gate. How good it felt to get out of the graveyard. "I like this wall," I said, running my hands over the rough surface. "It looks like it was built stone by stone centuries ago. A wall like this is even strong enough to hold back spirits." I looked up at the luxuriant bougainvillea spilling over the top. "And there is an affirmation of life."

"Or a symbol of death." Felipe plucked a spray. "As you see, the flowers are crimson, like blood." He pulled at the blossoms, tossing them lightly like confetti into the air.

I shook my head emphatically. "I've had enough of that scary stuff for one night. Today, I walked past our little chapel. It will be perfect for us."

Felipe took my hands in his. "Let's sit here for a minute on the grass," he suggested, his eyes serious.

My heart began to thump. "What's wrong, Felipe? Is there a problem with the divorce?"

His smile was tender. "No, *mi corazón*. There is no problem. Soon I'll be free to marry you just as I have always wanted. Ever since I first saw you it's been like that." He lightly kissed the palms of my hands. "But I have been selfish. It was wrong of me to keep you all to myself. Your mother, your family, should share in our happiness."

A chill swept over me. "San Francisco. You want us to be married there, don't you?"

"Exactly. How did you guess?"

"It's a very popular suggestion. First President Obregón last month, then Valencia del Valle last week."

"Really? *El presidente* suggested it . . . how perceptive of him. I don't know why we didn't think of it sooner."

"Well, I do! We want the people of Yucatán to be part of our ceremony, part of our love as they will be part of our lives," I reminded Felipe. I took his hands in mine, looking into his eyes. "It's what we've planned all along. We can go to San Francisco anytime. Our marriage is planned for the first of January in Mérida."

"We will still begin the New Year together, but in San Francisco."

"No, Felipe."

"Yes, Alma."

"Are we arguing?"

"No," he answered firmly. "Two people who have been through as much as we have do not argue."

Just as I was about to respond, Felipe's driver pulled up opposite us and signaled. Beside him was Jorge, Felipe's secretary. They both looked concerned; I assumed it was the traffic. The road was clogged with carriages, *fortingas,* and vendors pedaling large tricycles. Then I saw another car behind the first, following closely. The occupants were in uniform, cartridges worn bandolier style across their chests. They were holding guns. Not bodyguards! Felipe had always disdained protection, choosing to walk unarmed among his people. I searched his face anxiously for some clue. His expression was bland as he walked me to the first car, but his eyes avoided mine. After opening the back door for me, he went around to the front and conferred with Jorge for a moment. Their voices were too soft to make out.

Felipe walked back to me, his mouth set now in a reassuring smile. It didn't fool me. I'd seen him signal to the guards behind us. I touched his arm as he slid in beside me. "What's going on? What were you talking to them about?"

"Only confirmation of your passage on the *Woodrow Wilson*. You will leave Friday. I think you will enjoy the voyage through the Panama Canal."

"But we planned to do that together someday!"

"We will still do that together, on our way back from San Francisco. I will join you there next month."

"Felipe! There's something you're not telling me."

"*Pues,* perhaps," he conceded.

His voice had changed, was lighter now, almost playful.

I tried to read his expression in the dim light. "You've got to tell me what's happening!"

"Not now." He shook his head. "Later." His eyes were gentle, almost happy as they met mine. "I have planned a surprise for you . . . for us. Something that should please you very much."

28

Pixan-Halal

The morning headlines were dreadful. My coffee cooled as I glanced anxiously from one story to the next. Fighting had broken out in the streets of Mexico City. Obregón faced challenges, left, right, and center: restless *campesinos,* reactionary priests, army dissidents, remnants of the old guard. Everyone knew Felipe's loyalties lay with the beleaguered president. I worried that these sentiments would further weaken his position with the henequen planters.

Somewhere in the Gran's leafy courtyard, two parrots knocked a squawk back and forth. Mocking. Raucous. Those damn birds. How ugly they sounded. I reached for a croissant and began to spread guava jam across the buttery pastry.

"Enjoying your breakfast?"

I looked up to find Jorge approaching my table.

"Not really," I admitted, nodding at the paper. "Have you read the latest?"

He shrugged. "President Obregón has fought his way out of worse situations." His young face broke into a happy smile. "I have *real* news for you, good news. Don Eduardo's lawsuit has been decided in his favor. No prison, not even a fine."

I breathed an audible sigh of relief, but hesitated. "That decision will make a lot of people angry."

Jorge shrugged again. "A lot of people are always angry. You have more important things to think about. His Excellency awaits you in Chichen Itza. He has asked me to escort you there. You are to pack a small bag and come with me now."

Just then, Blanca appeared in the archway, smiling brightly. We'd planned a morning trip to the marketplace, where I hoped to find gifts for my family. Laughing happily, I waved her away. "Take the day off, have fun. We'll shop when I come back, sometime . . ." I jumped up, gulping the last of the coffee. It had been two days since I'd seen Felipe. There'd been only brief telephone calls, his tone affectionate but evasive. My departure was only two days away. Now, this unexpected outing . . . I was ecstatic.

If my first drive to Chichen Itza had dragged, this one was interminable. I remembered back to when Felipe had driven from Mérida nearly every day hoping to see me. So often I'd evaded him. We'd been like children playing at hide-and-seek. So much precious time wasted. Impatiently I watched as row upon row of henequen plants gave way to dense jungle stretching to infinity. Curiosity about Felipe's plans for our rendezvous vied with an almost frantic eagerness to be with him again.

Jorge and I livened the tedium with speculation about Don Eduardo's lawsuit. The Mexican government had decided that as legal owner of the property, the *don* had a right to dispose of its contents as he saw fit—even if that meant sending priceless treasures out of the country. It was a landmark case that would, I knew, be cited and disputed, perhaps for centuries, but what mattered to me was the knowledge that my friend was off the hook. The hacienda was close to Chichen Itza; Felipe and I must certainly visit Doña Celestina. With the suit so favorably resolved, perhaps she'd forgive me. But would the Maya ever forgive Don Eduardo? The doubt nagged at me.

We drove on and on and on for possibly two hours before Jorge slowed down. He seemed to be searching for something. Just what I couldn't imagine. The road was only a tiny ribbon, the jungle pressing in on us from all sides. "Where are we? What are you looking for?" I wanted to know.

He turned, smiling broadly at me. "You will soon find out." His eyes narrowed, scanning the curtain of green on either side of us. Then, apparently finding what he was looking for, Jorge eased the car onto a narrow shoulder. Jumping out, he hurried around to open the door for me. The jungle pushed toward us, the air spicy, musky, ripe, and sweet—odors of rampant growth rooted in decay. Where were we? As I looked at Jorge in bewilderment, the dense shrubbery parted and Felipe stepped forward.

"What's happening?" I gasped, throwing my arms about him. Beneath the starched pleats of Felipe's shirt, I heard his heart beating.

"I told you I had a surprise." He smiled and took my hand. "Wait and see."

Felipe led me along a dense trail overgrown with roots. Once, despite his help, I stumbled headlong and found myself at eye level with a caravan of leaf-cutter ants each carrying a parasol of green. Here and there a toucan with a banana-yellow beak fluttered through the still leaves. Branches closed in around us, black against the filtered light.

We emerged into a clearing. Men, women, and children came at us from every direction, cheering, chanting, blowing on conch shells, drumming, pelting us with blossoms. Women carried trays of sliced watermelon, mango, and papaya. I smelled pork roasting.

"What is this?" I gasped.

"The villagers of Na Balam, my people, are preparing a feast." Felipe held me at arm's length for a minute, smiling broadly. "Our wedding feast."

"But, Felipe, we've been so careful . . . word will get out. You know it will. People in Mérida will find out."

"I don't care. This is our wedding. Nothing and no one can take it from us. Not ever."

I looked at him, speechless, as more flowers were strewn in our path. Across the clearing stood two large mahogany chairs. Even in this steamy jungle setting, the lavish carving and red velvet upholstery looked regal. Feeling like the heroine of a film fantasy, I crossed the clearing and seated myself. *Was this happening to me?*

Platters of fruit and roasted pork appeared. A graceful, white-haired woman in an elaborately embroidered *huipil* knelt before us. She wore a jade necklace about her throat that could have been in a museum. The priestess—I think that's what she was—smiled, a brilliant, almost heartbreaking smile, and handed Felipe an intricately carved gourd. He tipped his head back, drank fully, then passed it to me. "It's *balche*," he explained. "Try some; I think you'll like it."

I took a sip, fiery hot, strangely sweet. I did like the taste, but drank little. The spectacle going on all around me was intoxicating enough. Drums rolled and then were silent. A hush fell over the crowd. Even the jungle was still. Our servers fell back, creating a pathway. Slowly, regally, an elderly figure in a jaguar-skin loincloth stepped forward. I moved closer to Felipe as the old man's eyes, clouded by cataracts, searched mine. I met his gaze for what seemed an eternity. The man's gnarled hand passed lightly over my face, then touched my head. Was it a benediction?

The elder, some sort of chieftain, I judged from the reverence reflected in the faces of those around us, said something in Maya. I turned to Felipe. He smiled back, his eyes shining with happiness and pride.

"Ek Tun is the direct descendant of our high priest at the time of the conquest. He blesses our union and has honored you with a new identity. Your name, your Mayan name," Felipe clarified, "is now Pixan-Halal."

My throat tightened. "Does it have a meaning?"

"Yes," Felipe said, "a very special one. *Pixan* means Alma—or soul. *Halal* is a reed that grows along the water's edge."

Ek Tun bowed low before me, smiling solemnly. He took my hand and placed it in Felipe's. The priest spoke again, more words I didn't understand. Felipe answered him, then leaned over and kissed me.

"You are my bride," he said. Taking my hand in his, Felipe raised our arms in a salute to the assembled crowd. My eyes stung with happy tears as loud cheers sounded from every direction.

Ek Tun departed as majestically as he had appeared. Drums pounded again, laughter and shouts of joy rang out as dancers darted into the clearing before us. Lithe and nubile, they dipped and swayed to a voluptuous rhythm.

Its message was clear: courtship, conquest, and fertility. Their movements left little to the imagination.

A sensation of heat flooded my limbs and face. I turned to Felipe and saw that he was watching. My body throbbed with longing. His arm slipped around my shoulders, but just then a small group of women detached themselves from the crowd and approached us, heads bowed deferentially. Two of them pulled me gently forward, bidding me with gestures to go with them into the darkening jungle.

Felipe's smiling nod indicated that I should obey. Reluctantly, I left his side and stood up. Two of the women took my hands, leading me away from the clearing. Some of the terrain looked vaguely familiar, but how could I tell? The trees and underbrush blended together into a tangled mass, thick and almost impenetrable. We rounded a curve and there in a clearing before us towered the pyramid of Kukulkan.

"You want me to climb that?" I gasped.

My attendants smiled sweetly and nodded. The two who'd been walking with me started up the massive stone steps, pulling me along with them. Another walked behind me. From time to time, she touched my back reassuringly, a gentle reminder of her support if I needed it. They must have found their climb tediously slow for their companions, more attendants, who carried cloths, basins, and mysterious covered baskets, easily passed us and were waiting at the top when I struggled up the last step.

Panting, I lowered myself, but wasn't allowed to linger long . Gently, but insistently, the women raised me to my feet and led the way to the small temple at the pyramid's center. Though the sun was just setting, torches had been secured to the walls. One woman deftly took hold of my sailor blouse, nimbly slipping it over my head. Another unfastened my skirt and lowered it to the floor, leaving only my pink chemise and step-ins. Before I knew it, they'd removed them as well. Shivering despite the heat, I stepped back. We're all women, I reminded myself, but still wondered if my pale body looked strange to them. Two of the women approached with basins of water and began to bath me. They were sensitive but very thorough. Later, as they patted me dry, I felt rather like a baby, precious and treasured.

After they'd enfolded me in a towel, their leader, an older woman, short and square with the classic Mayan nose, gestured for me to lie down on the altar, which had been covered by jaguar skins. The woman's strong brown hands moved over me, massaging my skin with yellow clay.

"This sacred, I bring from Tikul," she explained in a slow, halting manner.

My skin tingled, pleasantly at first; then the stinging began, like tiny ants biting me everywhere. I twisted this way and that to escape the sensation.

"*¡Un momento!*" she admonished. "The clay fights old skin. Soon pain be gone. Relax," she soothed, "relax." Her tone, soft and crooning like a mother to a child, helped. Some. I still didn't like it, didn't want to continue. Pulling myself up, I looked about for a garment to throw on.

"*¡Paciente!*" Her low, almost guttural voice droned as her hands moved over me. "We prepare our brides in this way."

Prepare our brides. I liked that.

Slowly, subtly, as the stinging had begun, it subsided and finally ceased. The old Mayan woman slathered me with honey, massaging my arms, my thighs, my breasts. How delicious the thought of being prepared for Felipe's love. Perhaps somewhere he was being prepared for mine. The masseuse wiped away the honey, applied a layer of rich cream, working it into my skin, then sprinkled me with rose water. My skin felt like silk, every pore alive.

A delicate scent surrounded me. Opening my heavy eyes, I saw blossoms everywhere, their petals floating downward like scented snow, the tiny temple filled with flowers—white, pink, peach, and crimson—a bower of love. One by one, my softly giggling attendants disappeared into the night. Beyond, through the open doorway, I saw the moon, ripe and luminous.

Felipe entered the small temple silently, walked to the altar where I lay waiting. As he lowered his lips to mine, I breathed in the scent of his hair, tasted the sweet salt on his neck. Slowly, he moved his hands, his fingers twining themselves in mine. And for that moment everything stopped. The warmth of him against my skin, the torchlight dancing over the surface of his cheek. Somewhere in the dark jungle below birds and insects sang love songs, then lullabies.

An owl hooted once close by. I thought I heard cries far in the distance but ignored them. Dawn was breaking when at last I raised my head from Felipe's chest and looked toward the temple's entrance.

"I don't want to go away—not ever," I said, as he pulled me toward him.

"Don't talk, Alma, not now." His mouth covered mine. I tasted the honey on his lips, felt the petals still clinging to our damp bodies. The scent of roses and his own musky smell overwhelmed me.

It was Felipe who spoke again later. The sun, by then, had risen.

"Now," he whispered softly, his lips caressing my throat, "we are truly married in the sight of Kukulkan."

I sighed, looking into his eyes. "This is wonderful, but I want the world to know that we belong to each other. I want to be married in a church."

"And I, *mi corazón*, want that as well, more than you can possibly imagine." He took my face in his hands, looked directly into my eyes. "We will have it, too, I promise you."

I caressed his cheek gently, then forced myself to pull away. So difficult. I willed my body to get up. Standing beside the altar where he still reclined, I spoke the words that nearly strangled me. "My ship leaves tomorrow."

"As if I needed a reminder, but it is the only way—for now."

My attendants had left us provisions, offerings to our love. The previous night we'd discovered champagne cooling, bright ceramic platters filled with fruit and cheese. Now, I found pitchers of water. Gratefully, I splashed the contents of one into a bowl and bathed. Nearby, I saw a *huipil* hanging from a carved Chac snout and put it on.

Felipe smiled. "Now you are truly Pixan-Halal, a Maya—one of us."

I gave him a shaky smile. "I guess this is my wedding gown."

"For the time being." Felipe took a tangerine from the plate and peeled it for me. "Have some wedding breakfast."

I nuzzled his hand, opened my mouth for the tangy segment he fed me. Felipe turned, picked up a water pitcher, and poured the contents down over his shoulders.

Slowly, I walked the few steps to the temple entrance. Though still early, the sun was bright, steam rising up off the jungle, lush and wondrous, like green fire. "It's another gorgeous day in paradise," I called over my shoulder,

Antoinette May

moving out onto the parapet. As I waited for Felipe, I absently studied the emerald landscape below. Off in the distance something caught my eye.

"Felipe!" I cried out. "Come here quickly. Look, isn't that smoke?"

In an instant, he was at my side. "*¡Madre de Dios!*"

"What is it? Where's it coming from? Oh, no, it can't be—"

Felipe put his arms around me. "I'm afraid, yes. It is coming from Don Eduardo's hacienda."

"We've got to help!" I gasped, starting toward the pyramid's ledge.

"No, Alma," Felipe pulled me back, steadying me. "It is too late. There is nothing that we can do now, nothing that anyone can do. Look," he said, pointing. The smoke had already turned to flames and as I squinted into the distance, I saw men with torches, dozens of them. They were destroying Don Eduardo's home, destroying his life.

"It's my fault," I sobbed. "I did this to him."

"No, my *peregrina*. It is no one's fault," Felipe laughed wryly, "unless you blame that cursed well."

· 324 ·

29

Home Again

San Francisco rested on the edge of adventure, whispering of exotic, far-off places, possibilities just beyond reach. Returning now after so much had happened
felt dreamlike, everything old, new again. The Golden
Gate silhouetted against the setting sun, Coit Tower en-
shrouded in mist. Postcard clichés, but so beautiful. I'd
forgotten that beauty. Now I longed to share the poet's
"cool, gray city of love" with Felipe.

The entire Sullivan clan, with their assorted husbands, wives, and children, was at the dock when I arrived. Muriel, the youngest, strikingly pretty now with
her long blond curls and the Sullivan baby blues. Prescott,
that bratty kid, almost a young man. I'd hardly touched

dry land before they surrounded me, hugging, holding, chattering, questioning. It warmed my heart but I wanted Felipe there, too, sharing this family world that had never before seemed important.

Mama was Mama, planning, taking charge. Crammed in beside me in the backseat of Walter's red Ford, her admonishments started before the dock faded from view. "Don't you dare elope—not like last time. I suppose you'll want to be married at city hall, but surely we can have a little reception afterward at the house."

"It won't be anything like last time," I told her. "I want a church wedding, maybe at Mission Dolores, with a reception. I want a big wedding cake and lots of champagne. I want a rehearsal dinner, too. The Old Poodle Dog would be nice. Mama, I want it all."

She just stared at me, silent. Florence and Muriel shrieked, "Alma, what's come over you?"

As the old Buchanan Street house came into view, I struggled, at a loss for words. "With Sam . . . it felt almost embarrassing to be doing anything so ordinary as getting married. Picking up a license, saying a few words, were formalities to be gotten through as quickly as possible so we could start our new life. With Felipe, I want everyone to know. I want to be married in a church so even God will know."

"Jeez! Alma! Calm down." Prescott, sitting on the other side of me, looked mortified.

Everybody laughed, including me. "I guess I have changed."

"That's an understatement," Muriel commented. "Soon you'll be wanting babies."

"Oh, I do want babies," I assured her. "One, anyway, right away."

"Alma, look at me," Mama insisted. "You didn't get sick in Mexico, did you?"

"Yeah, sick in the head," Prescott said as we turned into the driveway.

"You haven't met Felipe yet," I reminded them. "You'll love him."

"When is this paragon arriving?" Mama asked.

"Soon," I assured her.

Felipe had promised to leave Yucatán before the month was out. I waited eagerly for the cable announcing his departure date. In the meantime, there was plenty to keep me busy. I had stories to file for the *Times*, an article on Yucatán to write for the *News Call*. I spent the money as fast as I got it. When Sam and I were married, we threw a few things into an overnight bag and drove down to Santa Cruz for a hurried weekend. It would be different with Felipe. I wanted a real trousseau with all the trimmings. Mama and I made trip after trip to City of Paris, a grand old store dating from Gold Rush days. I loved imagining generations of brides shopping there. Now I was one of them. I bought chemises and peignoirs, laces and satins. Why deny myself anything?

Mama was determined to make my wedding gown herself. I wanted white, she wanted blue. "This is a second wedding. You know how people talk. . . ." I wanted a veil, too, but Mama put her foot down. "Impossible! You've already had your miracle. I never thought Father Sanchez would allow a ceremony at Mission Dolores, but then he always did have a soft spot for you. Saving that Ruiz boy didn't hurt any, either. His Mexican parishioners think you're some kind of saint. But a virgin's wedding dress?"

We compromised on cream *peau de soie*. It took days to find the perfect pattern, a *Vogue* original. The fashionable dropped waist was accented by a single satin rose that matched another on my headband, resting low on my forehead in a manner that was all the rage. If my gown wasn't the traditional one I longed for, its lines were chaste and elegant.

"You'll be beautiful, Alma," Mama assured me. "This 'Feeleep' person, whoever he is, will be proud of you. I only hope he'll love you as you've always deserved to be loved."

Hearing a catch in her voice, I looked up from the pattern table. Mama was busily polishing her small gold-rimmed spectacles. Her eyes glittered with unshed tears. "I'm the lucky one," I said, hugging her impulsively.

"Isn't he taking a long time to get here?"

"Just a few more days, Mama."

Chilly air gusted in our faces as we left the store. Fog surrounded us, thick and coiling like cigar smoke. We splurged on a taxi—the first time since Papa left.

Christmas crowded closer. Our tree was up, reaching nearly to the ceiling of the old Victorian house. Everywhere I looked my sisters had draped holly wreaths and mistletoe. Carolers stopped often at our doorstep. Nervous reminders of the approaching holiday. Felipe had promised to be in San Francisco by December 15. Where was he? My brother Walter had reserved a room at the Palace for an engagement party. As the day approached with no news of an arrival date, he quietly postponed it. The old gang at the *News Call* threw a bash for me at the Press Club instead. The toasts were touching, so much warmth and caring—if only Felipe had been there to meet my friends. Alone in my room that night, I reread his daily letters, remembering his massive self-confidence, the feel of his arms about me, repeating his words: "December 20 at the latest, my love—if I have to swim."

December 21 arrived, the winter solstice. Mama brought up coffee on a tray; tucked in beside the napkin was a letter from Felipe. The doubt I saw in her eyes mirrored my own.

I tore open the envelope. Four sheets of closely written script fluttered out. "My little *peregrina*," he'd written, "you are like a brilliant hummingbird, always in flight, always busy, stirring things up and writing them down. Our life will never be boring. If only we were together now . . ."

If only.

"Any news?" Mama asked.

"None," I said, dropping the letter despondently. This was to have been our first Christmas together. What was wrong? Why had he ignored the questions in my letters? Try as I might to shut out the doubts, fear crept in.

Everyone was so happy for me, so intrigued and excited by my famous fiancé. Prenuptial festivities accelerated wildly. There wasn't just one shower, there were many. Friend after friend, sister after sister hosted kitchen showers, linen showers, lingerie showers, lunches, brunches, and teas. "You'll need a whole boat of your own to take all this back to Yucatán," Muriel commented as she helped me box up the latest gifts. Heady moments to be sure, but Felipe's absence sapped the joy.

I moved through the revelry as though in deep twilight. Some part of me proceeded on cue, smiling, laughing, dimly aware that lights glowed, children sang, presents were wrapped, then unwrapped. Finally, it was Christmas night. The last gift had been put away, the last dish dried, and the cupboard closed. Outside, tired carols echoed. Our house was silent, Mama and Prescott asleep, the rest of the family long gone. I sat alone by the dying fire. Felipe's letters had stopped, my urgent cables went unanswered. Something was terribly wrong, but what more could I do? Yucatán was far away. Sobbing softly, I climbed the stairs.

On the silvery San Francisco afternoons that followed, I climbed Telegraph Hill and watched fog settle over the bay until wet mist met the sea and the whole city seemed to slip underwater. Then I'd slowly walk home praying that there'd be a letter waiting for me. There never was.

Four days after Christmas, I returned home to find a message from Fremont Older. His voice sounded tense when I called him back. "Better come down to the paper right away. Things look bad in Mexico. Obregón's archenemy de la Huerta seems to be calling the shots. Another revolution could break out any minute."

I caught a cable car downtown to the *News Call*, where my old boss waited in the doorway. "Communications with Yucatán are severed," he told me, "but rumors are beginning to filter in through Cuba."

I stationed myself in front of the teletype machine, the only source of international news, while a string of copyboys kept the coffee coming.

The story came in fits and starts: "According to sources in Mexico City, de la Huerta's rebel forces formed an alliance with hacendados in Yucatán. The federal garrison there has been replaced with a contingent of troops from northern Mexico." I gasped when I saw the name of their commander, Colonel Juan Broca, the rich landowner who'd sworn to kill Felipe. I was terrified.

The teletype clicked away the minutes, the hours, and finally the days while I remained powerless to do anything. Felipe was no warrior; he was a man of peace. Now, not only must he wrestle with his principles, but also the knowledge that his civilian militia, grossly underarmed, was no match for Broca's well-equipped army.

As the days dragged on, I lived at the newspaper, Mama or Mr. Older sitting beside me. I lit one cigarette after another. When the ashtrays overflowed, and I was alone, my brother, Prescott, appeared, a different Prescott than I'd known before. Silent, solemn-faced, he took my arm with the authority of a man, pulling me to my feet, leading me away from the teletype, out of the building, onto a cable car, and back up the hill to our house.

After a few hours of sleep, I'd rise despite my exhaustion, and return to the *News Call.* Bits of information trickled back from one source and then another. The teletype's *rat-a-tat-tat, rat-a-tat-tat,* like machine-gun fire, tore into me as I waited. Deadly silence and then a few sudden spurts and finally a brief headline:

governor carillo puerto's agent in new orleans seeks guns, ammunition

I breathed a sigh of relief. Felipe was defending himself. A Cuban correspondent cabled that Obregón had been assassinated and de la Huerta proclaimed president. Obregón, our only possible ally, dead! De la Huerta was an evil man and an avowed enemy of Felipe's. I'd hardly had time to register that frightening development before a Mexico City journalist denied it. An hour later, the assassination story was identified as a rumor planted by hacendados, but then an even more terrifying story was confirmed: Colonel Broca, a far more outspoken adversary, had persuaded de la Huerta to offer a $250,000 reward for Felipe, dead or alive.

As I sat, almost overcome with horror, the teletype's incessant clicks mocked me. News was breaking everywhere, correspondents hammering out stories around the world, clogging the wires, but nothing came through from Yucatán. A day passed, then another. If Felipe were dead I'd know it, I told myself again and again.

On the third day, a frightful account was filed by the *News Call*'s man in Havana. Trembling, I tore off the sheet. The words swam before my eyes. *Flight only hope . . . Governor escapes Mérida with three of his brothers and six chief lieutenants . . . Moving northward . . . dead of night. . .*

The machine went abruptly silent. Hours dragged by, then finally another burst from the teletype:

governor carrillo puerto disperses troops. "machetes no match for guns." vows to return with modern weapons.

I sobbed quietly, imagining the scene. I had seen Felipe with those people, remembered so well the loyalty and devotion that flowed both ways.

The following morning another pieced-together account arrived. Felipe's party had reached the coast and waded out to a launch. The men settled down, believing themselves on their way to safety, but the boat merely bobbed in the water. Blaming a disabled engine, the captain waved a lantern toward shore. A signal for help. Within minutes a squad of soldiers came into view. Felipe's men wanted to shoot it out, but he, realizing they were hopelessly outnumbered, ordered them to hold their fire. Felipe and his small party were forced off the launch and marched back to Mérida.

"There must be something you can do," I pleaded, turning to Mr. Older, who stood at my side reading the report. Fremont Older, editor of a great newspaper, was a strong man with friends in high places. Surely there were telephone calls he could make, telegrams he could send to power brokers in Washington.

"I'll try." He smiled; his hand squeezed my shoulder. I pretended not to see the doubt in his narrow gray eyes.

"How long will it take?" I asked, sick with dread.

He shrugged, reluctantly admitting, "I don't know. Your governor's too liberal to be popular in Washington. Politicians read dollar signs and little else. The cordage industry has a strong lobby. You know their links to the hacendados. I'll call in every favor, but I can't promise anything."

More news came, a freelance writer from Mexico City with what appeared to be an inside track. Who did this stringer know? I wondered. According to the journalist, an attorney representing a group of planters had offered Felipe safe conduct out of the country in exchange for $125,000. A cruel hoax, of course. Felipe's private funds, money with which he'd sought to buy arms, had been seized when he was captured. Felipe had no money, even if he'd been willing to accept such an arrangement. And what irony, the ransom was half the sum posted for his death! When Felipe scorned the impossible offer, the hacendados summarily announced that he and his party would be brought before a court-martial.

I could so easily imagine Felipe's bravery as he faced the court, refusing to make a plea. I could almost hear the dignity in his voice as I read the printed words: "I am the governor of this state. I do not recognize your court. I will be judged only by my people."

Mr. Older read the story with me. "He's a brave man."

"He's a dead man," I cried, tears streaming down my face. "They're going to kill him."

Mr. Older ground his cigar into the dish and got up. "Surely one of those Washington bastards can do something." He turned on his heel. A glass door slammed so hard I thought it would shatter.

Face in my hands, I sobbed. I don't know how long I sat there, barely aware of the jumble and clatter going on around me. The teletype machine started and stopped. Tough-guy reporters brought coffee, offered food I couldn't bear to look at. Mama and Prescott came again and again, pleading with me to go home with them. Finally, Mr. Older returned, took me by the shoulders, and raised me to my feet. He put his arms about me, soothed me like a little girl. A sickening shock went through my body.

"It's over, Alma." Mr. Older's rough voice was soft in my ear. "Ochs called from the *Times*. He got a cable from Colonel Broca in Mérida. That son of a bitch is damned proud of what he's done, wants the whole world to know about it. He took Felipe and his men to some cemetery outside of town, stood them against a wall, and shot them all."

Again Yucatán

On January 13, 1924, a short item appeared in the *News Call*:

Alma Sullivan Reed, of this city, fiancée of Governor Felipe Carrillo Puerto of Yucatán, yesterday received confirmation of his assassination at the hands of rebels. The communication received by her declared that Governor Carrillo Puerto, his three brothers, and other loyalists had met death from the revolutionaries. The governor, Mrs. Reed said, had come to be known as the Abraham Lincoln of Mexico, by reason of his efforts to free Indian slaves and improve their conditions in the southern republic.

Mr. Older's simple statement said it all. Felipe had been Yucatán's governor for a mere twenty-two months. When his term and his life ended so abruptly, he was thirty-eight years old.

In the dark, desperate days that followed, I barricaded myself in my bedroom, unable to talk to anyone. Submerged in an endless twilight, I wondered if I would ever see the sun again or even want to see it. Somewhere outside the dark circle, Mama, Prescott, all the Sullivans, closed ranks, shielding me from the curious, canceling reservations, allowing me to grieve.

My thoughts returned often to President Obregón, our host of the previous autumn. His profuse condolences had been cabled to me in care of the *News Call* almost immediately after Felipe's death.

Mr. Older sat quietly as I folded and then unfolded the cable to look one last time. "Obregón appears quite fond of you."

I nodded absently. "I suppose he is. We lived through some exciting times together." The cable crackled softly in my hands as I replaced the missive in its envelope. How long ago those gala evenings at Chapultepec Palace seemed now. "He was such a spellbinder, so witty, I tended to forget those awful war stories."

"They say he sizes up a potential battlefield at a glance, and then, months later, positions his forces to take full advantage of that terrain."

"Are you thinking . . ." I paused, not certain that I wanted to ask the question, or face the possibility. "Are you thinking that he used that same memory to size up a political opponent—to size up Felipe?" I stopped for a moment, unable to go on, then looked up, staring into Mr. Older's gray eyes. "Do you believe that in the end President Obregón brokered some kind of deal with Colonel Broca? Do you believe," my voice had sunk to a whisper, "do you think he sold Felipe out?"

"Obregón's been under fire from the United States since the beginning. Washington's as greedy as the Mexican oligarchy, demanding the same economic concessions the old dictator gave. Now there's new pressure from cordage interests—people we know favor Colonel Broca and the henequen planters. How easy for him to rationalize . . . perhaps all the excuse he needed."

A feeling of nausea swept over me. "You think President Obregón never thought of Felipe as a friend at all, just another rival to be eliminated."

"Perhaps men like Obregón can't afford the luxury of friendship."

Two weeks after Felipe's assassination a cablegram somehow found its way to me at the *News Call*. Addressed only to PIXAN-HALAL, SAN FRANCISCO, the cryptic message read: I HAVE SOMETHING FOR YOU. There was no signature.

Felipe! Was it possible that he lived? Could the execution have been some kind of dreadful hoax? Was my lover in fact alive, hiding in the jungle or a prisoner in some hacendado's dungeon? One thing was certain. I must return immediately to Yucatán. If Felipe was alive, I had to find him. If not . . . no matter how terrible the truth, I needed to learn it for myself.

"You can't go back!" Mama exclaimed. She was at first horrified, but quickly took another tack: "And just what will you use for money? You've spent every penny you earned."

"Almost," I agreed, "but I was able to return a few things to the stores and there's still a check due from the *News Call*. That will tide me over if I'm careful."

She grasped my shoulders, forcing me to look at her. "You're risking your life. You know that, don't you?"

For the first time since Felipe's death, I laughed. What life?

Relentless, the de la Huerta forces fought on, threatening to destroy Obregón's government; the *News Call's* teletype machines clattered incessantly. Their staccato pronouncements mattered not at all to me now. Whatever they said, I would take the train to New Orleans, then sail to Yucatán on the first boat allowed through the blockade into that beleaguered land.

The whole family assembled at the old station on Townsend Street to see me aboard the *Daylight Limited*. Amid much fuss and chatter, they settled me into the corner of a Pullman car. Beside my small bag were magazines and books, fruit and candy. At the last minute, when Mama wasn't looking, Mr. Older, who'd come, too, tucked a flask into my handbag. "You never know when it might come in handy," he said, patting my shoulder.

The locomotive snorted, gave a sudden jolt, then slowly began to move. The family hurriedly clambered off, Walter and Prescott supporting Mama, who sobbed openly. Hairpins slipped from her hair, the silver roll that anchored her hat coming undone. "I'll never see you again," she wailed.

"You will, Mama, of course, you will," I promised, leaning out the open window. I forced a confident smile, but my thoughts drifted to an early mentor at the *Call*, Ambrose Bierce. What had the crusty old journalist said before his trip south? "To be a gringo in Mexico is euthanasia."

For him, the words proved prophetic. Ambrose had never returned from his sortie into the revolution. No one knew his fate. Ambrose had simply disappeared somewhere in Mexico. Euthanasia. I had smiled at Ambrose's cynicism; now I felt a personal warning in his words. Why worry about a lingering old age? Still, as the train gained momentum, I thought eagerly of Yucatán. Felipe was waiting for me, I told myself; he *had* to be there.

Other times I doubted. If my lover was truly alive, why didn't I *feel* his presence? I must discover the truth for myself.

Soon I passed through the orchards of the Santa Clara Valley. Spring had come late that year. The sky was gray as a pewter platter, but on either side as far as I could see: the pink confetti of cherry blossoms. Finally, the track turned westward, snaking its way through coastal mountains that recent rains had transformed to emerald. Within a month those sweeping mounds would resemble nothing more than great dun-colored lions crouched to spring. I loved the amber beauty of California, yet on this day felt soothed by the rare expanse of tender green.

Night had fallen by the time I reached Los Angeles. A porter helped me to change trains; soon I was settled once again and heading eastward. In the dining car as though from some great distance I observed gleaming silver, heard the chime of crystal, the sound of muted laughter. Hardly had I seated myself before a waiter appeared with a silver tray, on its bright surface a folded note. Reading it quickly, I looked up. At the far end of the car, a man, seated alone, waggled his fingers at me. A cocktail? I shook my head, felt the pain of solitude, and held it in my heart.

At last the train pulled into New Orleans, with its narrow streets, brilliant flowers, and filigreed mansions, so like Mérida, yet not Mérida. When would the blockade lift? How long must I wait? Time passed slowly, days of sipping chicory coffee on the riverbank, nights alone on the balcony of my pension, listening to the muted wail of a saxophone somewhere in the distance.

Mexico's struggle continued. Some seven thousand people dead. Then, as one bloody headline followed another, Obregón pulled ahead. With weapons supplied by the United States, acting to protect its oil interests, *el presidente* was slowly crushing the de la Huerta rebellion.

One morning I came home to find a note addressed to me on the hall tray. Someone had called from the Ward Line. The blockade had been lifted. A ship sailing tomorrow for Progreso had an available cabin.

I was the first passenger aboard.

How slowly the shipboard hours dragged. On the second afternoon as I sat idly thumbing through a magazine, I looked up to see a deckhand staring at me. Aware that I'd seen him, he put down his mop and walked shyly forward.

"*Por favor, señora*. I am Guillermo Martinez," the slender, almost frail, young man introduced himself. "Felipe Carrillo Puerto was my benefactor."

Trembling, I motioned for him to sit beside me.

"I am the oldest of six," he explained. "My family is poor. When I wanted to become a doctor someone suggested that I apply to the governor. His Excellency's office was packed with supplicants. Even the president of the Socialist League waited for an interview. Hours went by. Finally His Excellency came out and apologized. He couldn't see anyone else that day. It had taken all my courage to go there; I knew I would never return. I couldn't hide my tears. Perhaps His Excellency felt my desperation. I knew a miracle had occurred when he gestured to me, just me, to come into his office. I told him my story. There had been hundreds of requests made to him, but for some reason, he agreed to give me thirty pesos a month until my education was completed."

Touched by Guillermo's story, I patted his arm. "You are working as a deckhand now—but Felipe is alive. I'll find him. I know I will. He'll help you again."

Guillermo shook his head sadly. "The governor is dead. Everyone knows that. But his faith has inspired me; I will go back to school one day." Guillermo paused, his young, unformed face serious. "The governor was my hero. I followed him everywhere. Once, I was in the shadows outside your window at the Gran while His Excellency's mariachis serenaded you. Yours was *un amor de calido*."

I felt the color rush to my face. A steamy romance. Is that how the people of Mérida viewed us?

The boy continued, his mind filled with his own memories. "Another time, after you had returned to your home in the United States, I was in a cantina sitting near the governor when the mariachis began to play 'La Peregrina.' There were tears in his eyes. He missed you very much."

Guillermo struggled to compose himself. "You must be prepared. Though most in Yucatán regard you as a heroine, there are angry ones who hate you."

"Why? What have I done but love him?"

"It's the old legend. He was like Kukulkan . . . tempted . . ."

I thought back to the day—was it only a year before?—when I'd sat atop the Temple of Kukulkan listening to Felipe recount the legend: *Kukulkan could not resist her. . . . The god abandoned everything, his heart flew out of his body. . . . He never returned.* Something had warned me then. Why hadn't I heeded that warning?

"There are many stories, rumors spread by hacendados," Guillermo continued. "They say that when His Excellency fled, he carried the state treasury with him to bring to you in San Francisco."

"Those rumors are insane! The money was meant for arms. Surely anyone who knew Felipe would also know that."

"Anyone who wants to know it."

Felipe had always walked a tightrope. Had I caused him to lose his balance? The tale was a blatant lie, yet the link to me . . .

"It *is* my fault." I said, more to myself than to the thin young man beside me. "But I will find Felipe. He's alive. He must be alive."

Guillermo's velvet eyes were dark with sympathy. He shook his head emphatically. "You will never find His Excellency in this life. But do not think his death was your fault. It was his own *destino*."

*E*s *La Peregrina. La Peregrina. Peregrina . . .*" The words followed me. People pointed, stared; others looked the
other way. It was as though the citizens of Yucatán had
been waiting for me, had always known that I would return, that I had to return. But who had sent me the cable?
How was I to find that person? Would he, could he, lead
me to Felipe?

One evening as I lingered over coffee in the garden of
the Hotel Gran, a lone guitarist somewhere in the distance
began to strum "La Peregrina." It happened everywhere I
went. They meant well, I supposed, but the pathos . . . I
stood up to leave, was fumbling for change, when a voice
behind me called out.

"Alma! Don't go."

I turned at the sound.

A pair of creamy arms lightly dusted with freckles
grabbed me in a warm embrace. "Alma, Alma, what can I
say? I'm so sorry, so very sorry."

"There's nothing you can say, Ann." I fought the lump
rising in my throat and held her back at arm's length. My
friend glowed, giving off little sparks of energy and excitement. I wouldn't reveal my quest. Something told me
that Ann would only dash my tenuous hopes. I forced a
smile. "So, you've come back to Yucatán."

"Yes, more funding, another dig," she grinned. "We
work from dawn to dusk. Earl and I were lucky to get

an overnight leave. We're in Mérida to pick up supplies. I heard you were in town and came looking."

"Lucky for me." I hugged her hard. "But I'm surprised you're here. It's still so unsettled, angry riots every day."

Ann shrugged. "Not much affects us in the back country. Though it was strained in the beginning. The Maya villagers were frightened when we returned. They believe Felipe's death was a punishment from the gods."

"The gods! I haven't heard that one before."

"It's hard to understand everything our workers say, but apparently they thought he was punished for bringing scientists to their ruins. The witch women say that if he'd offered an animal sacrifice, as they advised, everything would have been all right."

"As though Felipe would ever have done that!"

"We did."

"You're joking! I can't imagine Sylvanus—"

"Well no, not Sylvanus. One of the workmen shot a deer. There was a little ceremony and then we all had deer stew. It's quiet now. Why don't you come back with us? We're doing some exciting things. Earl and I are excavating a ruin of our own. The Maya call it the Temple of a Thousand Columns. You wouldn't believe it. Every day we dig up a new one and try to put it in place. They go on forever. Who knows, maybe there really are a thousand of them."

"Hard work must be good for you. You look fabulous."
I meant it. "I can see that life's going well for you and
Earl."

"Oh, it is! We're uncovering wonderful things." Ann
hesitated, a rueful smile on her lips. "Of course, it's clearly
understood that they must *all* remain in Mexico. We've
your story to thank for that. Archaeology will never be
the same."

"Maybe that's good."

Ann smiled again. "I don't think you'll get anyone at
the Peabody to agree."

I laughed heartily for the first time in how long? It
felt good, but there was a question I was dreading to ask.
"How is Don Eduardo? Felipe sent men to put out the fire
at the hacienda—we had to leave—he was determined
to protect me, to get me on that damn boat home. I never
heard what happened."

Ann shook her head sadly. "The hacienda's a ruin. Only
the walls remain. The Maya workmen have built little cottages on the grounds for the archaeologists. That's where
we're staying, where everyone will stay from now on."

"And Don Eduardo's library?"

"Completely destroyed. You wouldn't know him. The
library was his life. Don Eduardo aged twenty years in a
day."

Pain pierced my heart. I thought I had no tears left; I
was wrong.

That evening the composers of "La Peregrina" visited me at the Gran. Luis Rosada de la Vega, who'd written the lyrics, held my hand in his as he reminisced. "Once Felipe had spoken to me of his feelings for you, the song wrote itself."

Waves of sorrow washed over me as I imagined Felipe planning the surprise, remembered my joy upon hearing the music that first night in the midst of a violent hurricane. I wanted to think that the song would live on as long as there were mariachis.

"Can you tell me anything about Felipe?" I pleaded, looking from one to the other. "That's why I've come back to Yucatán. I heard the awful story, of course, but are you certain that it's true? Is there any chance that he may be alive somewhere—a prisoner, perhaps?"

"My dear, my dear," the musician Ricardo Palmerin shook his head sadly. "We were part of a large group—a mob, you might call it—who went out to Panteón General a few hours after it happened. Hundreds of people came from everywhere. We couldn't believe it either, but none of us will ever forget what we saw. The blood, the bodies . . . News wire services wouldn't run the pictures outside the country, they were too gruesome, but our papers ran them for days—it was a massacre, hideous . . . hideous." For a moment Ricardo sat quietly, face buried in his hands. "Later," he continued at last, "we carried the bodies away. They lay in state. Everyone came. And then there was the funeral; Rosada and I were pallbearers. Now our Felipe lies in peace only a few feet from where he was shot."

"'La Peregrina' was almost the last sound Felipe heard," Rosada added. "He thought the court-martial a sham and refused to testify, all the while trying desperately to save the others. 'They were merely doing their duty,' he reminded his captors. 'Do what you will with me but spare my brothers and friends.' Felipe's plea was ignored," de la Vega picked up the dreadful story, his face downcast. "The governor was returned with the other prisoners to their cells. During the night, soldiers outside his window taunted him by singing a whiny parody of 'La Peregrina.' At dawn the ten men were led from the prison and driven through the streets of Mérida to Panteón General, where they were lined up against the wall."

Palmerin's eyes were dark with sorrow. "I'm sorry, my dear. We shouldn't have come. This is too much for you to hear."

I shook my head. "I wanted to know everything. I had to; that's why I came back to Mérida."

I sat quietly for a time, overcome by memories. "The cemetery," I murmured, remembering marigolds reflected in torchlight, burning copal, peppery and piquant, mariachis singing their souls out, and Felipe's arms around me. The wall I had thought strong enough to hold back spirits had claimed his. The Day of the Dead ghosts had enjoyed yet another joke, this one on me.

"Yes," Ricardo nodded, "that's where it happened. I heard the story from a soldier the next day. Sick with shame for his part in it, he told me that a squad of nervous riflemen had been moved in for the kill. Ignoring the bribe-taking Colonel Broca, Felipe walked past them to a young soldier. 'Please see that Señora Reed gets this,' he said, handing him the ring that was to have been yours.

"Felipe bade good-bye to his brothers and friends. The colonel gave the order to fire. Bullets shattered plaster as the soldiers blasted over the heads of the prisoners. In a rage, Broca screamed to the riflemen in the second rank to cut down the soldiers of the firing squad. Standing over the bodies of their comrades, the second squad executed the ten men, who stood with their backs against the wall."

Rosada broke in: "Desperate to get word to you, we sent a boy to swim out to an English ship with the request that a message be sent."

My voice constricted to a whisper, "PIXAN-HALAL, SAN FRANCISCO. I got it but by then I'd already heard about the assassination. I couldn't believe it. I thought—I hoped—that the message was from Felipe. I wanted so much to believe that he was still alive."

Ricardo took my hand. "Alma, *mi* Alma, I am sorry that we gave you hope when there is none. Our messenger was only a boy—a brave boy ready to swim out into hostile waters—but he knew no English. We simply wanted to let you know that we have the ring, the ring that Felipe meant for you. A soldier brought it to me and I have been holding it for you, waiting for you to come back to us." He took a small pouch from his pocket and gave it to me.

My hands trembled as I slid the gold wedding band onto my finger.

The next day brought a cable from Mr. Ochs urging that I remain in Mexico to cover the archaeological scene. Impossible, I cabled back. The wounds cut too deep. Someday I might return to seek out the hundreds of hidden sites dotting Felipe's beloved land. Perhaps. It would not be soon.

Mama had written almost every day, her question always the same: When was I coming home? When indeed? My money was almost gone. I could remain in Mérida no longer, nor did I want to. Where did my future lie?

The next morning another cable solved the problem. Mr. Ochs was back to me with a different assignment. Tunisia. Some archaeologists were digging up Carthage. Rumor had it that the site was cursed. Did I want to take it on? Why not? What was a curse to me?

I hired a *fortinga* to take me out to the graveyard. Asking the driver to wait, I approached the bullet-riddled wall slowly. It was exactly the spot where Felipe and I had paused to make our plans after leaving the cemetery. I'd felt so happy then, so safe, until I saw the armored car, the bodyguards. Felipe must have known then that an uprising was coming. How lightly he'd spoken when all the while everything he'd fought so hard to achieve teetered on the brink of ruin. He'd tried to shield me from danger and I had reacted like a foolish girl. How could I have been so blind?

There were other mourners present, mostly women, all in black. I felt their eyes on me as I touched the wall, still stained with blood.

"La Peregrina," someone said. "It is La Peregrina. She has come back to him." Quietly they followed me into the cemetery, kneeling near me at the gravesite. The concluding words of the song echoed in my heart as I placed a single red rose on the tomb.

> Traveler of the enchanting face,
> When you leave my palm groves and my land,
> Don't forget—don't forget—my land.
> Don't forget—don't forget—my love.

"I will not forget," I whispered. "I will never forget."

A Good Life?

SAGE

The galley proofs of *La Peregrina* came late one rainy April afternoon. How exciting to see my printed words at last. They awaited my final scrutiny, the last task before publication of my book. I called Mark, full of eager anticipation, but his response was slow, his voice labored. "I'm . . . happy for you, babe. This is . . . what you've been waiting . . . for."

A warning chill went up my arm. "Are you okay?"

"Yes . . . fine . . . just a little tired."

"I'll be right there," I told him. "I'd have left earlier but the carpet cleaner came late. He was just leaving when the mail truck drove in. I'll hop in the car right now."

"No, Sage. Don't do that," Mark's voice was firmer now. "You'll hit the rush-hour traffic. It's raining hard, the roads will be slippery. Stay home and work on your galleys. Read carefully. Come tomorrow and bring them then. . . . I'd like to see . . ."

I glanced out the window. It was raining hard. Perhaps he was right. I'd been making this hour-long commute each day for so long; I dreaded going out. "All right— I'll be there first thing in the morning and stay all day," I promised, trying for the lilty note he usually responded to. "Tomorrow is supposed to be clear and sunny. I'll wheel you out onto the terrace. We'll have lunch there."

"Good. A long . . . sunny day . . . together. Nice."

That chill again. "Mark, are you sure you don't want me to come now?"

"Yes, I'm sure. Come tomorrow. Don't forget the galleys. I want you to read to me. See you in the morning, babe." A click and he was gone.

I hesitated, hand clenched around the receiver. Should I call back? The proofs, full of promise, spilled from their envelope. I wanted to build a fire, brew tea, settle in. The first galley page cried out to be corrected. Read me! Read me! Then I thought of my husband as I'd seen him the day before, dark shadowed eyes, skin almost translucent. He said he was tired; maybe he wanted to be alone.

The galleys won. I read page after page, relishing the look of my work in print as though I'd never published a word before. It was after six when Mews's hungry me-ows roused me. I fed her quickly and settled back in my chair by the fire. At nine I broke for a bowl of soup, a glass of wine. I thought of calling Mark but decided against it, fearing the possibility of waking him. I didn't quit reading until my eyes blurred. It was nearly twelve. Reluctantly I set my work down and went to bed. Sleep came instantly.

The ringing phone pulled me from my slumber, strange dreams—rain falling on Mayan carvings, ferocious profiles, feathered plumes. I fumbled for the receiver beside my bed. The clock's illuminated face read three. *I knew then.*

By the time I reached Ravenswood, Mark's body had already been removed. Standard procedure, I was told. His bed was empty, the mattress rolled back, the walls bare. That awful emptiness, as though he'd never been there. Mark's possessions—clothing, pictures, books—in the hallway in two cardboard boxes. The floor director pointed them out to me. "Your husband died peacefully," she assured me. "The night nurse was in to check on him minutes before. His breathing had grown very heavy. Finally, we think, he was just too tired to go on."

So that's the way it was. After all my efforts to be there for Mark, in the end he died alone. I had let him down. In the busy days that followed, I tried not to think about that, but the reality was never far from the surface. I had sensed a warning and ignored it. I would have to live with that for the rest of my life. Mark had been a major part of my life for so many years. Now, besides the guilt, I felt an aching void, a sense of loss that I could never before have imagined. Mark was *gone*. Sometimes I wanted to die and yet felt hunger and thirst; my heart continued to beat out the seconds of my so-called life. He was lost and I was left—so alive that I could almost feel my hair and nails growing. How could it be?

The wake we held at Mark's house—I had never come to think of it as mine—was well attended. The same crowd who'd celebrated his big sixtieth bash was back in force. This time Kevin and Lance also managed to round up Mark's ex-wife and two former girlfriends. Mews, that little flirt, went from lap to lap, wrapping them all around her fluffy paw. Favorite tunes played on the stereo, toasts were drunk, reminisces exchanged, a gentle roast. Mark would have loved it.

Finally only the "family" remained; we sat around looking at a house that hadn't had much attention in recent years. To satisfy the terms of the will, it would have be sold. To get the best price, it required a face-lift. Kevin's and Lance's wives were full of ideas. Unfortunately, they were nowhere close to the same ideas. They had each begun to stake out territory, were counting silver, evaluating artwork. These were ugly days and would only get worse. I longed to escape.

Mark was lying paralyzed in a convalescent hospital when we married a little over a year ago—yes, I'd fulfilled my bargain. Everything the way he wanted. It had pleased Mark to think of me living in his house. I believe he wanted to imagine me somehow an average wife, just waiting for him to come home. To humor Mark, I'd moved in and eventually become used to rattling around in the mini mansion where I'd spent happier times with him. Now I felt desperate to get away from the silent reminders—if only for a little while. But where to go?

The next day an out-of-the-blue e-mail answered the question for me.

Are you the Sage Sanborn who's writing a biography of Alma Reed? If so, let's talk. I knew her.

The sender signed himself: MikeAldrich@unisono .net.

Knew Alma? That would make him older than God. The e-mail was a joke of some kind, had to be, but I couldn't ignore it. Unisono was a Mexican Internet carrier. Mike Aldrich, whoever he was, lived south of the border. To my surprise, Google revealed him to be a writer, a Latin affairs expert with numerous articles to his credit. He also headed a small PR company in Mexico City. Since Aldrich looked legit, I responded. Two days later he replied with an apology for not getting back to me sooner. He'd been at Chapultepec Palace supervising photo shoots. Mexican fusion food and haute couture. What would Obregón think of his hard-won citadel now—a museum used for promotions.

Okay, so now I knew Mike Aldrich was for real, but what—if anything—did he know about Alma? In the course of setting up a meeting, a temporary plan for myself evolved. Nothing or no one required my services in the near future and I was sick to death of the bickering going on around me. Why not make a short pilgrimage to the place I'd grown to love? Aldrich, it appeared, was spry enough to have a tight schedule. We agreed at last to meet in the bar of the Mexico City airport where I'd be changing planes en route to Mérida and he'd be about to start off on a press junket to Cuba.

I entered the bar literally holding my breath. It was like meeting a legendary figure from another time. Could Mike Aldrich really have known Alma Reed? *My* Alma Reed? I looked about the room. It could be any airport bar: people talking intently or not talking at all, poring over the paper or gazing off into space. The man in brown wearing a yellow carnation who'd promised to meet me there was nowhere in sight but I did manage to spot an empty table. My margarita had just arrived when the mystery man appeared in the doorway.

Mike Aldrich looked tall and broad as he shouldered his way toward me. A thick thatch of salt-and-pepper hair topped his ruddy, weathered face. "You don't look old enough to have known Alma Reed," I told him and meant it.

Smiling, Aldrich signaled for a drink. "It's this way," he said as he settled down across from me at the small round table. "When she was very old and I very young, we worked on the same newspaper."

"Really?" I tilted my head, regarding him inquisitively. "Was it the *Mexico City Dispatch*? I know she worked there later, was working there when she died—right?"

Aldrich reached for an ashtray and pulled a battered cigarette pack from his shirt pocket. "That's right. I quit Columbia when I was twenty, came down here and landed a job on the only English-language daily in town. Alma was a stringer there. The *Dispatch* suffered—still suffers—from the same attrition rate as most expat papers. Within a year I'd been ratcheted up to the editor's slot. I was her boss."

"And Alma?" I tentatively tasted the salt around the rim of my margarita.

"This was back in the sixties. They would have had to be pretty desperate to hire a woman in those days—sorry about that." He smiled at me in a manner that didn't appear sorry at all. "It was before PC. Besides, even without the gender thing, she was pretty long in the tooth to run a paper."

"How old?"

"Pretty old." This time Aldrich's smile was rueful. "Around seventy—like me."

"You're still going strong."

"And so was she. You should have seen her. Knock-out blue eyes, mesmerizing. You could not help but stare into those eyes—a bit like yours," he added, studying me appraisingly.

When I didn't rise to the bait, Aldrich went on. "Alma was a demon even then. She'd been writing her column for ten years by the time I met her. She continued it for seven more—right up till the day she died. Art and archaeology mostly, and interviews—colorful personalities that drifted into her life. Alma knew everyone, had a gift for pushing beyond puffery, the PR flak."

I nodded, fascinated with his story, how it jibed with my own findings. "Truman Capote was intrigued with her, I understand—and Budd Schulberg."

Aldrich smiled, as though remembering scenes from long ago. "Capote came down here and spent the whole day. Took her out on the floating gardens. We thought maybe he'd write a book about Alma. Budd Schulberg was keen on the idea, too, for awhile, but neither of them ever did anything with it."

"How did you learn about my book?"

"I was in Yucatán on a story a while back. There's quite a social community down there, lots going on. Interesting expat crowd in Mérida; you'd fit right in. I'll give you some names, phone numbers. People were talking about this pretty gringa who'd been asking questions. Introduce yourself around next time. The *La Prensa* gang was all agog over you."

La Prensa! Again I saw those terrible headlines. "You wouldn't believe the pictures I found in their file—the blood, the mutilated bodies. How could Alma have ever gotten over what happened to Felipe?"

"In some ways, she never did." Aldrich lit another cigarette from the end of the first. "In other ways it was only the beginning for her."

"I've come to realize that," I said, regretfully. "My book is finished, you know. I mailed the galley proofs back to the publisher on the way to the airport this morning. Unfortunately, News Call Press was only interested in Alma's California ties, her early years on the newspaper. They couldn't ignore Felipe—such a dramatic story— but my biography is part of their California writers series. Who knows, perhaps I'll expand the story for another publisher later; such things happen. I know there's much more to be said about Alma."

"You should," he encouraged me. "The Felipe part was just the beginning."

"Was there ever another man?" I asked, thinking first of Mark and then of David.

"Lots of them, but not in the way you mean. She had many young artist and writer friends, but I don't think anything went beyond friendship. Felipe Carrillo Puerto was a hard act to follow."

"Still," I countered, "she did move on with her life. I loved Alma's book on Mexican archaeology, a good work, well written, excellent research." I studied him curiously, hoping for an answer that had plagued me. "Why do you think the critics were so harsh?"

Aldrich shrugged. "Perhaps they were jealous of her notoriety, or maybe she'd just beaten them to the punch—written their book before they could. Who knows about those things?" He lit another cigarette. "The book sales surely didn't change her life. Alma lived mostly on the edge—seemed to like it that way. The *Dispatch* paid her a pittance, but then, fortunately, she got involved with a bunch of underwater archaeologists—amateurs mostly, but enthusiastic. One real rich guy funded it. Archaeology was his passion, Alma his charity. She wrote press releases for them on a retainer basis. That and her newspaper columns kept her going."

I shook my head. "Sounds sad."

Aldrich laughed. "Alma didn't think so. You wouldn't either if you'd seen her apartment out in the Colonia district. It was stuffed with Oriental rugs, copper pots, artifacts from all the digs. And photographs, photographs all over the place, autographed by anyone who mattered in those days. There were paintings, too, and lots of sculpture—gifts from artists she'd helped launch. After a while some of those gifts must have been worth a fortune." Aldrich bent his head back, blew some smoke rings, his eyes seemingly lost in thought. "Alma had great parties," he said at last. "Everybody went. It wasn't a bad life at all."

Perhaps not. . . . Just what was a bad life? Indeed, what could be called a good one? I leaned back, too, took a sip of my margarita and savored it. Why did the first one on every trip always taste the best?

D riving from Mérida to Chichen Itza I planned my own life, at least its immediate future. The will had made it abundantly clear that I was to have not only half of Mark's monetary estate but any of his furniture or personal effects that I wished. I didn't wish much—Mews, of course, the Waterford martini pitcher, the desk and chair I'd used so often, and a painting that Mark had insisted on buying in Rio because he thought it looked like me.

I'd rent a small apartment in the city, probably Telegraph Hill, most certainly with a view. I'd wait there until the will was probated and my book published. Then move on . . . but where and to what?

For now, I looked forward to climbing the Temple of Kukulkan, to leaning against the wall of the small temple at the top as I used to do. Perhaps the future would reveal itself to me there. Once, I recalled, it had—in a sense. I remembered David as he'd appeared to me, poised on the top stair, tall and lean and trim. I had thought of him, longed for him, so often in the past year. After Mark's death, I'd thought more than once of calling him but couldn't bring myself to do it. Too soon. Later, perhaps. . . . Later for sure, but not now.

I'd booked a room at the Mayaland Hotel; Hacienda Chichen had too many memories. Maybe I'd walk over later and have dinner. Possibly they'd remember me and sing "La Peregrina" one more time. Pulling into the Mayaland's drive, I signaled to a bellman. Quickly, I filled out the registration, and sent my small bag out to the miniature jungle lodge that would be my room for the next two nights. The park would be closing in an hour. I wanted time to walk there and, most particularly, to pay homage to Kukulkan.

I half ran the short block to the park entrance. My pyramid was so close. I rounded the path and there it was. "Oh!" I literally cried out in shocked dismay. The Temple of Kukulkan had been cordoned off with ropes. Tourists stood off at a distance, trying to take pictures, but no one was allowed to climb. I ran forward, out into the center of the park, and looked in every direction. At the far end I saw Ann Morris's Temple of a Thousand Columns. I'd never mount those stairs again to throw my arms around the great columns, nor would I pose before them for the ultimate vacation photo. Well, not for more than a minute anyway. People did, from time to time, sneak under the ropes that now barred access to all the ruins. I saw them, but I also heard the whistle blowers who seemed ever alert. How could they do this?

I began to cry, all the tears I hadn't shed before. The awful finality of Mark's death, my own guilt, and now this travesty. With the flourish of a pen some official had blocked off the access to history—modern as well as ancient. No more would people exchange pleasantries on the stairs or at the summit. That panting, puffing camaraderie that had bound and sustained decades of visitors was gone. What must Felipe think of his industry without smokestacks now? The pyramid's days of talks and trysts were over.

Thoughts of David and our time together in Yucatán haunted me as I walked back to the Mayaland. I wanted so much to tell him what had happened. He was the only one I could tell now, the only one who would understand. My tiny cabin had no Internet access, so I hurried into the main hotel to a large room set aside as a business center. It was a pleasant place with Catherwood prints on the wall, Mayan artifacts on shelves, and women in pretty embroidered *huipiles* dispensing coffee and margaritas. I chose the latter. Within seconds I'd logged on and was typing jaguarpaw@aol.com. The first part of the message was easy:

David: Two sad things I must tell you. Mark is gone. He was brave and dear to the end. I am in Chichen Itza now, devastated to find that the pyramid—our pyramid—has been roped off. No one can climb there anymore.

I hesitated over what to say next. What was there to say? Plenty. But *how* to say it? I typed: "I'd like your shoulder to cry on." Then quickly deleted it. What was I thinking of, it had been more than a year. I gulped the margarita and typed: "Are you still there? I am." Barely, I thought, and clicked the mouse. No taking it back now.

Dinner was a desultory affair. I couldn't bring myself to walk over to the hacienda, and most of the Mayaland guests left early for the Sound and Light Show. That was one way to obscure the offending ropes. It would be too dark to see them.

I had another margarita and walked back through the rustling blackness to my small lodge. It was mostly screened, letting in the exotic noises that I loved. Frogs and crickets were my companions through the night as I lay awake thinking about Mark and David. Slowly, I was beginning to forgive myself. Maybe I had never been there for Mark, not when he died, not when he lived, but surely I had tried. I had done my best. On some level Mark must have known that, perhaps still knew it. Time now to move on. I hoped—prayed—that David might be part of that.

The next morning I went directly to the business center. This time it seemed an age before I was able to connect and then log on. When the screen at last came into view I saw that my message to David had bounced; jaguarpaw@aol.com was no longer a valid address. What did that mean?

I could wait and call David when I got home . . . but I didn't want to wait. I wanted more than anything to hear his voice now. I wanted to tell David that our pyramid was history. If anything could give him a sense of fleeting time, that would. I was free at last; we had waited long enough.

Phone calls from Mexico cost a fortune, but wasn't this worth a fortune? I picked up the phone and an English-language operator got me to NIH in no time. It took longer to get David's extension, but I did. The phone rang and rang. Would I have to spill my guts to an answering machine? No, someone was picking up.

It wasn't David. "Dr. Winslow is away," a man's voice informed me. "May I take a message?"

"Tell him that Sage Sanborn called. I'm in Yucatán, staying at the Mayaland. The number is—"

"It may be a while," he stopped me. "Dr. Winslow is out of the country."

"Really! A new assignment?"

"No, actually, he's on vacation—as a matter of fact, his wedding trip."

It was as though a knife had been plunged into my heart. The phone slipped, but I somehow retrieved it. "His wedding trip!" How naïve of me, so foolish to have imagined—"How nice." I smiled automatically into the receiver. "In that case, no message. I'll call him later with my congratulations."

I hung up the phone, nodded to the attendant, and slipped out. Leadenly I walked the short distance to the park. It was very early. Perhaps for just a few moments I'd have the ruins to myself. That was not to be. As I approached the gate, two snorting tour buses pulled up. A stout woman in white with a whistle around her neck jumped out of the first one and hurried to the ticket booth. Her charges, a large group of Germans, disembarked in quick order and assembled behind her. As I waited for my own ticket I watched them step into line. She was leading them off to the right, toward the Temple of Kukulkan.

"Why did you do it?" I asked the gatekeeper. "Why are the ruins roped off? *¿Porque estan cerradas ruinas?*"

He smiled broadly, showing a set of sparkling white teeth. "To keep you safe." He pronounced each word slowly, distinctly, and, I thought, proudly.

"*Claro.*" I nodded, but I didn't understand. I never would. Once inside, I took the path to the left. Was there anywhere else to go? Moving faster now I passed bright T-shirts strung on clotheslines, vendors hawking key chains and statues, blankets and ashtrays. Noise all around me— the first customer of the day. Incredibly raucous; but, as I continued, the sounds gradually faded until all was silent. I was used to that. Often in the past I'd watched visitors step to the Sacred Well's edge, gaze into its murky depths with a fearful curiosity, then draw back, their voices instinctively lower. A sense of mystery, of horror even, pervades, surviving the passage of centuries.

On this morning I had the site to myself. Thus far the well remained free of the offending restraining ropes. But how long could that last? I sat down a few feet from the cenote's rim, settling back against the crumbling remains of a low wall. There it was: the Mouth of the Well of the Wizard. At a moment like this when everything had gone wrong, it was hard not to think of the well's ancient curse. Don Eduardo had been warned that anyone taking treasure from the cenote would lose the thing he loved most in the world. Perhaps the archaeologist had convinced himself that the loss of his hearing was forfeit enough. Chac had decreed otherwise. In the end Don Eduardo lost everything. What did Alma think when she extracted her own treasure—the story that would make her famous? Had she believed herself immune?

What had I imagined? Every biography is in some way an exploitation. Hadn't I reinvented my heroine? Biographers face constant choices. What to say, what to leave unsaid? Alma's discovery of the cenote's treasure was a high point of her life. It was also the centerpiece of my book. I, too, had paid for my tiny bit of plunder. Ixchel alone knew how much I'd already sacrificed; only she could feel the aching void I suffered now.

Alma had lost the thing she loved best in the world and yet survived. Mark had joined Felipe in that same unknowable place; and now David, too, was dead to me. I had to step forward alone to claim my future as Alma had once claimed hers. Chichen Itza, for all its timeless magic, had been dragged into the twenty-first century, a place where safety and correctness rule. One thing I knew: Alma would not have accepted such banality. I wasn't going to, either. I would create my own world, just as she had created hers.

EPILOGUE

"Alma Reed wasn't the first woman to go to Mexico to forget a man. She won't be the last. Still, it's her story that became a legend." I set the book down and looked out over the bookstore audience. "I thought it was time someone told Alma's story right," I explained to them. "Why shouldn't that someone be me, a wanderer like her? A reporter, too."

Once, seeking to banish some forgotten doubt about my abilities to write the biography—write it right, that is—Mark had said those words to me in his inimitable my-Sage-can-do-anything way. People disappear when they die; Mark had disappeared from my world. His quizzical smile and ready laugh were gone now as surely as his flesh and bone, but his spirit remained. I knew it. Studying the many faces before me, I longed to see his among them. No shade appeared, but I did feel Mark's essence guiding me, challenging me, as he had so often done.

It was a good crowd. I was lucky. The Book Place had promoted my signing well. What we'd thought of as an obscure little biography had pulled a large audience. They listened attentively when I read two short excerpts, no shuffling, not much throat clearing. Now the crowd was full of questions.

"What happened to Alma? Did she go to Carthage?" a trim, outdoorsy woman asked from the front row. She must have come early; there were no seats left. People were crowding in the entryway, leaning against bookshelves and walls. *A standing-room audience.*

I smiled at her. "Alma went to Carthage and a lot of other exotic places before opening a gallery in New York."

A man rose, long hair, broad shoulders. "Is it true that the artist Orozco was her protégé?"

"He certainly was. Thanks to Alma, Orozco went home to Mexico famous. She discovered him and many other talented men and women. She showcased Mexican artists."

A younger woman, also in the front row, looked up from her notes, shoved up her glasses. A student reporter, I guessed. "What about that well—those sacrificial virgins—isn't there supposed to be a curse?"

I paused a moment, recalling the gaping water pit surrounded by lush tangled growth, saw again the sheer perpendicular sides, and far below, the turgid, green water. "The well has a tragic history, we know that much," I told her. "Many skeletons were found at the bottom. Were they virgins? Storytellers find the possibility romantic. The site itself is so chilling, it's easy to imagine a curse. No doubt about it, the *cenote* has claimed its share of martyrs."

The store manager came to my side. "Ms. Sanborn can answer one more question and then it will be time for her to sign copies of *La Peregrina*." She gestured, smiling at the pyramid of books beside me.

I looked out over the crowded room. Many in the audience smiled back, old friends who'd turned out tonight to offer moral support. I saw a smattering of street people, too, clearly looking for a clean, comfortable place to sit. Still, the majority of the audience seemed to have been drawn in by the book itself, genuinely captivated as I had been by the fantasylike life of Alma Sullivan Reed. "Instead of answering a question, let me give you a postscript. Alma went back to Yucatán one last time—after she died. She's buried there, next to Felipe in Panteón General, the cemetery where he was slain."

There was an audible sigh, so romantic. The manager returned with a pen, which she placed before me. A line began to form, people moved forward to have their books signed. "¡*Buenos Viajes!*" I wrote. It sounded better than "Happy Trails." After a time the pen foundered. Out of ink. I fumbled through my tote bag for another.

"May I offer mine?"

I looked up at the sound of a familiar voice, caught my breath in surprise. "David!"

"I saw the notice of your book signing in the *News Call*."

"What are you doing in San Francisco?"

"Spending a couple of nights on the way to our next assignment—Micronesia." He paused a moment, looking at me. "Sally, my wife, is a biostatistician."

"Congratulations." I glanced down at his gold wedding band. Smiling, I took the pen. "Is she here? Some friends are having a party for me after the signing. I'd love to meet her, love to have you both join us."

He shook his head regretfully. "I'm sorry. She's back at the hotel; we have an early flight—four a.m." He moved closer, looking intently into my eyes. "I can see that you're fine. Success obviously becomes you." He glanced now about the crowded room. "I don't see Mark. How is he?"

"I've been alone for six months."

"And you didn't call! You didn't let me know?"

I said nothing. What was there to say?

David raised a sandy brow. "Clearly, I'm not your romantic revolutionary hero. I'm not your Felipe Carrillo Puerto."

"I'm not Alma Reed, either." My eyes strayed back to his wedding band.

We were quiet after that, both of us trying to ignore the impatient, grumbling line behind him. "I stopped by the Compass Rose Room last night," David said at last. "It isn't there anymore."

I nodded sadly, considered telling him about the roped-off pyramid but decided against it. "Good luck with your new assignment," I said instead.

"What's next for you, Sage?"

"Lots of things." I felt a rush of excited expectation as I thought of all that had happened in the past few months. "I'm moving to Mérida next week. I bought a house there. Some say Villa Aurora was to have been Felipe and Alma's home. *¿Quien sabe?*" I shrugged. "All I know for certain is that it's old and beautiful—and thanks be to Ixchel—has modern plumbing. I love it! I've made some new friends down there. We're going to start an English-language newspaper. And if that doesn't keep me busy enough, I've an idea for a novel—always wanted to try my hand at fiction. What better time than now?"

A man leaned forward, placing a book into my hands. I shrugged at David, smiling. "I learned a lot from Alma. Endings are a big part of history." Opening the book, I scribbled another *Buenos Viajes*. As I returned it, I looked back at David and smiled. "Maybe the best part, because they open the way for new beginnings."

AUTHOR'S NOTE

I heard the tale of Alma Reed and Felipe Carrillo Puerto while researching a guidebook, *Yucatán: A Guide to the Land of Maya Mysteries*. At first I was incredulous. It sounded like an opera plot. Things like that just don't happen to real people. But they did. Alma and Felipe were indeed legends in their own lifetimes and even now their stories are widely remembered

A few years after Felipe's death, schools, streets, and even a town were named in his honor. Today one sees statues and murals of him throughout the state. Most revere the former governor as "the Abraham Lincoln of Yucatán."

Alma survives in the beautiful song "La Peregrina," which Felipe commissioned for her. It's a mariachi favorite everywhere. After Felipe's death, Alma had a rich and varied life, first reporting on archaeological discoveries in Tunisia, Greece, and Italy, and then operating an art gallery in New York. She was a patron of many talented artists and introduced José Clemente Orozco to the world. Alma never married. She returned to Mexico when she was sixty and spent the last seventeen years of her life as a reporter on the *Mexico City News*.

Today, her body lies beside Felipe's in Mérida's largest cemetery.

TIMELINE

JANUARY 1542—Mérida is "founded" by the conquistador Francisco de Montejo, on the ruins of an ancient Maya city.

NOVEMBER 8, 1874—Felipe Carrillo Puerto is born in Motul, Yucatán.

1876–1910—The dictator Porfirio Díaz rules Mexico.

JUNE 17, 1896—Alma Reed is born in San Francisco, California.

1910–1920—Porfirio Díaz is exiled and revolution engulfs Mexico.

1920—After brutally eliminating his competition, Álvaro Obregón becomes Mexico's first president.

Timeline

1921—Alma Reed is instrumental in passing a bill raising the execution age in California from fourteen to eighteen.

FEBRUARY 5, 1922—Felipe Carrillo Puerto becomes governor of Yucatán.

FEBRUARY 1923—Alma Reed accompanies the Carnegie archaeological team to the ruins of Chichen Itza in Yucatán. She discovers that more than $2 million in treasure has been stolen from a sacrificial well. Her exposé appears in the *New York Times*.

JANUARY 3, 1924—Felipe Carrillo Puerto, governor of Yucatán, is executed.

1928—Álvaro Obregón is shot by a Catholic zealot who believes him to be the Antichrist.

1950—Alma Reed is awarded Mexico's highest civilian award, the Order of the Aztec Eagle.

NOVEMBER 20, 1966—Alma Reed dies on Mexico's Independence Day.

OCTOBER 22, 1967—Alma Reed is buried beside Felipe Carrillo Puerto at Panteón General in Mérida.

ACKNOWLEDGMENTS

To Vern Appleby, Gerald Stoner, and John Wilson, who each in his own wonderful way provided the spirit. To Ann Axtell Morris, whose delightful children's book, *Digging in Yucatan*, provided the spark. To Ana Argaez, Ruth Shari, and Jim Budd whose enthusiasm and practical assistance made *The Sacred Well* possible. And finally to Lucy Sanna who "got it" from the start.

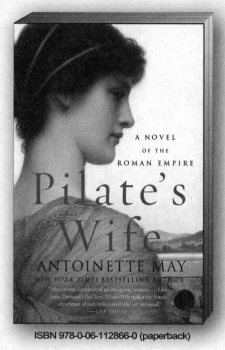